LOVE UNTAMED

A DIAMOND CREEK, ALASKA NOVEL

J.H. CROIX

DEDICATION

To my readers for such phenomenal support and for making this journey more fun that I could have imagined! And always...my husband for supporting the work of my dreams.

Sign up for my newsletter for information on new releases & get a FREE copy of one of my books!

http://jhcroixauthor.com/subscribe/

Follow me!
jhcroix@jhcroix.com
https://amazon.com/author/jhcroix
https://www.bookbub.com/authors/j-h-croix
https://www.facebook.com/jhcroix

CHAPTER 1

ne-year prior

The rain came down so hard, the windshield wipers could barely keep pace. Susie Hammond glanced over at Jared who sat silently in the passenger seat. He was soaked through and yet managed to somehow seem unperturbed. Her emotions on the other hand were in turmoil. She tried to tamp them down, but waves of anxiety, fear—and inconvenient desire—crashed inside. Jared had been quiet since they'd dropped off Tess and Nathan at Tess's hotel.

She thought back to when Hannah called her early this evening and broke the news that Jared, Luke and Nathan hadn't been heard from and were overdue at the harbor for their return from a routine fishing trip. She'd looked outside and her heart had stuttered. Kachemak Bay was barely visible in the heavy rain that fell and the mountains were invisible. Wind blew in window rattling gusts. Storms off the coast of Alaska could be vicious and made more so by the unforgiving conditions. On a perfectly calm day in the summer, the chances of survival in the ocean were slim without quick rescue.

Susie had done what she always did—tucked her worry away and went into action. Jared, Luke and Nathan Winters were three brothers who ran a guiding business in Diamond Creek, Alaska. Luke was married to her friend Hannah, while Nathan was dating her other friend Tess. As she'd sat waiting with her friends, Hannah, Emma and Tess, Susie's mind kept turning to Jared. Against every shred of sanity she had, there was an undeniable draw to him and it drove her batty. Jared was exactly the kind of man who would push her over the edge—detail oriented, always together, never messy, always calm—and so damn sexy she could barely look at him sometimes. Knowing he was out there in the wind and rain seemed to have flipped a switch inside. All those feelings she'd managed to keep at bay created an internal tumult.

Susie had stood in the lashing rain with her friends as the helicopter landed, the whir and whack of its blades swirling the rain around them. Even though she'd personally spoken to the harbormaster and knew the Coast Guard had reported all on board were safe, her heart kicked into gear while she waited for the passengers to disembark from the helicopter. Jared had stepped out after Luke, tall, dark and dripping with water. She hadn't been able to stop herself from pulling him close for a hug. "You're soaked. We need to get you dry," she'd said.

Jared had pulled back and looked down at her, his piercing green eyes a flash of color in the dark rain. He chuckled. "Dry would be good about now."

Susie fought her urge to fret over him. He was soaking wet and shivering, and he was laughing about it. *He's okay. You said you just wanted to know he's okay. Clearly, he is. What are you freaking out about?* He was okay, and she was still off kilter to the point that emotion welled in her chest. Her emotions made no sense, and she wanted them to stop. Now.

After a visit to the hospital for Jared, his brothers and the passengers on their guided trip to get cleared, Susie had taken charge of Jared, Tess and Nathan, while Emma brought Hannah and Luke home.

"Damn, this rain isn't letting up." Jared's voice cut through the quiet in the car.

Susie glanced over. "Definitely not. I'm glad you're not still out on the water. How are you feeling?"

Jared shrugged. "Like a drowned rat. I'm relieved the family with us is okay. I was pretty worried about their daughter. By the time the Coast Guard got there, she was shivering so hard, her teeth were chattering."

Susie nodded. "Sounds like she'll be alright." Tears threatened to spill over. *Get a grip. Jared is just Jared. You're freaking out because he's your friend. That's all.* She squinted through the rain running down the windshield, trying to ignore her feelings. No matter what she told herself, she'd been scared to death until she knew Jared was safe. And now that he was here beside her, she didn't know what to do with her feelings. To say it was awkward didn't quite capture it.

"Is this your road?" she asked. Though she'd been to the house Jared shared with his younger brother, Nathan, it had been awhile. Since Luke had married Hannah and moved out, she'd had less of a reason to stop by with Hannah.

"That's the one," he replied.

When she came to a stop in the drive, Jared looked over, his inscrutable eyes flashing with something she couldn't define. "Why don't you come in? Give it a few minutes and see if the rain lets up before you head home."

Susie felt her head nodding before she could think. The house was quiet, the rain and wind muted inside. Jared adjusted the thermostat. Only then did Susie realize she was shivering. He turned on the television, said he needed a quick shower and disappeared, leaving her to wonder what the hell she was doing here. She idly flipped through the channels and was about to leave him a note and get out of there when he returned to the living room.

Her pulse ricocheted. He leaned against the small island separating the kitchen and living room. He'd changed out of his wet clothes into navy sweatpants and a black t-shirt. The soft cotton clung to his fit, muscular build. She didn't know if he did, but she'd bet money he worked out. Though he lived a life that kept him fit as a commercial fisherman and fishing guide, he hummed with a leashed energy. She couldn't imagine him being still for too long. She glanced over, carefully keeping her expression bland while her pulse pounded and that inconvenient desire coursed through her.

Susie stood and walked to the kitchen. "I should go," she said, her words coming out stilted. She needed to get the hell out of there before Jared picked up on the riot of emotions. *This will pass. It's just because you were afraid he might die. And because your friends were worried and it's some kind of contagious thing where their worry stuck to you.*

"What are you shaking your head for?" Jared asked, a small smile playing at the corners of his mouth.

She looked over at him and wished she didn't like what she saw so damn much. On top of his deliciously built body that she itched to touch, he had those amazing green eyes, wavy black hair and chiseled features with a full mouth. As both of his brothers did, he also had dimples. So when he flashed that small smile, his dimples came with it. And since when were dimples so sexy? On Jared with his serious, intense eyes and not too frequent smile, he went from handsome to swoon-worthy because they were so unexpected.

She felt the blush heat her face. She'd shaken her head without a thought passing through. She tried to pass it off. "Oh, just relieved you're all okay. It's not looking like the rain will let up."

Jared pushed away from the counter and came to stand in front of her. She could have sworn she felt the heat of his body. His damp curls caught flecks of light. She heard him take a deep breath. Her heart started beating faster.

He swore softly and moved so swiftly, it took her by surprise. Since it seemed she'd lost all capacity for clear thought, the only thing that didn't surprise her was she couldn't seem to think straight. All she knew was one minute he stood before her and the next, his hand was in her curls. She opened her mouth to say something and his lips landed against hers, his tongue stroking deeply. The desire she'd been trying so hard to keep tamped down roared to life, spiraling through her with such force, she was lost. Every fiber of her strained toward him. One of his hands slipped around her waist, tugging her tight against him. The feel of his muscled body against hers stoked the fire inside of her. Slick heat built in her core. His hand slid down and caressed her bottom, pressing her against his arousal. No surprise, but he was clearly well-endowed. The length and heat of his hard shaft pressing against her cleft was so delicious, all she wanted was to tear his clothes off and have him inside of her.

His lips left hers and traveled in a heated and frantic pass down her neck. He tugged at her damp blouse, tearing the top buttons apart. Her breasts were visible, barely restrained in the black lace bra she wore. He muttered an imprecation as he undid the clasp holding her bra together in front. Her breasts spilled out, and Jared wasted no time. His lips closed over a nipple just as his knee shifted between her thighs, pressing against her. He alternated with soft licks and suction. Her nipples peaked to an ache. Her hips moved of their own accord, riding his thigh, desperately seeking release.

Jared abruptly pulled back and said her name. She opened her eyes into his piercing green gaze. "Do you know how long I've wanted to do this?" he asked in a whisper.

She swallowed and shook her head, unable to form words.

"Too long," came his raspy answer. His eyes flicked down to her breasts. Her nipples were damp from his attention and pebbled in the cool air. Her breasts were heavy and full. She'd always wished to be thinner, her curves usually seemed too much. But now, with him looking at her breasts with that heated gaze, she felt so wanted that she wouldn't change a thing. He cupped her breasts with both hands and leaned forward to lave one nipple and then the other, slowly grinding his thigh against her. She was so wet, she feared he could feel the moisture through her jeans.

When he softly bit her nipple, she suddenly broke out of the heated moment and pushed away. She opened her eyes to find him looking back at her, once again, his eyes inscrutable. Questions tumbled through her and she ignored them. She couldn't believe what had just happened and had no idea what to do with how she felt. "I...um..." she started to speak and stopped when she tripped over her words. "I have to go," she finally said abruptly.

"Susie..." Jared started to say.

As soon as he spoke, she got angry, furious with herself for wanting him so much she'd made a fool of herself.

"What the hell was that about? I'm not like those idiots who moon over you. I'm definitely not your one night stand to make you feel better after you almost drowned," she said, her voice strident and loud, even to her. She quickly tugged her clothes together, shoving her breasts back into her bra and buttoning her shirt. She grabbed her purse and gave her raincoat a shake before putting it on. She couldn't even look at him again.

"Do you have to get angry right off the bat?" Jared asked, his eyes flashing.

She didn't look up. "Shut up." She raced out the door. She heard her name once more as she ran through the rain. When she slammed her car door, she saw him coming through the rain toward her. She started her car and shifted into reverse before he had a chance to reach her. Her headlights illuminated him in a glittering arc through the rain as she backed up rapidly.

CHAPTER 2

*P*resent

Susie pushed through the door at Sally's. It was raining, so she was meeting friends for an early dinner. Sally's was a Diamond Creek fixture, an old renovated barn that had long been an established restaurant and bar. She shook her brown curls, raindrops flying when she did. She strode quickly over to the dining area, searching out her friends.

A good hour later, Susie was wondering how much she could take from Hannah and Tess about Luke and Nathan, their respective husbands. Hannah, Susie's best childhood friend, had married Luke Winters, and Tess had married his younger brother, Nathan, after meeting him on a fishing trip to Alaska last year. Susie loved to see her friends happy, so she just might have interfered a little. But if she'd known how much they were going to drone on about how awesome their husbands were, she would have reconsidered. There was also the inconvenient fact that Jared was the older brother to Luke and Nathan, so it was difficult to avoid him. She thought she'd done a good job of hiding how she felt about Jared, but it was becoming increasingly difficult. Especially since that damn kiss last year. Just thinking about it aggravated her still. She didn't like letting anything get the best of her, and she'd been an idiot to let that kiss happen.

After Hannah made a sly comment about Susie being the one to set Hannah and Luke up, Susie harrumphed and took a swallow of beer. "Maybe I can see a good thing coming, but that doesn't mean you have permanent permission to drone on about how great he is."

"It bothers you because you can't keep your eyes off Jared and won't admit it to save your life," Tess replied with a sly grin.

Susie choked on her beer, grabbing a napkin to wipe her chin. Emma gave Tess an admiring nod. "You may be kinda new around here, but…wow…that took nerve." Emma was Hannah's older sister and had moved to Diamond Creek a few years ago. Their parents had given Emma up for adoption, and many years later, Emma had started searching for them. Unfortunately, she never met her biological parents because they had died in a plane crash in rural Alaska. But she'd found Hannah and decided to move here. She was more low-key than Hannah and Tess, but probably sharper than all of them as she was a therapist. Her sly sense of humor tended to sneak up on others.

Hannah bit her lip and shook her head. Susie glared at them and hoped they didn't notice the blush creeping up her neck. Tess had zeroed in on an uncomfortable truth—Susie barely could keep her eyes off Jared whenever he was around, and it drove her nuts. Even when she wasn't thinking about it, she'd catch herself looking at him. It didn't help that he was ridiculously sexy. Matters made worse by the fact that they were not cut out for each other. Maybe that one kiss had been mind-blowing, but Jared had never even hinted it happened. He was cool, calm and collected. *Stop thinking about him! He doesn't matter. Right, you only wish.*

"What?" Hannah asked, feigning innocence. "You're happy to dish it out, you'd better be ready to take it."

Play it cool, do NOT let them see you sweat this. Susie straightened her shoulders and glanced around the table. "I'll have you know that while I won't deny Jared is handsome—that whole damn family is—I can certainly keep my eyes off of him. Plus, can you imagine me with someone that uptight? That man seriously needs to loosen up."

"And maybe you're just the girl for the job," Tess said.

Susie thought she might get skid marks on her tongue because she had to bite it so hard to keep from swearing. If she didn't want the whole world to know Jared pushed her buttons and then some, she couldn't go around losing her temper just because her friends teased her about him. She rolled her eyes at Tess. "I'm sure I could be the girl for the job, but it's not one I want."

Conveniently, the waitress arrived to deliver their check. Susie took the moment to take a faux bathroom break and gather herself. She was not up for parrying about Jared tonight, not when her friends were uncomfortably close to the truth. By the time she returned to the table, she managed to make her excuses and get the hell out of there.

As she drove home, she wondered how to stop feeling the way she did. Before her fated kiss with Jared, a teensy tiny part of her might have admitted she was more attracted to Jared than anyone before. But then…the kiss. *Oh, that kiss.* It had been over a year and not a day passed that she didn't think about it. Jared irritated the hell out of her half the time, and the other half—holy hell, all she did was fantasize about him. Then he just had to go and be an amazing kisser.

When she pulled up in front of her house, she banged her forehead on the steering wheel. "Damn, damn, damn." She lifted her head, brushing her unruly curls out of her face. All by herself and she was blushing like crazy. She needed to talk to someone, but doing so meant sharing a few details she'd rather not. She was the strong friend, the together friend, the one who played matchmaker and who always had a quick comeback. The only friend who had glimpsed the *her* underneath all that was Hannah, her best friend since elementary school. But Hannah had missed a few details while she'd been out of state at graduate school and grieving the death of her parents. And Susie hadn't quite found the time to fill her in.

The main detail being that Susie had somehow never managed to lose her virginity and here she was thirty-one years old. Oh and this might have happened because she narrowly avoided getting date-raped by some asshole who slipped something into her drink one weekend when she was in Anchorage. Up until then, she'd had been a fun-loving flirt. Perhaps she'd made it a little further than most with regard to her virginity, but it hadn't been because she was uptight. Just because she was choosy.

But her choosy radar must have been turned off that night. She'd thought Tim was cute and fun. He was of one of the common tourist types that visited Alaska—outdoorsy, and handsome. She'd been up in Anchorage with her mother and decided to stay an extra night to stock up on shopping. Nothing cued her that Tim might not be a decent guy. Until she woke up, woozy, out of it, and with him tugging her jeans off. Though she couldn't even see straight, she fought like mad. She knew to this day she was lucky he didn't care to fight too hard to rape her because she might be feisty but she barely topped five feet. She came out of it with a few bruises while he left her hotel room swearing, bright red scratches on his face.

That had been the last time she'd been anywhere close to being intimate with a man. She hadn't meant for it to be like that, she just couldn't seem to let down her guard. She'd convinced herself being single was a choice of freedom and tried to ignore the corner of her psyche that doubted her instincts and shied away from intimacy. She was strong and independent. Though she was more romantic than most, she focused all that energy on her friends, committed to making sure they weren't dumb enough to let the good guys blow by. Until Jared came along.

Susie swore and climbed out of her car, stomping into her house. She bought this house herself when she moved back home after college. Diamond Creek was home and always would be. Her parents would have been happy to let her stay with them as long as she wanted. But she had needed to make it on her own. Reeling from anger at herself, frustration that she hadn't the courage to track Tim down and press charges, she'd thrown herself into making an independent life for herself. A few years later and she was known as the best accountant in town and had her own home. It was a small, cedar A-frame with purple trim and a wrap-around deck. As with almost every house in Diamond Creek, it had a lovely view of Kachemak Bay and the mountains across the water.

Diamond Creek was situated on the shores of Kachemak Bay, one of Alaska's coastal jewels and a massive tourist draw from spring to fall. Kachemak Bay detoured off the Cook Inlet, an inlet that stretched from the Gulf of Alaska in the Pacific Ocean to the bustling port of Anchorage. Anchorage was the hub of Southcentral Alaska. The Kenai Peninsula sat south of Anchorage, and Diamond Creek was located toward the southern end of the peninsula. Susie was an Alaskan girl, through and through. She enjoyed trips to Seattle and just about anywhere, but Diamond Creek was home. She savored the wild edge, the immense beauty, and the independence and quirkiness that Alaska fostered in people.

Susie shook her raincoat and hung it on the small coatrack by the door. She flicked on a few lights and glanced around. It was cold, dark and rainy, and she was glad to be home. Realizing her feelings for Jared might be obvious to her friends made her want to jump out of her skin. How could she explain why it would never work with him? And why, oh why, did he have to be the man who made her think twice about her plan for being permanently single?

There was a soft scratching at the door. She flung it open to find her cat, Jasmine, looking irate and wet. Jasmine raced through the door, promptly jumping on the kitchen counter and shaking. Susie found Jasmine last spring when it was still too cold at night. After a few hours of wondering what was scratching under her porch in the night, Susie shined a flashlight underneath and found Jasmine, then a kitten, shivering. Jasmine was a smoky gray feline with a streak of feistiness tempered by her sheer adoration of human affection.

"Jasmine, you're soaked! I didn't know you were out all day." She went to the small laundry room off the kitchen and grabbed a towel, briskly rubbing Jasmine with it. Jasmine purred like mad, rubbing into the towel, her irritation at being outside instantly gone. Her gray fur tufted up all over once she was dry.

After changing into warm, dry clothes, Susie curled up on the couch and flipped through the channels, Jasmine snugged up against her side, purring audibly. Thoughts of Jared crept into her mind, and Susie sighed.

CHAPTER 3

$\mathcal{J}$ared tossed a salmon toward the cooler.

"Dammit, Jared! How about you actually look next time you throw a fish?" Nathan exclaimed.

Jared turned to look and burst out laughing. Nathan was seated on the bench beside the cooler in question with a salmon on his lap.

Nathan shook his head and chuckled. "You're lucky I'm a good sport. Getting a slimy fish on my lap means I'll stink the rest of the day."

Jared shrugged. "Sorry 'bout that. Didn't realize you were right there. Should I point out it's kinda hard not to smell like fish when you're fishing?"

Nathan rolled his eyes. "For you of all people to say that when you make it seem like fishing isn't even messy. If I threw a fish on your lap, you'd be pissed, so you might as well appreciate my good attitude. You're the master of tidy. You manage to avoid the slime. Don't pretend like you don't either. I don't know how you pull it off."

Jared merely shrugged again. No need for him to agree with Nathan when it was obvious. He took good care of his gear and if any fish slime got on him, he hosed it off as soon as he could.

"You wanna grab a bite at Sally's when we get in with the crew?" Jared asked, moving on from the errant salmon throw.

"Sure. Tess'll probably want to meet us there. That okay?"

Jared nodded. "Of course."

He looked away, moving to step behind the steering wheel. They were coming in from a two-week commercial fishing run for sockeye salmon. He and his brothers ran a commercial and sport fishing business, The One that Didn't Get Away. They usually took the crew out for dinner when they got back to harbor after the longer runs. Jared looked ahead at the shores of Diamond Creek. Otter Cove Harbor was visible now. The town's boat harbor was tucked into a small cove. Wooded hillsides rose up around the cove, spruce trees marching up the mountains behind. Diamond Creek was built into the hillside and looked out over Kachemak Bay. He glanced behind him. Mount Augustine, a volcano, sat in the distance, silent and majestic.

A few hours later, he pushed through the swinging door into Sally's, which was bustling tonight. He'd called ahead and reserved a big table for the crew. He was halfway through his hamburger when he saw Tess making a beeline for Nathan. Susie walked behind Tess. All he had to do was see Susie, and it was as if someone flicked a match in the air around them —it crackled and sizzled. Heat crept through his body, and his pulse shifted gears. His body had all kinds of ideas about Susie, no matter how many times he tried to talk his body down.

Relationships were messy. He liked his world to be sensible and predictable. The mix of someone else's emotions in his daily life invited mayhem. He'd tried it before, and it had been…discombobulating. He'd even come close to getting engaged, an experience that illuminated how confusing emotions could be. Trying to make sense of it made him tired and feel half-crazy. He found being single to be much simpler. He could live life on his terms and not worry about how someone else felt.

And Susie. Well, she'd take messy to a whole new level. She was brash, funny, assertive and so damn sexy he could hardly stand it. About a year ago, he'd lost his mind and given in to what he'd wanted to do for too damn long. He'd kissed her like his life depended on it. And not a day passed since then that he didn't think about it.

"Hey there," Susie said.

Her brown eyes were wide and bright, always with a glint of knowing, like she could see right through him. Her brown curls were just…wild. They tumbled every which way, bouncing around her shoulders. She swiped one out of her eyes, looking at him expectantly.

He bought some time by taking a swallow of beer. He needed a minute to try to get his mind off how damn sexy she was. "Hey there. How's it going?" he finally asked.

Susie shrugged. "Fine. Just fine. Did you get the spreadsheet I sent over?"

Jared had to force himself not to stare at her breasts. She was all curves. The night he'd kissed her, before he could stop himself, her luscious breasts were in his hands. And even now, a year later, all she had to do was get anywhere near him and his hands practically itched to touch her. *Get a grip. This is Susie. You do not want to get tangled up with her.* About that point, he realized he'd yet to answer Susie's question.

"Just got in from fishing today. I'll check my email tonight and catch up. What did you send over?" he asked, trying to tamp down the irritation he felt. He was irritated with himself for constantly feeling off kilter with her, which in turn made him irritated with her. It was as if she held the secret key to make him lose his cool.

Susie's eyes searched his for a moment, a flicker of confusion in them. "It's the quarterly report you asked me to send," she said pointedly. "You wanted me to change the spreadsheet layout, so I did." She shook her head, releasing her breath in a huff.

He was fairly certain his blood pressure literally rose. As usual, he wanted to do one of two things: swear and walk away from her, or grab her, drag her out of here and finish what he started that night. But because Susie was who she was, his sister-in-law's best friend and a good friend of practically everyone he knew, including himself, he couldn't do either one of those things. He took a few swallows of beer and a deep breath instead.

"That I did. Forgot for a minute there. All I've been thinking about is fish," he finally replied. When he looked into her eyes, his heart pounded, and he was damn glad he was sitting down so no one would notice that he was hard as a rock.

Susie nodded and gave him a bright smile that looked a tad forced. "Of course. Fish, fish, fish.

Anyway, when you get a chance, let me know if the spreadsheet is set up the way you wanted." She glanced down the table. She started to move to the other end. "Call me about it if you need any other changes," she said, not bothering to look his way again.

Jared breathed a sigh of relief when she moved out of his immediate vicinity. When he and his brothers first moved to Diamond Creek, they'd gotten to know Susie pretty early on. Jared had thought she was cute because she was. Those wild curls, laughing brown eyes and curves were cute... and sexy as hell, but he tried not to think about it. She'd become a friend over time and ran an accounting business, By the Numbers. She was a bang up accountant—detail oriented, a math whiz, computer savvy and ruthlessly efficient. Not to mention that she beat him at his own game half the time. Whenever he asked for something, such as the spreadsheet in question, she'd have it to him sooner than he asked and better than what he wanted. Somewhere along the way, his unwanted attraction to her bloomed before he noticed it.

Luke sat across from him, chowing down fast. He looked up and chuckled.

"What?" Jared asked.

"Whenever Susie gets anywhere near you, you get irritated about nothing. And then she walks away and you can't stop looking at her," Luke said with a sly grin. "Like now."

Jared realized he was staring in Susie's direction and whipped his head back to face Luke. "Seriously, dude? Don't you have anything better to do other than watch me?"

Luke kept on grinning. "Not when watching you get all twisted up over Susie is more fun."

Jared had to force himself to take a deep breath and not take the bait. He took another bite of his hamburger.

Luke's eyes sobered. "Just joking around. But seriously, Hannah thinks Susie's got a thing for you. Maybe you won't admit it, but she's pretty awesome. About the only woman who doesn't drool over you around here."

Jared rolled his eyes. "Women don't drool over me."

Luke shook his head. "You choose to ignore it, but it doesn't mean it's not happening. Come on, man. You're like candy because you're so unavailable. I've told you for years that your rule about no relationships is stupid."

"Yeah, yeah. You've pointed that out. I'm not like you and Nathan. Relationships are messy. I'm fine by myself."

Luke gave him a long look. "You know, I was as committed to staying single as you are. And for similar reasons, so I get it. Maybe the details were different, but you weren't like this until you got burned by Jen. Seeing as you're only two years shy of forty, you might want to move on one of these days."

Jared swallowed and stared at Luke. "What the hell? Do we have to have a deep conversation right now? My age has nothing to do with this. Jen is old news. I got over her years ago. What makes you think she has anything to do with anything now?"

Jared shoved his annoyance with Luke down. He wanted to tell him to shut the hell up, but that wouldn't help matters. Jen was his ex from back when they lived in Seattle. He'd been set to ask her to marry him when she'd broken it off, offering the contradiction that he was 'too intense and held too much back'. She also claimed she wasn't ready for commitment. Jared didn't like to talk about it, but it had hurt like hell. He meant it when he said he was over her. But a few years of avoiding serious relationships made him see how much easier it was. His mother had finally stopped dropping hints and seemed to have accepted that he planned to stay single and be the favorite uncle to their grandkids.

Luke eyed him and shrugged. "I'm not saying you're pining after Jen. Just that after she broke it off, you changed. You'd never been into the casual thing before and since then, it's the only thing you'll consider and barely. I think maybe you think it's easier. That's all."

"It *is* easier," Jared said flatly.

Luke chuckled. "In some ways, maybe. Look, I didn't mean to turn this into much. Just thought maybe…nothing," he said with a shrug.

Conversation moved on. A bit later, Jared realized his eyes were following Susie as she left. He'd never admit it, but Luke was right. He couldn't seem to keep his eyes off of her, even when he tried. And damn if that didn't annoy him. He prided himself on being in control. Susie tested that simply by existing.

THE FOLLOWING MORNING, Jared stood by the windows in his small cabin and looked out over the bay. He'd moved out of the home he used to share with his brothers when Tess moved up here. Nathan had tried to talk him out of it, but it didn't make sense for Nathan to move when the last thing Jared needed was that big house all to himself. He'd rented a cabin down the road. It was small, practical and came with an astounding view of Kachemak Bay. The back of the house faced the view and was floor to ceiling with windows. The cabin was a small gambrel style home. It consisted of a basic kitchen and living room area with a bathroom downstairs and an expansive loft upstairs that served as the bedroom. It was open, airy and bright with more than enough space for him.

The wind was up this morning, white caps dotting the water. Clouds scuttled across the sky, coasting in front of the mountains across the bay. His yard was a small patch of grass surrounded with fireweed that would bloom in late summer. He sat down at the kitchen table and flipped open his laptop. He plowed through some email and opened the spreadsheet Susie had asked him about last night. It was precisely as he'd requested.

And for some reason, that annoyed the hell out of him. Luke had gotten under his skin last night. Between his irrational attraction to Susie and Luke noticing it, Jared wanted to do something to shake it off. So he was annoyed at Susie over a spreadsheet. *Now that's irrational. Get a grip.*

He stalked into the kitchen and poured a fresh cup of coffee. A few sips later, he talked himself out of asking her to make more changes. *To a spreadsheet.* His mind went from spreadsheets to Susie's curls and curves. He swore, set his coffee down and went to change to go for a run.

A solid hour later, he slowed his pace as he approached his cabin. He'd taken off on one of the longer loops he ran through a few local trails and connecting roads. He waved when he saw his friend Travis drive by and walked onto the back deck. The run had barely started to burn off his restless energy. What he couldn't figure out was why his mind jumped on the hamster wheel of Susie so much these days. He didn't like to admit it, but he'd wanted to kiss her for quite some time before he'd given in last year. He didn't think he would have were it not for the circumstances. Hours of holding it together in the driving rain out on rough seas had worn his defenses down.

By the end of the long afternoon and evening, when Susie drove him home, he wasn't thinking straight. So he'd let his impulses get the best of him. Susie had been so damn tempting, he couldn't resist the urge to lose himself in her heat and lush body. Oddly enough, the first few times he saw her afterwards were a little awkward, but he managed to play it cool and not dwell on it. But lately, his attraction to her had burrowed under his skin. He couldn't shake it off. He grabbed his gym clothes and took off. If a run couldn't turn his mind off, maybe lifting weights would.

CHAPTER 4

Susie glanced up from her computer when the door to her office opened. Jared stepped inside and closed the door behind him. Her heart started pounding. She forced herself to take a slow breath. Her reaction to him was getting ridiculous. Somehow she'd managed to get her feelings under control for a while after that kiss last year, but lately, she was losing the battle. Jared wore faded black jeans and a black t-shirt that fit his muscled build like a glove. His piercing green eyes met hers. She instantly felt pinned by his gaze. That annoyed her. She stood abruptly, needing to move to fling off the desire that thrummed through her anytime he was near.

"Hey there, I didn't know you were stopping by. Did you need something?" Susie knew she sounded prickly and wished she didn't. She was annoyed with herself for being so damn attracted to him that it had to come out somewhere. Because she sure as hell couldn't act on how she felt. That was out of the question. Not to mention, she was pretty sure Jared wasn't interested. Maybe he'd seemed interested that rainy night, but since then, he'd been cool and collected whenever he was near her.

Jared came to a stop by her desk and placed a manila envelop on her desk. "Thought I'd drop off our receipts from last month," he said simply.

Nonplussed, she stared at the envelope for a long moment.

"That okay? I usually drop them off every month," Jared finally said when Susie didn't reply.

"Oh, right," she finally said, fighting the blush she felt creeping up her neck and face. "Sorry. I was in the middle of working on some stuff and wasn't too focused." She fought to collect her thoughts. "Have you heard anything about Emma's ex?" she asked, figuring this topic might be the cold water she needed to get her desire under control.

Emma's abusive ex-husband had recently shown up in town after he'd gotten wind Emma was involved with someone else. Though Emma wasn't ready to admit it, Trey was perfect for her—sexy, smart, an awesome single father and he adored her. Susie was doing her best to interfere and make sure Emma realized she and Trey were meant for each other while this mess with her ex was getting in the way and scaring her. Susie and the rest of Emma's friends had been keeping an eye out for her ex. Along with everyone else, Susie was impatient for him to be located and arrested. Jared was one of the most plugged in, keeping tabs with his friend who was a local cop and keeping the rest of them in the loop. Of course, Jared just had to go and be about as nice as a man could get when it came to stuff like this. He was protective of friends and family and went out of his way to help without any hesitation.

Jared shook his head. "Trey's about out of his mind. I just told him he could stop by here to meet me. He says Emma is insisting on staying away from him because she's worried about Stuart. Could you maybe talk some sense into her? Trey's pretty much a goner when it comes to her."

Though Susie agreed with Jared on this and had made the same point to Emma, it rankled her that he would ask her to talk to Emma about it. "Look, let Emma figure this out on her own. She's pretty freaked out about everything. I'm sure Trey means well, but it's not like she's staying alone. She's been at Hannah and Luke's place and knows she can stay with me anytime."

Jared's eyes sharpened. "All I'm saying is maybe she could cut Trey a break and try not to shut him out."

Susie didn't know why, but she wanted to argue. "And all I'm saying is let her figure this out her own way."

When she'd stood up, she'd walked around to the side of her desk. She hadn't noticed she was so close to him. Jared's eyes caught hers. His green gaze was bright. His chest rose and fell in a deep breath. He leaned forward, his face coming within inches of hers. "Why the hell do you always have to argue with me?"

Having Jared this close to her set off flares of heat inside. Flustered and flushed, she tried to gain control of the situation and didn't back down. "Why the hell do you always think you're right?" she countered.

Her heart pounded, her pulse careened and that oh-so-inconvenient desire thundered to the fore. She started to say something when Jared's lips came down on hers. What started hard and fast slowed when her mouth opened under his. The anger she felt morphed into a heated, intense passion that enveloped them. He traced her lips, searched inside her mouth. His tongue stroked deeply, tangling with hers. She strained toward him and gasped in his mouth when he slid his palm down her back to cup her bottom and tug her against his arousal. Heat swirled in her center, slick moisture built in her core. The sheer relief of finally giving in to what she wanted ruled her body. She forgot she was angry, forgot all the reasons why Jared was *not* a man she should allow this to happen with, and tumbled headlong into sensation.

Jared's mouth left hers as he trailed heated kisses down her neck. His hand slid up to cup one of her breasts, her nipple pebbling against his palm through the thin blouse she wore. "Dear God, Susie," he whispered, his voice raspy.

She was so desperate to feel his body against hers that she tore at his t-shirt. Jared suddenly tensed and froze. As he did, she heard footsteps approaching her office. She shoved away from Jared. He took several quick steps back, his eyes pinned to hers, his green gaze piercing right through her. She knew...just knew... her desperation was written all over her face. She wanted to run and hide. Her only saving grace was that Jared looked as rattled as she felt.

Trey stepped into her office, glancing between her and Jared quickly. For a split second, Trey looked curious, but he masked it quickly. She barely heard Trey's greeting to Jared and had to force herself to focus. When Jared commented that he'd talked to Darren earlier, she jumped in. "You did? Please tell me he said he can do something about that asshole," she demanded and then glanced to Trey. "By the way, I know we've met before, but I'm a friend of Emma's. You should know that I'll personally kick your ass if you hurt her." As soon as the words left her mouth, she wondered why she had to start there. She was so discombobulated with what just happened with Jared, she wasn't thinking clearly.

Trey looked taken aback. Before Trey could reply, Jared cut in. "For God's sake, Susie, lay off it. I told you, he's a stand up guy. Not to mention, he knows I think of Emma as family. He'll have me to answer to as well, but how about we not start off with a threat?"

Susie had to bite her lip not to reply to Jared. She knew she'd kind of jumped down Trey's throat, but the last thing she needed was for Jared to get on her case about it. To make matters worse, Jared seemed to gather himself after snapping back at her, which pissed her off. She couldn't even look at Jared right now and kept looking to Trey to keep her eyes anywhere else. The conversation continued and she somehow got through it. To keep her hands busy, she started pointlessly shuffling papers on her desk, trying to tamp down the seething she felt inside. Her anger with Jared swirled in the cauldron of desire she felt, both feeding into each other. Trey finally left.

"What the hell is wrong with you?" Susie asked, letting loose with her anger. She strode up to Jared, her finger pointed at him. Jared took a step back, which satisfied her immensely.

"What are you talking about?" he asked in return.

"You. Jumping on my case for telling Trey he'd better be good to Emma."

"You told him you'd kick his ass, which is ridiculous. Trey's a good guy. He doesn't deserve you treating him like some schmuck."

Susie knew Jared had a point. Even worse, she'd jumped on Trey because her frustration with Jared had nowhere else to go in the moment. As was the case with everything that had anything to do with Jared, her annoyance crept up a notch. She whirled away and stalked over to her desk again. "Fine. Whatever. Did you need something else before you go?"

She turned to face him again, lifting her chin and willing her eyes to be steady.

For a quick second, she saw uncertainty in Jared's eyes, but he masked it quickly. He appeared to be considering his words. When he finally spoke, he said, "Nope. I know you're pissed with me, but you should understand. You're protective of your friends, and so am I. Difference is, I'm not as blunt as you, and I give people the benefit of the doubt."

His words simultaneously infuriated her and made her wish she wasn't so obvious. *Get a grip, Susie. Don't let him see how pissed off you are. That'll only give him the upper hand.* She held his gaze, hoping the unstable combination of anger, uncertainty, confusion and yearning she felt didn't show. "I know," she finally replied. "Will you call me if you hear anything?" She hated asking him, but if anyone would keep her up to date, it would be Jared. Emma would mean to, but she was so caught up in what was happening, she wouldn't necessarily think to call.

Jared nodded brusquely. "Of course." Without another word, he turned and left.

She collapsed into her desk chair and willed her heart to slow down. She was hot all over. She brushed her curls out of her face and stared blankly at her computer screen.

* * *

THE FOLLOWING MORNING, Susie walked into the kitchen at her parents' house to find her mother chopping a huge pile of fresh basil. Her parents' dog, Dante, slept in the center of the kitchen floor. Dante was a large, shaggy brown dog who looked to have some German Shepherd in him, but it was anyone's guess. He stood to greet Susie and then promptly settled back on the floor with a sigh.

Her mother, Faye, looked up with a warm smile. "Hello dear. I'd give you a hug, but I'm right in the middle of this," she said, gesturing with her chopping knife.

"I can see that. What are you doing with all that basil?"

"Making pesto. We'll have some fresh, and I'll freeze the rest. This looks like a lot, but once it's chopped, it seems like hardly anything," Faye replied.

Susie had inherited her brown curls, brown eyes, and curves from her mother. Faye's curls were shot through with silver now, but just as wild as Susie's were. She had also inherited her tendency to be bold from her mother, but she'd yet to develop her mother's soft touch. Faye had a way of making blunt comments with a subtlety that Susie envied. Susie knew she often let her emotions get the best of her, as she had yesterday with Jared. She flushed.

"Where's Dad?" Susie asked.

"He's down at the hospital for yet another meeting

about the budget," Faye said with a sigh as she transferred chopped basil to a bowl.

"Oh he complains about it, but you know Dad would go bonkers if he wasn't working at all."

Faye had retired as a schoolteacher a few years back and now volunteered on various community projects, along with keeping busy with her gardening every summer. Susie's father, Patrick, had been one of the main family doctors in town when she was growing up. He'd retired from practicing medicine, but he still worked part-time in the hospital administration.

Faye smiled softly. "That he would. I almost did myself. It's good to keep busy." Faye finished chopping the basil and quickly rinsed her hands in the sink. "Coffee?" she asked, glancing to Susie.

Susie nodded and went to sit at the small round table in the kitchen that overlooked Kachemak Bay. The view from her childhood home was so familiar she had it memorized. Yet she never tired of looking. Her parents' home was further east than hers with a clear view of one of the glaciers across the bay. When she was a little girl, she thought the eerie blue glow of the glacier was magical. The glacier flowed between two mountains, its light a stark contrast to the dark green mountains. The wind was up today, the water choppy in the bay.

Faye set a cup of coffee in front of her and joined Susie at the table. "So what brings you over today?"

Susie shrugged. "I thought I'd just pop in and say hi." What she didn't say was that she felt out of sorts and didn't know where to turn. This *thing* with Jared was driving her near to distraction. Yet she couldn't bring herself to talk about him with her mother. Nor could she bring herself to talk about what really weighed on her, which was how the hell she'd ended up a virgin at her age and what to do about it. She'd never considered herself a prude, the opposite really. But somehow here she was, her mid-thirties looming in front of her and she knew if she got involved with anyone, they'd be surprised. She hadn't meant to shut down after the almost date-rape incident in Anchorage. But she'd gone from a girl who loved to flirt, tease and have fun to one who generally avoided flirting and lived vicariously through her friends when it came to romance.

For a while, she'd convinced herself that would be okay. But now…this out-of-control attraction she felt for Jared was making her question herself. To make matters worse, she could hardly stand that it was Jared who was throwing her into this internal turmoil. If she wasn't a virgin, she thought perhaps she could burn off this insane lust for him with one wild one-night stand. But the whole virginity thing made that idea a little more awkward than she could tolerate.

Faye tilted her head and eyed Susie speculatively. "You've got something on your mind," she said matter-of-factly.

Susie sighed and took a sip of coffee. A raven called outside, another returning the call in quick succession. A burst of magpie chatter interrupted the ravens. Dante ambled over to the windows to investigate. Susie glanced out the window and back at her mother. "Would it break your heart if I stayed single forever?" she asked.

Faye gave her a sharp look. "It wouldn't break my heart, but I'd be a little sad. I want you to be happy, and I'm not one who thinks the whole marriage thing is for everyone, but you were always a friendly sort and not exactly a loner. So I've worried that you haven't even dated in the last few years. But if you're happy on your own, then that's all I want for you."

Susie tugged on one of her curls, pulling it out and letting it bounce back. "I'm not unhappy. And it's not exactly easy to find someone around here," she said wryly. Desperate as she was to talk to someone about Jared and her inconvenient virginity, the thought of trying to have the conversation with her mother was a bit too much.

Faye shook her head. "Funny you say that when you're busy setting up all your friends," she said with a chuckle. Her gaze sobered. "Are you sure you're okay?"

Susie nodded quickly. She took a gulp of her coffee and looked out toward the bay, the icy glacier glittering under the bright sun. Tears pressed behind her eyelids. Because she wasn't okay, she was out of sorts.

"I'm okay. It didn't bother me when I turned thirty, but now I'm questioning everything. Maybe it's an early mid-life crisis."

Faye shrugged and smiled. Susie sensed her mother knew there was a bit more going on, but if there was one thing her mother knew, it was that Susie didn't handle being pressured well. So she was pretty darn good at giving Susie space.

Susie shifted the conversation to gardening, a surefire topic to keep Faye occupied. A while later, she drove down the hill toward town, feeling a little better after seeing her mother.

CHAPTER 5

Susie swung her faded blue hatchback into the parking lot at her office and walked inside. She rented the small office smack in the middle of town. It was an old renovated one-bedroom house. She used what was once a living room and kitchen as the space for her desk and for meeting with clients. The single bedroom served as storage for filing and office supplies. The only other room was a tiny bathroom. She quickly checked her email and began working on monthly reports.

She was so focused that she jumped when her office door opened. Hannah strode in and promptly sat down in one of the armchairs across from Susie's desk. Hannah was her oldest friend. They'd become fast friends in elementary school when Hannah's family moved to town when she and Susie were six years old. For most of her life, Susie spoke to Hannah almost every day. The only break in this happened when Hannah was away at graduate school. Susie missed her like crazy and worried, but she'd never doubted Hannah would come home and their friendship would be just what it had always been. That's what happened, except for the fact that Susie hadn't gotten around to filling Hannah in on the almost date rape and the fact that Susie was an accidental virgin. It wasn't like Susie had been keeping it from Hannah, it was just that so many other things were happening, it never came up. If Susie was honest with herself, she might have to admit she didn't mind that there was always something else to talk about.

"How's it going?" Hannah asked, brushing her long, dark hair away from her face. Hannah's tall frame slouched elegantly in the chair. Her blue eyes flashed when she smiled.

"Fine. Just busy working on reports. What are you up to?"

"Going crazy worrying about this thing with Emma's ex. Luke's getting updates from Jared practically every hour for me. How the hell can it be that easy to hide in Diamond Creek?"

Susie hit save on the report she'd been working on and closed her laptop. "I've been wondering the same thing. Have you talked to Emma today?"

"Did you forget she's staying with us?" Hannah countered with a grin. "She's as okay as she can be. I think. She's all worried about Trey and keeps talking about how she should've known better than to get involved with him. Then Luke tells me Jared says Trey is head over heels for her, and it's breaking his heart she won't stay with him. I'm trying to let her figure it out."

"I'll talk to her. She's being ridiculous," Susie said flatly and then realized she'd said the opposite to Jared yesterday. Irritation with him flashed through her. It drove her crazy that he made her feel so contrary. The mere thought of him elicited the memory of their kiss the other day—delicious, intoxicating and maddening. Instantly, she flushed and went quiet.

After a long moment, Hannah's voice broke into her thoughts. "You okay?"

Susie felt herself start to nod and then stopped. She absently tugged on a curl and bit her lip. She desperately wanted some advice on what to do about Jared, but she was conflicted because it meant admitting her friends had been right about her attraction to him. She groaned inwardly. She needed advice more than her pride at this point.

"Not really. This is going to come out of left field, but here goes. Jared's driving me nuts. I don't know what to do and you all were kind of right the other night that I might…" Susie paused to take a breath, felt her flush deepen and knew her face was bright red "…kind of notice him. The problem is he's all wrong for me, and you know it as well as I do. Not to mention that somehow I'm still a virgin and if I wanted to just have a one night stand to get him out of system, it won't work because he'll be expecting me not to be a virgin and then it'll be awkward and I don't know what to do."

The words tumbled out of her mouth so fast Susie couldn't stop them. Hannah's mouth opened and closed. Once Susie finished, she put her face in her hands and groaned.

"Well, all right then. This is obviously bothering you. I'm guessing you need someone to talk to," Hannah said softly.

Susie nodded and lifted her face. Hannah's eyes

held no judgment, no teasing, just understanding. Susie burst into tears and nodded.

Hannah knew her well enough to stay quiet for a few minutes. After the initial burst of tears, Susie grabbed a tissue and blew her nose, finally getting the courage to look at Hannah again. Hannah gave her a small smile, her blue eyes warm.

Susie took a deep breath. "It has been on my mind. A lot has…"

"You mean more than you being totally into Jared and you forgot to mention you're still a virgin? Not like you had to tell me, but once upon a time you would have," Hannah said softly.

"It kind of happened by accident. Which makes it even more embarrassing," she said with a sigh.

Hannah tilted her head. "What's embarrassing about it?"

Susie shrugged. "I don't know. Thirty-one seems kind of old to be a virgin. And for all the wrong reasons. I mean it's not like I was saving myself, or anything. Just that the right person never came along and then…"

Susie shifted in her seat, crossing and uncrossing her legs, tugging on a curl, and closing her eyes for a moment. She wanted to tell Hannah about what happened in Anchorage, but she didn't want it to become a 'thing.' But then she wondered if not telling anyone about it had made it more of a 'thing' than it needed to be. Since it was a secret, it seemed so much bigger. She thought about how she felt when Emma finally told them about her abusive ex-husband and how it had made her sad Emma had thought she needed to keep it a secret. Secrets were never a good thing. But Susie hated, oh how she hated, anything that made her feel vulnerable.

Glancing up, she saw the worry in Hannah's eyes and knew if she didn't explain, it would sit like a stone in her consciousness. A flash of irritation rose inside, that prickly feeling she got whenever she knew she needed to do something but didn't really want to. If there was one thing Susie was good at, it was blurting things out, so that's just what she did. "While you were gone after your parents died, I almost got date-raped. Some jerk I met at a bar in Anchorage put God-knows-what in my drink, and I woke up with him tearing my clothes off. Asshole was damn near close to raping me while I was unconscious!" Susie paused for a breath after the words flew out her mouth.

Hannah's eyes widened and teared up. Susie plowed ahead. "Don't worry, I stopped him, but it took a few kicks and scratches. Anyway, right about then, I'd been determined to find the guy to get the albatross of my virginity off my neck, but that pretty much put the brakes on it. It's not like I meant to, just seems like I haven't been interested in anyone, not even a little, since then…and now there's this thing with Jared. Oh my God, I can't believe I told you about Jared." It occurred to her that she was more uncomfortable talking to Hannah about Jared than about almost getting raped. She supposed the upside to that was she obviously wasn't too messed up over it. As for Jared, well that was another matter altogether.

Hannah sat quietly. Susie sighed. The relief she felt at telling Hannah everything was huge. She felt less irritable than she had in weeks.

Hannah eyed her for a long moment. "I'm sorry I wasn't here for you when that happened. I had no idea..."

Susie shook her head. "It's okay. You weren't here—literally. You had a lot more going on after your parents died," Susie replied quickly.

Hannah shook her head slowly. "Maybe I did, but it would have been okay for you to talk to me, to ask for help. I'm sorry you didn't think you could."

Susie felt restless even though she was relieved to have finally said something. What she couldn't quite say out loud was she hated the feeling of helplessness that washed over her whenever she thought about what happened. And she knew she'd been lucky. Aside from being completely freaked out to wake up half out of it with Tim crawling all over her, she hadn't been raped. But she still felt helpless because she couldn't undo the sense of trust that had been wiped out of her in one fell swoop. She glanced out the window of her office, which faced Main Street. Behind the building across the street, Kachemak Bay glittered in the bright sun, the mountains tall and quiet in the distance on the far shore.

Hannah's voice broke into her thoughts. "So if I get this right, some asshole slipped something in your drink, but you woke up in time to get him off of you?"

Susie nodded, tears tight in her throat.

"Is this why you haven't dated anyone since I've been back? I've asked you a few times, but you're pretty good at brushing me off."

Susie thought for a moment, feeling compelled to try to explain better. "It's not like I'm afraid every guy I meet is going to pull something like that, it's just I kind of lost interest after that."

"Except for Jared," Hannah said with a quick grin before she sobered again. "Look, you don't have to talk more about it, but maybe you should talk to someone about what happened. Emma could recommend someone for you."

"I thought about it, but honestly I'm okay. I was totally freaked for a few days, but the worst part didn't happen. I don't have nightmares, I don't think about it much. If it weren't for the fact that I'm still a damn virgin, I probably wouldn't even connect it to anything. It just happened at a bad time and then after that, no one else came along that I was interested in. And here I am now…"

Hannah was quiet for a moment. "Okay. I know as well as anyone that good friends can get you through anything. If you want to talk more…"

Susie interrupted her. "I know. I think what bothered me was I hadn't told you about it. I'm relieved I have now. As for Jared, now I could use some advice there. I can't believe I'm saying this," she said with a sigh, dropping her face in her hands. When she looked up, she knew her cheeks were flaming. "Why, oh why, does he have to be the first guy in too long to make me notice him?" she asked, throwing her hands in the air.

Hannah chuckled. "Because that's how it works. We don't get to pick the ones who are convenient and easy. Plus, I happen to think you and Jared might make a good couple."

Susie's mouth fell open. "You have got to be kidding."

Hannah shook her head. "I'm not. Seriously Susie. You're both smart as hell. You've said it yourself— Jared needs to loosen up. He won't do that with some woman who's all nicey nice. You don't need some guy who's going to cower the minute you get in his face. Jared won't. Even if you bitch about him, you're friends. You respect him and he respects you. And admit it, you think he's handsome as hell," she finished with a grin.

If possible, Susie blushed even harder, but she'd already fessed up about Jared so she didn't shy away. She shrugged sheepishly. "I'd have to be blind not to notice that. But as you've pointed out many times, the whole damn family is good looking," she said with a roll of her eyes. "Have you and the girls been gossiping about this?"

Hannah laughed. "The most we've ever said about it was the other night at Sally's with you right there. We're not blind either. It's plain as day you can't keep your eyes off Jared, and his eyes are glued to you when you're around."

Susie's head whipped up. "They are?"

Hannah's threw her head back, laughing harder now. "Oh yes! He may not be ready to admit it, but he's into you too."

Susie considered telling Hannah about the two kisses she'd shared with Jared, but she wasn't quite ready. "Even if he's into me, he's all about not having a relationship, so it doesn't really matter. I'm telling you, if I wasn't a virgin, I'd go straight to his house tonight and have an amazing one-night stand."

Hannah gave her a hard look. "For starters, why are you so determined it could only be a one night stand? And if that's really all you want, who cares if you're a virgin?"

Though Susie loved Hannah, sometimes she hated

how fast Hannah zeroed in on the questions she'd rather not answer. So, she glared at her.

Hannah threw her hands up. "What? Those are obvious questions."

Susie wrinkled her nose. "Because even though you seem to think Jared and I could be a couple, I don't think it would work. He drives me insane. *Insane*. So if I could just get this little attraction thing out of the way, it will go away. And I don't want him to wonder why I'm a virgin. It's an accident, but he'll probably read all kinds of things into it, and I don't even want to go there. So let's just forget about it. I'm sure this…" she paused and waved her hands "…thing will go away. It has to. I see him all the time, and it's not like I can avoid him."

Hannah lifted her eyebrows, her gaze skeptical. "Well, we agree on one thing. You can't avoid him. As for the rest, I'm not so sure. You're the one who always insists on being honest, so that's all you're going to get from me. How much will you bet on this?"

"Bet on what?" Susie said, her annoyance with Hannah growing by the second.

"That 'this little attraction' isn't going away anytime soon," Hannah said with a wide grin.

Susie grabbed a pen from her desk and threw it at Hannah. "No betting. Now I finally told you about it, that should do the trick. It'll be gone tomorrow."

Hannah's grin stuck as she stood up. Susie could hardly stand it for Hannah to be so confident about Susie and Jared that she wanted to bet on it. She swallowed her annoyance and shook her head at Hannah.

"We'll see. Anyway, I'll call you if I hear any news about Emma and you do the same. K?" Hannah asked.

Susie stood and came around her desk, following Hannah to the door. "Of course."

Hannah turned before she opened the door, her grin gone. "I know you said you're fine, but if you need to talk again, I'm here."

Susie nodded. "I know you are."

Hannah reached over and tugged her into a swift hug before turning to go. Susie watched her drive away before turning to stare at her desk. She couldn't get it out of her head that Hannah thought she and Jared would make a good couple. Since everything that had anything to do with Jared annoyed the hell out of her, this did too. Susie swore and grabbed her purse, stomping out of her office. She had no destination in mind, but she couldn't focus on numbers right now. Not when all she could think about was the way Jared felt against her body, all coiled tension and hard muscles.

CHAPTER 6

"Hey Jared, toss me a towel," Luke called out to him.

Jared grabbed the towel from the back of his chair and swiveled to toss it in Luke's direction.

Luke wiped his face and threw the towel on a nearby bench. He'd just finished helping a customer bring in a king salmon, which had put up quite a fight. They were out on a guided fishing trip with a group of staff from a tech company. The tech company in question had arranged several trips as some sort of morale building activity for their teams. Jared wasn't so sure what he thought about the idea since some of the staff were clearly not too thrilled about fishing.

Jared held the steering wheel loosely in his hands. They'd anchored to fish for a bit earlier and then put trolling lines out for the ride back to the harbor. The day was gorgeous – the sky clear and bright with a soft breeze. The sun struck sparks off the water. The mountains looked lush with the deep green spruce forests coating their flanks. A gull called as it flew by.

"Hey, take a look over there," Nathan said.

Jared turned, his eyes following Nathan's point to a pod of orcas curling across the top of the water in the distance. They were more commonly known as killer whales in most areas, but in Alaska, they were referred to as orcas and were revered among local Alaskan Native tribes. There were a few oohs and ahs among the group. Nathan went into tourist guide mode, explaining there were known resident pods of orcas that frequented the coastal waters in Southcentral Alaska. No matter how many times he saw them, Jared found orcas amazing. They tended to swim in unison, so the entire pod undulated in rhythm across the surface, a flash of black and white followed by the cut of their fin through the water.

As he turned away, he caught the gaze of one of the women in the group. She'd flirted with him off and on all day, accidentally brushing against him, making ridiculous comments about his fishing skills and so on. Normally, Jared would be happy to enjoy a night or two with a tourist. His preference for keeping boundaries clear in relationships, namely that there wouldn't be a relationship, was much easier if the other person didn't even live in town. The woman in question was beautiful—long blond hair, blue eyes and willowy figure. Yet he didn't even feel the slightest attraction to her. Objectively speaking, he could appreciate her. He tried to conjure some interest, but his brain instantly summoned Susie whose luscious curves filled his mind the second he thought of her. His thoughts took his body right back to the other afternoon when he'd kissed her again. What Susie did to his body made him almost lose his mind. Just the thought of her, here now while he was driving a boat filled with people in the middle of the ocean, made his heart race, his breath become shallow and his cock hard.

Jared took a quick gulp of air and forcefully shook his head. He could *not* get a hard-on right now. He glanced over his shoulder. "Hey Luke, you mind driving for a bit?"

Luke looked up from where he was seated on a bench, untangling some fishing line and putting away hooks and other gear. "Nope, not at all." He had a puzzled look on his face, but he quickly got up and came to take the wheel. Jared knew Luke wondered why he was asking since Jared almost always drove, but he wasn't up for explaining. He just needed something to do with his hands to get his mind off of Susie.

Jared immediately picked up what Luke had been doing, relieved at how maddening the tangled lines were. Being forced to pay attention to the minutiae provided a respite from thoughts of Susie, and he managed to get his body under control.

* * *

JARED WALKED down the dock toward the parking lot, the last to leave the boat today. Luke and Nathan had helped the group get their fish ready to be taken over to the Fish Factory for flash freezing and shipping. Jared had stayed behind to tidy up the boat and make sure it was moored properly. It was late afternoon, the sun beginning to arc down from its peak in the sky. A salty breeze blew across the harbor. He paused at the top of the dock to look out beyond the harbor into the bay. He still wondered if he'd ever tire of the view and was fairly certain he wouldn't.

He and his brothers had relocated their commercial fishing business up here from Seattle after a few salmon runs when they'd collectively fallen in love with the area. They'd grown up in Seattle and inherited their father's love of fishing. Diamond Creek had the hustle and bustle of tourist season tempered with peace and quiet in the winter. Jared savored living on the edge of wild. He'd always loved the outdoors. Growing up, he'd thought he would take over his father's aerospace engineering business. Though he started the college track to head in that direction, his father had taken him fishing one afternoon and bluntly told him he didn't want Jared thinking he expected him to take over the business. His father, Matthew, was a relentlessly hard-worker and the success of his business was a source of pride for him.

Matthew and Iris, his mother, were college sweethearts. While Iris supported Matthew in everything he did, she was a schoolteacher and valiantly believed children should try to follow their dreams. Matthew believed the same. He'd given Jared a long, hard look. "You don't love engineering. You'll do it because you think you should. Because you're a good boy like that, always were. Don't. If there's one thing I worry about with you, it's that you take life a tad too seriously. If you don't do something you love, I'm worried you'll get even more serious. Maybe you don't know it yet, but I take one look at you and I know what you should do. It has to be something to do with the ocean. Anytime we're out on the water, I know you're where you need to be. So stop thinking I want you to take over my business. I already have a plan to sell it when the time's right."

Jared had been stunned and relieved. Tears had

pricked behind his eyes when he'd looked back at his father. Matthew had tugged him into a swift hug and then handed him a fishing rod. Not long after that, Jared persuaded Luke and Nathan to start their commercial fishing business in Seattle. After several years of fishing in Alaskan waters and visiting Diamond Creek every time, they decided it made more sense to live here and visit Seattle, rather than the other way around. He hadn't regretted the decision for a minute since. Once they'd gotten settled here, they'd added guided fishing tours to capture the tourist income here and keep them busy between commercial runs. In winters, they plowed snow and laid low.

An eagle lifted from a dock piling where it had been perched, its wings casting a shadow across Jared. He followed its flight across the harbor where it landed on the far side on a spruce tree on the edge of the cliffs that curled around the harbor. He turned and walked to the parking lot. When he entered the lot, the woman who'd been flirting with him most of the day approached him.

"Hey Jared, a couple of us were thinking of heading out for drinks. Didn't know if you'd be interested in joining us," she said. She smiled up at him, her blue eyes blatantly raking over him.

For the life of him, Jared couldn't recall her name at the moment, nor could he summon even the slightest interest in her. He wished he could, as he'd love to find someone to flush his recent obsession with Susie out of his mind. As Luke pointed out, Jared might be happy to keep things casual, but he wasn't an ass. Hence, he couldn't consider going for drinks with a woman whose name he couldn't remember and when he made a feeble attempt to dredge up some attraction, Susie instantly filled his mind. So he smiled and shook his head. He even offered a few suggestions for places they could go and then went on his way.

Driving toward home, he saw Susie walking into the post office. The mere sight of her hijacked his body and next thing he knew, he'd pulled into the parking lot and was walking into the post office. *What the hell are you doing?* His mind had a quick reply. *Checking the mail. I haven't checked it in days.* The other part of his brain chuckled. *Dude, you might check the mail, but that's not why you stopped. Susie is why you stopped.* Jared shook his head abruptly, a flush racing through him when he turned down the aisle where his mailbox was and saw Susie leaning over to tug mail out of hers.

She wore a gray skirt of some kind of soft gauzy fabric that twirled at the hem and hugged her deliciously round bottom. She'd topped this with a bright blue blouse that buttoned only halfway up over a tank top that stretched across her breasts—those breasts that Jared could *not* forget. It was no wonder she hadn't buttoned the blouse because Jared didn't think she could, her breasts filled every inch of it and then some. He didn't know how she pulled it off, but she wore a pair of Xtratuf rubber boots with the skirt. Xtratufs were an Alaskan favorite—relentlessly practical boots that pretty much couldn't be worn out. How Susie managed to wear them with a skirt and not look ridiculous, he didn't know, but somehow it added to her charm.

Jared forced himself to walk past her to check his mail. When he looked up from locking the mailbox,

Susie was leaned against the wall of mailboxes glaring at him.

"Were you going to say hi or just ignore me?"

Jared had to force himself to breathe. It was getting so bad, he was turned on by her being angry with him. And that aggravated him. Just being near her disoriented him so much that it pissed him off. He was a man who was always in control. Except, it seemed, when it came to Susie. She stood there—her wild brown curls all over the place, her eyes locked onto him, and her body...oh dear god that body of hers. What he wanted to do was walk over there, push her against the mailboxes, flip that skirt up and...

Oh my God, stop right there.

He met her bright brown eyes, which were, at the moment, shooting sparks in his direction. "Hey, didn't see you there," he replied.

Susie sighed elaborately. His irritation spiked. She rolled her eyes. "You didn't see me? Seriously Jared? There's no one else over here. It's just you and me. How could you not see me?"

Jared stood there, well aware she had a point. But he wasn't about to explain his thought process to her, especially when he couldn't seem to stop thinking about what it would feel like to have her legs wrapped around him. His eyes wandered to her mouth. She had full, bright pink lips shaped like a perfect bow. Her lips were like the rest of her body, lush and plump. He knew exactly how good they felt against his too. He was beginning to think he'd been possessed.

"Yoo-hoo," Susie said, waving at him.

"I'm here," he tried to focus on her face and rein his body in, annoyed that she noticed he wasn't really paying attention. Which, of course, served to notch his desire higher.

The pattern between them was so set—one of them would say something to set the other off, the other would lash back, and they'd both get irritated. For him, the irritation was flint to his lust for her. All he knew was he wanted her. He wanted to feel her anger because the fire that always flashed in her eyes turned into the passion he knew simmered just under her skin.

Jared was beyond reason at this point. He walked over to stand right in front of her. He felt the rise and fall of her breath. Her eyes darkened. He could see the beat of her pulse in her neck. He didn't hesitate when he reached his hand up to cup her cheek and slide it down along her neck, his thumb coasting over her pulse beat, which sped at his touch.

He waited for her to say something, but she didn't. A brief flash of vulnerability arced through her eyes. And damn if it didn't make him want to tell her he would never hurt her. Because he wouldn't. Ever. She was too much of everything that was good. And he knew her heart was gold. She was a good friend and loyal as they came. He wondered why another man hadn't snatched her up and held her close. As these thoughts passed through his mind, he realized he'd completely lost it because nothing made him think twice at the moment. He, who was determined never to touch another messy relationship, wasn't even pausing when he realized maybe this woman who had him turned inside and out might have some emotional underpinnings he hadn't considered.

He traced her collarbone, dipping down to follow the curve of her tank top. Her breasts rose and fell with her breath. He couldn't keep his eyes from falling to soak in the sight of her breasts, literally straining against the taut white cotton of her tank top. He almost salivated. His cock was rock hard. Her breath hitched. His eyes whipped up to see her tongue dart out to lick her lips. The reins on what little control he had were broken.

Jared leaned forward and kissed her. He tried to start slow, he really did, but this was Susie and she'd burrowed into his brain and body like no one else. Not to mention, she threw herself into everything and kissing was no exception. The moment his lips met hers, hers opened on a sigh and he delved into her mouth. She tasted amazing, honey with a hint of mint. And damn if she couldn't drive him wild with a kiss. Their tongues tangled. He tore his lips away, feathering them down her neck and across the tops of her breasts. He pressed into her, savoring her gasp when he shifted so his shaft nestled at the apex of her legs. He couldn't help himself and tugged her tank top down to find what passed for a bra, lacy and white, barely holding her breasts in. He leaned forward and laved one nipple and then the other through the lace. She gasped and shifted restlessly against him. He curled a hand under her knee to lift her leg so he could press even closer into her when he heard voices approaching them.

He'd completely forgotten where they were. The post office was one of the central places in town. Though it wasn't always busy, there was almost always someone there. He forced himself to focus and rapidly moved back, tugging her tank top up, regretting he had to stop. Susie's eyes were hazy and startled at once. She remained where she was, leaning against the mailboxes. The voices that had broken through the fog of Jared's sheer lust turned down the aisle before the one where they stood. He breathed a sigh of relief and glanced over at Susie. He didn't know how to read her expression. His best guess would be to call it guarded. Which was so unlike her, it worried him. He wanted to ask how she was, but sensed now might not be the time. But he wasn't going to simply walk away and pretend like *this* hadn't happened.

He cleared his throat. She looked up at him, her lips swollen from his kiss, making him want to kiss her again. Instead, he asked, "How about you come over to my place for dinner?"

He hadn't really thought through what he was going to say, but he knew they needed to talk and it needed to be somewhere they wouldn't get interrupted. Between the two of them, they couldn't go somewhere public without tons of interruptions, so his house seemed a safe bet.

Susie held his eyes for a long moment and finally nodded. She started to turn away, and he placed his hand on her arm. "Look, I don't know what to say right this second, but I figure we'd better try to talk."

Susie looked at his hand and then up at him. She wrinkled her nose. "I know. It seems like this…" she waved between them "…keeps happening. It's not exactly convenient," she said with a soft laugh, a blush staining her cheeks.

Though he still seemed to be momentarily possessed and downright unbothered by his raging, out-of-control attraction for her, he could agree it wasn't convenient. He nodded with a chuckle. "Maybe not. So, my place around six?"

"Should I bring anything?"

He shrugged. "Don't know. Hadn't really thought about it. I have fresh silver salmon from today. How about you bring whatever you'd like to go with that?"

Susie nodded, her curls bouncing. They turned to walk out together. Jared had to resist the urge to reach for her hand. Though he'd lost his mind, he had enough sense to know they were nowhere near hand holding.

* * *

SUSIE FILLED Jasmine's food bowl and made sure she had fresh water. Jasmine twined around her ankles, purring audibly. Susie walked to the couch and plunked down with a sigh. Her pulse pounded and the butterflies in her belly just wouldn't quit. Ever since she'd walked out of the post office, she hadn't been able to get settled inside. Jared had taken her by surprise. She looked out her front windows hoping the view would soothe her. Wispy clouds drifted across the sky. The mountains were as they usually were—quiet, still, and majestic. Dappled sunlight fell on their green flanks. She took a deep breath and wondered what the hell she'd been thinking when she agreed to meet Jared for dinner at his place.

She was beginning to realize that her flawed idea of a one-night stand to rinse him out of her system might be utter nonsense. They were on kiss number three now, each one ratcheting up the depth of her desire. She'd felt like a panting puppy when she walked out of the post office with him. She'd had to hold herself back from reaching for his hand. Jasmine leapt up beside her and immediately nestled against her. Susie stroked through Jasmine's thick gray fur and contemplated texting Jared to cancel. A night at home with Jasmine curled by her side looked appealing about now. She was terrified at whatever was happening with Jared. The feeling between them seemed to have a life of its own. She couldn't control herself with him. The second he touched her, she was lost. No man had ever made her feel so out of control. She was in over her head and needed to get out. She went so far as to pick up her phone before setting it down. She wasn't a coward, and she wouldn't back out. If only she could get her heart rate under control.

Get it together. You are not a coward, you can do this. You'll go over there and talk. You'll nip this in the bud and that'll be it.

The clock on her wall, a whimsical star-shaped clock fashioned of metal twisted into a curly star and painted bright yellow, told her it was almost six. One more stroke for Jasmine, and Susie stood to go. She left a lamp on for Jasmine and walked to her car, carrying a bag with salad fixings. A cluster of lilac trees weighted the air with their scent. As she drove down the hill the few minutes to Jared's house, she repeated the same thing over and over. *This'll be easy. Just tell him the touching and kissing has to stop. All we have to do is keep our hands to ourselves. Oh and don't make a fool of yourself.*

CHAPTER 7

Susie knew where Jared had moved after he moved out of the home he'd originally shared with his brothers, but she'd never been inside. When Tess moved to Diamond Creek to be with Nathan, Jared had insisted Nathan stay at the house. Susie, along with a few other friends, had helped move Tess into the house and Jared out of it. Her contribution for Jared had been merely to unload boxes onto the deck and drive away. When she pulled up at the small house, she glanced around. As with just about everyone in Diamond Creek, he had a breathtaking view. The small cabin was built into the hill that faced Kachemak Bay with the view tumbling wide open behind it. As she stepped onto the deck, she heard her name and followed Jared's voice. The deck wrapped around the house. She found him on the back portion of the deck, beer in hand while he turned salmon steaks in a pan of marinade by the grill.

Her breath caught in her throat and her pulse, which hadn't really slowed to normal since Jared kissed her in the post office, ricocheted to high speed. His black curls were damp. His piercing green gaze locked onto her, and she couldn't look away. He wore a pair of faded jeans that fit like a glove, molding to his lean body. A faded blue t-shirt hugged his torso. His teeth flashed in a grin.

"So you made it," he said, a question in his tone.

As usual, he instantly set her on edge. The fact that she couldn't get her body under control only increased her irritation. *Hands to yourself, hands to yourself...*

"Of course I made it. Did you think I wouldn't?"

Those ridiculously gorgeous eyes of his crinkled at the corners when his smile widened. He shrugged. "I wasn't sure. But I figured you'd be polite enough to call if you decided to back out."

Damn if he didn't make her want to argue. "But why would you think I wouldn't come? I said I would." She wasn't about to admit she had actually considered texting him to cancel.

Jared's easy grin tightened, and she experienced a flash of satisfaction. She was curiously pleased that he wasn't immune to her irritation.

He sighed and shifted his shoulders. "I wasn't sure because..." he paused, his eyes darkening as he gaze traveled over her. She hadn't even thought to change her clothes and still wore her gauzy gray skirt, bright blue blouse and tank top. She had ditched her boots for a pair of strappy sandals at the last minute. His gaze heated her head to toe. By the time his eyes reached hers again, she knew she was visibly flushed. She was on the verge of needing to fan herself.

She lifted her chin and attempted to take the attention away from her. "You were saying?"

Jared didn't miss a beat. "I wasn't sure because we can't seem to keep our hands off of each other recently. I have to admit it kind of took me by surprise, but I've decided we just need to talk it out of our systems and clear the air." He set his beer on the deck railing and gave her an expectant look.

Susie prided herself on being blunt and direct, but for the life of her, she didn't know what to say. He seemed to think they'd just talk and it would go away. *Isn't that what you thought?* A corner of her mind mocked her while the rest of her couldn't think sensibly. If she spoke the truth, she would have to tell him he was driving her mad and she wanted him more than she'd wanted anyone. For a split second, she considering proposing her one-night stand plan, but she immediately shot the idea down because it required dealing with her inconvenient virginity. She finally decided she couldn't be a coward and met his eyes. She didn't know what she expected, but it wasn't understanding and a glimmer of concern. Which kind of made her want to slap him because it only made her feel more vulnerable. Her mantra about not making a fool of herself had been rendered completely useless.

Her pulse was flat out of control at this point and her sanity almost gone. With her emotions bouncing around and the sheer lust that seemed to take over the minute he was near, she couldn't think straight. Before she knew what was happening, she walked over to him intending to slap him—seriously—but when she got in front of him and started to open her mouth, he kissed her. Again!

Her anger dissolved into burning need. In seconds, she was on fire. The kiss started fast and furious, Jared stroking into her mouth without hesitation. Several breath-stealing moments later, he gentled his lips, tracing her mouth with his tongue, dusting soft kisses across her face and down her neck. By the time his lips met hers again, she was practically a puddle. His slow kisses seared her through.

A raven called nearby, a burst of magpie chatter following. The sounds broke through the trance she'd fallen into, and she pulled away. She gulped for air and stumbled back unsteadily, bracing her hands on the deck railing. Flushed, she looked out toward the bay. The cool air was a balm to the heat coursing through her. She didn't know what to say or do. She fought the urge to flee. The effect he had on her was mortifying. This was Jared for God's sake. Susie had no idea what Hannah was thinking when she said she thought they'd make a good couple. While Susie wouldn't argue for a second that there was passion between them—it was its own living, breathing force —Jared was so tidy and organized and calm and steady. Basically, everything she wasn't. They'd drive each other crazy and not the good kind of crazy.

Jared's voice interrupted her thoughts. "So that kind of got out of hand," he said wryly.

She looked up and met his eyes, her face burning. She was relieved to see he was flushed as well. He reached for his beer again, a slight tremor in his hand.

His gaze didn't waver. When she didn't say anything, he spoke again. "I don't know what it is with us these days. I'm not sure what I was thinking when I said we should try to talk about it because I have no idea what to say. I get near you and..." he paused and took a deep breath "...I kind of forget everything else."

Before an actual thought formed, she blurted out. "I say we try a one-night stand and see if that gets it out of our systems."

As soon as the words left her mouth, she couldn't believe it, but she didn't really want to take them back. She quickly rationalized he somehow wouldn't notice she was a virgin. And what better way to lose her virginity—with a man who got her so hot and bothered it would be guaranteed amazing.

Jared's eyes widened at her suggestion, and he was silent for a long moment. "What if it doesn't work?"

"It'll work," she replied with far more confidence than she felt. She'd decided that now she'd started down this path, she'd brazen her way through it.

Jared eyed her skeptically. "You seem pretty confident. I'd like to say I agree, but I'm not so sure. And here's the thing: you're my friend, I respect you. I can't treat you like a fling. Trust me, if I thought we could just go for it and have one fun night in the sheets, I'd be dragging you upstairs right now. But our kisses don't seem to point in that direction."

Susie flushed and realized her inexperience might show if she argued the point too much. And did he have to go and give her a vision of being tugged upstairs to his bed? She hadn't even seen his bedroom and now she wanted to just get right to it. Instead, she nodded. "Right. Maybe not. In that case, I don't know what to say. I mean, we can't be 'we.' I would drive you insane and not in the good way."

Jared was quiet for another long moment, which made her restless. She wanted him to agree quickly and then they'd decide to somehow ignore this raging lust between them. He met her eyes and she wanted to cry. He looked serious and like he actually cared. His shoulders rose and fell in a deep breath.

"Well, we seem to drive each other insane in the good way," he said with a wry smile.

Susie burst out laughing. It was so ridiculous they were trying to rationally discuss what to do about the fact that they couldn't stop kissing each other.

Jared chuckled and set his beer on the railing again before stepping to the grill. "How about we try to eat?"

She nodded, relieved to let the topic drop for now. Jared gave her a brief tour of his home, which was essentially a living room and kitchen area with a bathroom downstairs. He didn't take her upstairs to the loft area, which must hold his bed, though Susie couldn't see far enough beyond the railing to know. He got her set up in the kitchen where she prepped the salad while he went back onto the deck to grill salmon. The focus of something to do took her mind off the constant buzz of her attraction to Jared.

Somehow, they managed to behave like normal people for a little while. Susie thought maybe, just maybe, she'd gotten a handle on herself. Though it would have been lovely to eat on the deck, the mosquitos drove them inside. Somewhere between the salmon and her third glass of wine, she realized she was arguing with him over a spreadsheet. She'd handled the accounting for Jared and his brothers ever since they'd moved here, so she was quite accustomed to how precise Jared could be. In this case, he'd asked her if she could revise the reporting columns for expenses. She'd done exactly as he'd asked. But now, he wanted her to modify it again. Illuminating for her precisely why he drove her crazy—the not-good crazy. This is why they would never work.

She blew a curl out of her eyes. "Seriously? Again, Jared? I did exactly what you wanted. I even have the email trail to prove it."

Jared slanted his eyes at her. "I didn't say you didn't do what I asked. I said I reconsidered how I wanted the data organized."

"Oh. My. God. Do you do this to yourself too? Like rearrange how you organize the bathroom every other week?"

Jared glared at her. "You're an accountant. You should understand how important it is to like how you're looking at the numbers."

Susie felt a swell of joy. Jared finally looked annoyed with her, and she reveled in it. This—his eyes narrowed, a telltale tick of his jaw muscle—was how she preferred Jared. She knew how to deal with this. It gave her something to focus on other than how much her body wanted him.

"Of course I know how important it is, but you go overboard. Way overboard."

Jared looked away. After a long silence, he pushed his chair back. The scrape of the chair on the hardwood floor was loud in the quiet room. He silently gathered up their plates and carried them into the kitchen. "It's your prerogative to say I go overboard, but if it bothers you that much to change the spreadsheet again, I'll do it myself."

He set the dishes in the sink and turned to look at her, his green eyes bright in the fading light. In a flash, the desire she'd convinced herself was in hand flared again. She stood quickly, carrying her now empty wine glass to the kitchen. "Whatever. You don't have to do it. I will. It's my job. I was just pointing out your tendency to be…I don't know…too organized."

She set her glass by the sink and took a step back.

"Too organized, huh?"

Susie looked up and realized she might have miscalculated Jared's level of annoyance. His eyes were dark, his green gaze zeroed in on her, his intense, coiled energy coming off in waves. She took another step back, her hips bumping into the counter.

A heated silence wove around them. As he held her gaze for a moment, the air around them felt heavy —with unspoken and unexpressed want. His energy was potent. He shook his head. "Can't help myself," he said abruptly before closing the space between them in one quick stride.

His lips came against hers softly, but with such intensity it stole her breath. When she gasped against his lips, he pulled back a fraction. She opened her eyes to a haze of green. He searched her eyes for a breathless moment. Her pulse careened. She couldn't look away. His eyes fell closed, hers following, as his lips met hers again. He traced the shape of her mouth with his tongue. She was helpless to stop her mouth from opening to his. She wanted this *so* much, she couldn't stop.

Susie simply let go into the moment. She batted away the reflexive thought that she should stop this. Their tongues tangled while one of Jared's hands slid down her back to cup her bottom and tug her close. He brushed her curls back with his other hand, tracing her ear and sending delicious shivers down her neck. Heat built inside of her rapidly, flushing her inside and out. His lips followed a path down her neck, dipping between her breasts. He shoved her blouse off her shoulders.

She couldn't seem to get close enough. The feel of his body through the thin cotton of his t-shirt made her impatient. She slipped her hands underneath, sighing at the feel of his warm skin under her hands. His knee slid between her legs, the rough denim against the silk of her panties unbearably arousing. Her hips moved of their own accord, sharp spikes of pleasure arcing through her. She gasped when he rolled her nipple between his fingers.

His hand stilled. The haze that had overtaken her made it hard to focus, but she somehow opened her eyes. Meeting his merely ratcheted the heat inside— the intensity of his green gaze took her breath away.

He started to speak, but a mere rasp came out. He cleared his throat. "If we're stopping, we need to stop now," he said bluntly. He didn't move away. She felt the heat of his erection cradled against her hips. Need coursed through her. The last thing she wanted to do was stop. She glanced down. His hand rested on her breast, his thumb idly stroking her nipple through her tank top. Her nipple was practically begging for more, pert and tight in its bid for attention.

She looked back up into his eyes—stark desire reflecting back at her. Though she knew it wasn't sensible and probably completely insane, she simply didn't care anymore She wanted Jared with a force she couldn't deny. She shook her head.

Jared gave her a pained look. "Is that a no—we're not stopping, or a no—we're not doing this?"

"Not stopping," she whispered, a flush washing across her face.

Holding her eyes, he cupped her cheek and slid his hand slowly down the side of her neck, his thumb brushing across her pulse. He kissed her again, and she melted inside. She frantically pushed closer to him, tugging at his shirt. He pulled away and grabbed her hand.

"This way," he said.

Next thing she knew, they were in the loft. Just beyond the railing that could be seen from below lay his bedroom and a bathroom to one side. Unsurprisingly, the room was sleek and modern looking with basic black furniture and brushed steel accents. There were gobs of pillows on the bed, which surprised her. He moved quickly, tugging his t-shirt off and tossing it on the floor. Susie scarcely had time to admire the view of his bare chest, muscled and fit with a dusting of dark hair, before he advanced on her. She'd come to a stop by the edge of the bed. Somehow, she found herself seated on the bed looking down at Jared's black curls while he knelt in front of her, efficiently unbuckling the flimsy straps of her sandals and removing them. He paused to place a kiss on the inside of her knee, dallying with soft kisses to both of her legs for a moment, his warm palms sliding up her legs. Her fingers tangled in his curls. Moisture built in her core, and she felt herself spiraling. She experienced a flash of panic, that fear of being out of control, but before she could react, he'd pushed himself up and kissed her. Losing herself in his kiss, the panic receded.

Though she knew without a doubt her sheer burning want for him was a force to reckon with, she hadn't considered the benefits of Jared's relentless attention to detail and how such attention would drive her to a point of arousal beyond her control. He pressed her back into the lush pile of pillows on his bed and proceeded to lavish every inch of her—patiently and thoroughly. He traced her collarbone with his tongue while he slowly peeled her tank top off. With no hesitation, he flicked his fingers under the clasp holding her bra together. When the lace cups fell to the side, a small sound came from his throat. She managed to drag her eyes open to find his trained on her breasts. In slow motion, he leaned forward and set his thorough tongue to work, tracing circles around her nipples and softly nipping before his lips finally closed over one. She arched into his mouth, tangling her hand in his curls.

One of his hands slid down her abdomen, caressing its curve, coasting over the thin fabric of her skirt and sliding between her thighs to cup her mound. He didn't push her skirt out of the way, just held his hand still and firm over her. Liquid pooled inside and feverish want built higher. She shifted restlessly against him. She wanted to feel him against her. He still wore his jeans, and it felt as if there was far too much between them. When she reached for his zipper, he stopped her.

"Not yet."

A flash of anger rose. "Yes, yet," she replied.

He silenced her with his mouth, finally rolling atop her, giving her just enough of what she craved to ease the ache. The feel of his chest against her breasts was intoxicating. He rocked his hips into hers, the feel of his hard cock against the ache between her legs overwhelming. She bucked against him. He muttered an imprecation against her lips and moved swiftly, shoving off of the bed and tugging his jeans off. His boxers followed in quick succession. Susie barely had a chance to appreciate the sight of him fully naked and aroused before he was tugging at her skirt. She lifted her hips and shimmied out of it, leaving her in nothing but the tiny scrap of black silk that passed for panties. For a moment, she felt far more vulnerable than she wanted when he paused to look at her, his eyes darkening as they traveled down her body. She wasn't thin, nowhere near. She was curves and more curves. He knelt on the bed with one knee, his fingertips tracing her breasts and along the curve of her belly and hip.

He met her eyes for a long moment, and she prayed he couldn't sense the flicker of apprehension. Oh she didn't want to stop. They were too far in for that. And she wanted him with a ferocity that left her shaken. But she couldn't quite forget she was about to lose the one thing she'd accidentally hung onto. She hoped again he wouldn't notice. Before she could think too much, Jared shifted and began kissing his way up her body, starting at her ankles.

Passion flushed through her, her skin dampening in its sheen. His hands were everywhere at once, his lips making mischief all over her body. He paused when his lips coasted across her abdomen, quivers and shivers following every touch, and slowly pressed her knees apart, hooking a finger on the edge of her panties and dragging them off. She was dripping with need, almost incoherent, when he slid a finger inside her slick channel. She arched into him, the pressure inside building. Another finger followed. He established a slow rhythm, toying with her, plunging in and out, softly stroking across her clit.

"Jared..." she gasped.

"Yes?" he questioned, a little more in control than she wanted to hear.

So beyond control was she that she didn't even care. She just begged. "Please..."

Suddenly, his mouth joined his fingers, his tongue laving her clit while his fingers pumped in and out. She came in waves, convulsing around his hand. His mouth slowly stilled along with his hand, his lips moving to trace their way up her body. She tasted herself on his lips when he brought his to hers in another searing kiss. The utter decadence of having all of his body against hers was beyond incredible. She finally got to run her hands across his chest, stroke his muscled back and curl her hand around his cock—its warm velvet length pulsing in her grasp. He proceeded to recalibrate her yearning again. From the echoes of her orgasm, another began to build as he toyed with her with his fingers again, this time with soft strokes, the barest of touches, driving her close to her peak, but not allowing her to tumble over.

Jared paused to stretch across her, tugging open the drawer of a night table. Susie was so deep into the haze of desire, her mind didn't register the sound of the condom wrapper tearing. Suddenly, he was on top of her again, his elbows bracketing her head. The tip of his cock rested against her channel. The desperate need to have him inside of her was something she'd never experienced. Because while she may have been a virgin, she'd had plenty of foreplay. And she'd *never* been overcome like this, where the ache to reach completion was a throbbing instinct. His green gaze was a blur. He held her eyes for a long moment before bringing his lips to hers just as he arched his hips and slid inside of her with a swift surge.

Pain sliced through her and every muscle in her body tensed. She tried to breathe through it. He froze completely and lifted his lips from hers. She tried to school her expression to blank, but she didn't have time. He swore savagely and started to pull back.

"No!" she slid her hands down his back and held him against her.

"You could have mentioned you were a virgin," he said, his voice low and threaded with anger.

"It doesn't matter," she said defiantly. "Plus, it's too late now."

"Oh it's definitely too late," he said flatly.

Though his anger was clear, Susie wasn't sure if he was angry with her, himself, the situation, or all of the above. But even in his anger, he stayed firm inside of her, so she knew he hadn't lost his desire. She didn't want to explain, but she knew she had to say something.

"It wasn't like I was saving myself. It just kind of… happened. Don't think I'm going to be all gaga because you ended up being the one I lost it with. It just happened that way."

As she spoke, the pain was finally receding. She shifted her hips subtly to ease the pressure. Jared closed his eyes and took a slow breath, appearing to attempt to keep himself under control. He might not want to admit it, but she felt his hips move in reflex when she did. The tiny motion set sparks of pleasure alight in her again. Keeping one hand firmly against his muscled back, she slipped the other up and around the back of his neck, pulling his lips to her.

"Don't be a coward and back out on me now," she whispered against his lips.

"I'm not a coward, but we *will* talk about this later," he replied.

Susie tugged him closer and kissed him, hoping it would shut him up. Passion filtered around them again. Jared began to move in increments. Twinges of pain lingered, but slowly faded. He settled into their kiss, once again demonstrating his sheer mastery of the act. By the time his lips left hers to trace a heated path down her neck, she was gasping. He kept mostly still inside of her while his fingertips traced her breasts softly, making her desperate for the touch of his lips. Heat built in her core. Slick as she already was, she felt herself getting wetter as his lips finally closed over one of her nipples. He patiently laved and nipped both nipples, bringing her to the point that her head tossed on the pillows and her hips shifted restlessly against him.

She gasped his name and bucked against him. The pain completely gone now, she was feverish with want to achieve release. He slowly made his way back up her neck, cupping her cheek with one hand, his forehead falling against hers. Finally, finally, he began to slide in and out. She almost sobbed in relief. The feeling of him inside of her was so intense, she could hardly bear it. The contrast of his hardness to her softness—his cock inside of her, his chest against her breasts—made her almost delirious.

Jared had been mostly quiet, his responses physical rather than audible. But when he pulled almost all the way out and stroked in deeply… "Oh my God… Susie…" he rasped, his voice slurred. Through the haze of desire snaked around them, she arched against him, her legs curling around his hips, and pulled him deeper into her. He slipped a hand between them, his thumb stroking across her clit, and she shattered, convulsing around him. He drove deep in a final surge. She felt his climax as he pulsed inside of her before collapsing against her.

CHAPTER 8

*J*ared fell against Susie's lush body, barely able to catch his breath. After a long moment, he shifted so his weight didn't crush her, immediately missing the feel of her full breasts against his chest. He made do by dragging a hand down to curl under one of her breasts. The soft glow from a lamp he'd flicked on when they got upstairs glimmered against her damp skin. As the pulses of his orgasm faded, he found he didn't want to move away from her. The tight glove of her channel was better than anything he'd ever felt, but then he'd never been with a virgin. When he was younger, the last thing he'd wanted was to bear the burden of being someone's first. Too much pressure. So he'd dated older girls. His mind was still reeling from the fact that she was a virgin—*was* being the operative word now.

Her breath was slowing. He snuck a glance at her. Her eyes were still closed, which gave him a moment to observe her unguarded. Her brown curls were a riot on the pillows. Her lips were swollen from his kisses. He knew her body better by feel than sight, so he savored the view—her breasts were full, the soft pink of her nipples an unholy temptation, her rounded belly and hips were heaven. He didn't want to pull away, but knew he needed to. Though he was no expert, he knew she'd be sore. He'd tried to keep his pace slow and measured, but he'd lost all sense of control toward the end. That was a first for him.

He closed his eyes and took a slow breath. He'd been furious with her when he'd felt her arch in pain against him. She was so tight, tighter than he'd ever felt. He'd known in that instant she'd been a virgin and hadn't bothered to tell him. This, after she casually tossed out that they should have a one-night stand to get this out of their systems. As he'd predicted, he didn't think it would be so simple. Because if his body had anything to say about it, he could go for another round right now. He slowly shifted his hips to withdraw from her and roll away. He tossed his condom in the tiny wastebasket on the far side of his night table. When he rolled back over, he saw blood smeared on her thighs. Though his mind thought he should be angry, he wasn't. Oddly enough, he believed the gist of her explanation. She wasn't one to hold onto her virginity out of prudishness. Though he sensed there might be a bit more to the story, he wasn't up for pushing the topic just now.

Susie's eyes opened, and she rolled her head to the side. Damn if he didn't want to curl up against her and start all over. For once, her eyes weren't sharp and knowing. They were warm, brown and sated, and he simply wanted to tumble right back where they'd been. Susie with her defenses down was passionate beyond measure. If he'd thought about it, he could have guessed that. She felt things strongly—good and bad. That oomph was nothing but amazing when it came to sex.

With a shake of his head, he stood and strode into the bathroom adjacent to his bedroom. He returned to the bed with a warm washcloth in hand and carefully wiped the blood from her. She was quiet, a blush washing over her entire body. He tossed the washcloth in the sink. He paused to look outside. The sun had almost dropped out of view, a curve of red and gold crested the mountains. The light had faded, cool air blew in through the windows. He turned to the bed and gave a quick tug on the lightweight down quilt, yanking it from under her. She squeaked and glared at him.

"Hey!"

He chuckled. "Hey yourself. It's getting cool. If we don't get under the covers soon, you'll wish we had," he replied matter-of-factly as he climbed into bed beside her and tossed the quilt across them both. Warm summer days in Alaska quickly turned to cool evenings and even cooler nights. Jared liked fresh air, so he kept his windows open almost constantly in the summer.

He didn't want to think—at all. Because if he thought too much, it wouldn't help matters. Matters like the fact that he didn't even consider whether she'd stay the night, and the fact that he'd just had the most amazing sex of his life with a woman who drove him out of his mind. His penchant for control was lost at the moment. Instead, he curled against Susie, tucking her into his side, savoring the feel of her soft skin and curves.

"Jared?"

"Mmmhmm?"

"You said we had to talk."

"Changed my mind. We can talk later," he replied, not wanting to wonder if they'd just ruined a pretty good friendship and not wanting to even think about what it meant that he'd been the first for her. All in all, it was too much to consider when he'd rather lose himself in how good she felt. He promised himself he'd keep it under control, but he couldn't stop his hand from wandering over her body, savoring her softness and lush curves. He heard her breath start to slow and become even. He followed her into sleep with his hand curled around one of her breasts.

* * *

EARLY THE NEXT MORNING, Jared woke with Susie curled against him. Upon waking, he was already hard. Since he'd given up thinking he could control his body around her, he chuckled. He had a moment of consideration when he attempted to talk himself out of making love to her again, but he rationalized since they'd already blown through that barrier, no sense in not enjoying at least one more time before he had to face whatever it was he had to face because of this.

So he set himself to feast on her body. He heard her gasp when his mouth closed over one of her nipples and grinned against her skin. He knew she wouldn't admit it, just as he wouldn't to her, but he loved that he could make her lose control. She shifted at his side, her fingers curling in his hair. He kept moving, licking and kissing his way down her belly.

He slipped his hands around her hips, savoring their fullness. He slid one finger inside her channel, smiling with satisfaction at the slick moisture. She gasped his name. He'd never given a damn if women called him by name, but with Susie—oh dear God, it was gratifying. So he slid another finger in, testing her. She didn't flinch, only raised her hips to press into his hand. He set to work, bringing his mouth to join his hand, savoring the salty taste and sheer pleasure of watching her fall apart. Only after he'd brought her to orgasm once and to the brink several times did he slide up her body. Her eyes were wild—dark with passion and intent. She tugged him close and kissed him, like only she could, her tongue tangling wildly, nipping at his lips.

He was so lost, he almost forgot to put a condom on, but remembered just as he was about to shift his hips. He swore as he rolled to the side and fumbled in his nightstand, quickly putting the condom on. He forced himself to go slowly, concerned she might be sore. If she was, he couldn't tell. As he slid inside her, he felt almost drunk from how good it felt. Her velvet channel hugged his cock, clenching around its length. She curled her legs around his hips, urging him on. He bracketed her face between his elbows, keeping his weight off of her, but savoring the feel of her breasts against his chest as he stroked in and out of her. Her head tossed and he felt the pulses of her orgasm begin. He plunged into her heat, driving deeply, and felt his own release roll through him. He opened his eyes to find hers looking up. A flash of feeling washed through him, and he wanted to tell her it would be okay, but he didn't. Somehow, if they were just physical, he could keep himself from thinking too hard. He kissed her and shifted to the side. The only sound was their labored breathing, which slowed in unison.

Eventually, Jared pulled out of her and rose. In silence, she followed him out of bed. He didn't know why, but he couldn't find words. The intimacy woven around them was disconcerting. He thought perhaps he should say something, but silence was a refuge from how shaken he was by what had passed between them since last night. He ushered her into the shower and followed her in. They showered, not a word spoken between them. Downstairs, when they were both dressed, he finally spoke.

"Do you want breakfast?"

Susie shook her head, her curls bouncing. "I have to get home and let Jasmine out. I, uh, guess I'll see you when I see you."

He looked over at her, feeling uncertain and with no idea what to say. So he nodded. Susie turned to leave, and he followed her out onto the deck in front. Just as she started to walk down the stairs, he spoke.

"I guess maybe we should try to talk sometime soon."

Susie looked up. Her eyes were uncertain and vulnerable, and his heart clenched.

"Probably. How about we call it a day for now?" she asked.

"Sure. I'll, uh, give you a call soon," he replied, thinking he sounded like an idiot and feeling out of control. The calm, steady control he relied on was out of his grasp.

She nodded and briskly walked to her car. With a quick wave, she was gone.

* * *

JARED WENT THROUGH MOST of the day completely out of sorts. He couldn't stop thinking about Susie, which pissed him off. He'd gotten pretty comfortable with his situation of no serious involvement. It meant he didn't have to worry about someone else's feelings, or his own. In an effort to get her out of his mind, he went for a grueling run on one of the more difficult trails that carried him from sea level to nine thousand feet up and back down a mountainside. Utter fail on wiping Susie from his thoughts.

Next, he busied himself with a trip to the harbor to make a few boat repairs, and clean and organize gear. The sun was high in the sky, and it was approaching hot while he worked. He was glad for the break when Nathan stopped by to pick up a few things for storage.

"Hey man, how's it going?" Nathan asked as he stepped over the side of the boat, immediately flinging himself on a bench and lounging. As the youngest of the three brothers, Nathan excelled at making it seem like he wasn't doing anything. Jared knew the opposite to be true. Nathan was a tireless worker and rarely complained.

Jared sat across from him and tugged his work gloves off. He wiped his forehead on his sleeve and caught the water bottle Nathan tossed his way. "Thanks," he said before taking several swallows. "Going okay. How about you?"

"Good. Always good," Nathan replied with a grin.

"That's all you ever say since Tess moved up here." Jared experienced a flash of envy at how easily Nathan had settled into love and marriage. Nathan's relationship with Tess appeared uncomplicated and clearly made him happy. Jared wondered why it couldn't be like that for him with Susie and promptly wondered what the hell he was thinking.

Nathan's grin widened and he shrugged. "Yup. She's the best thing that ever happened to me. Seriously man. You should reconsider this whole ban on relationships you have. No sense to it, and you're missing out."

Susie flashed through Jared's mind again. For just a moment, he wondered what it would be like to wake up with her everyday. He swatted the thought away. "I never said I had a ban on relationships," he replied, cringing internally when he heard the defensiveness in his tone. "I only said relationships were messy."

Nathan grinned and nodded. "And the right mess is worth every minute. That's the part you gotta figure out. With the right person, it's all worth it."

"Won't argue with you there. Between you and Luke, that's pretty obvious. Not so sure for myself."

Nathan tilted his head, his grin fading. "Okay, I know I'm your baby brother so you don't have to listen to me. But maybe you should expand your horizons and open the door to the idea that it could work."

A flash of irritation rose in Jared. He tamped it down. "Expand my horizons?"

Nathan rolled his eyes. "Dude, you don't even look at anyone unless it's obvious they are totally cool with nothing more than a roll between the sheets. Any of those women who give off even the mildest vibe they might want more than that—you don't even consider. That's what I mean. Stop ruling people out. That's all."

Jared forced himself not to snap at Nathan. "Got it. How about we agree I'll try to 'expand my horizons,' but you back off and realize it might not be that easy?"

Nathan grinned and nodded. "Whatever you say. I didn't come here to lecture you. Let's get started."

In short order, they'd carried several loads of gear to Nathan's truck for cleaning and storage, and Jared started the drive home. As he drove through town, he found himself pulling into the parking lot at Susie's tiny office. An unfamiliar truck was parked there. Jared immediately wondered who it was and realized he was being ridiculous. It wasn't as if he and his brothers were her only clients. Walking into the office, he found Susie seated at her desk, focused on paperwork in front of her while a man Jared had never seen sat on the edge of the desk, looking way too comfortable. Before Susie looked up, she laughed at something the man said, which infuriated Jared.

"Hey there," Jared said.

Susie's head whipped up. She swiped a few loose curls out of her eyes, a flush staining her cheeks. "Hi. I didn't know you were stopping by," she said, her words measured.

The man remained seated on the edge of her desk and gave a small wave of greeting to Jared. "Dan Cantwell here, dropping by to discuss our accounts with Susie."

Jared nodded tightly. *Get a grip. You cannot be jealous of some random guy in Susie's office.* Incredulous didn't quite capture how he felt. He realized he hadn't replied and forced himself to speak.

"Jared Winters," he said with a nod toward Dan. "Do you, uh, live around here? Don't think I've seen you around before." He knew it was ridiculous that he had to know, but this guy was more comfortable than he wanted any man being with Susie. He wondered if he'd truly lost his mind. He knew before it even happened that it would be a mistake to let his attraction to Susie get out of hand. It had officially gotten out of hand. Here he was, attempting to clarify just who the hell this guy was so casually sitting on Susie's desk. He knew damn well it wasn't someone she was having sex with because before last night, she'd been a virgin.

Dan, oblivious to Jared's mental gymnastics, shook his head. "Nah. My wife and I live down the road in Homer. But I work on the North Slope, so I drive through Diamond Creek every other week. Susie's the best accountant around, it's worth a stop," Dan replied with a grin.

The North Slope was shorthand for working on the Alaska pipeline. The money made the travel worth it, so many people traveled up for two weeks of work and returned home in between. Jared could care less where Dan worked, but he was relieved, and simultaneously annoyed with himself for being relieved, to learn that Dan was married.

He nodded and forced himself to make casual conversation. "Susie's definitely the best accountant around. Speaking of..." he glanced at Susie. Her expression was guarded. "Have you had a chance to tweak that spreadsheet?" As soon as the question left his mouth, he recalled she'd gotten annoyed with him about the spreadsheet in question last night.

She nodded tightly. "Already fixed it."

Dan glanced at his watch and stood up. "I gotta get going. Have to catch my flight in Anchorage." He looked to Susie. "As always, thank you! Joan said to tell you that your mother's zucchini was amazing."

Susie rolled her eyes and laughed. "Glad she enjoyed it. I spend half my summers trying to pawn my mom's zucchini off on people, so it works when it's appreciated."

Dan said his goodbyes and left. The room fell quiet once Dan left. Susie stood and walked around her desk to the file cabinets. She put some files away and walked back to her desk, pausing at the side.

"Did you need something?" she asked, her words sharp.

Jared looked at her and wanted two things at once: to run out of the office and forget everything that had passed between them last night, and to drag her against him and tumble right back to that place between them. Her curls were wild, but then they always were. Her brown eyes were looking back at him with a hint of annoyance. Damned if he could explain it, but somehow when Susie was annoyed with him, he got annoyed with her and that instantly morphed into desire. He forced himself to focus.

"Just what I said. Thought I'd stop by to see if you fixed that spreadsheet."

She sighed. Loudly. "Let's be clear. The spreadsheet didn't need to be fixed because the one I set up before was precisely to your specifications. Which," she pointed a finger in his direction now, her brown eyes flashing, "…you emailed to me, so there's no point in arguing because I can show you the emails for proof. So nothing needed to be fixed. You're just picky and you change your mind. But because I'm a nice person and I try to take good care of my clients, I already made the changes you asked for this morning. So if that's all you need from me, you have an answer," she said with flourish, bringing her hands to her hips and arching an eyebrow.

Jared was so annoyed with her, he was speechless. His cock was also rock hard. His eyes honed in on her plump lips. Before he could think clearly, he'd taken two strides and leaned forward. "That's not all I need," he said bluntly before kissing her.

Susie pushed at him, tearing her lips away. "What are you doing?! We're in my office. Plus we have to talk..."

Jared cut her off with another kiss, savoring how pliant her lips were under his. He pulled away briefly. "I don't care if we're in your office. And we can talk later," he said, grinning when her eyes flashed. But she didn't pull away when he brought his lips to hers again. He loved, absolutely loved, how she threw herself into kisses. There wasn't the slightest bit of hesitation from her. Her mouth fell open and her tongue went wild against his. He threaded his hand into her curls. He groaned at how good it felt for her soft curves to meld against his body. Just as he slid his hand down over her bottom, he heard the sound of a car. Susie instantly stepped away. He took another few steps back and leaned against the wall nearby, forcing himself to breathe slowly and get a hold of himself.

Emma walked into the office. "Hey, hope it's okay I just stopped by," she said.

Jared was relieved Susie managed to respond. She nodded, almost too emphatically. "Of course! What's up?"

"I think I saw Greg in the parking lot at the grocery store. I tried to call Trey but he didn't answer and..."

Jared went into action. His lust for Susie was instantly doused. He quickly pulled his phone out and called Darren, a friend and local cop. Before Emma could even ask what he was doing, he started talking. "Hey Darren, it's Jared. Calling because Emma says she just saw her ex in the parking lot at the grocery store."

"Got a car description?" Darren asked.

"Car description?" he asked, glancing at Emma.

Emma quickly described the car. Jared repeated the information to Darren and hung up. He pushed away from the wall. "Gonna head over there myself. If he hasn't left yet, I can follow him." He looked to Emma. "Between Trey, Darren, me and my brothers, you can call any of us. Anytime."

Emma nodded. "I know. I just hate this."

"We know you do, but stop worrying about accepting help. You're family to us. Listen to Jared. Call me, call any of us whenever you need to," Susie said firmly, reinforcing one of the characteristics he appreciated about her. She was the best kind of friend —loyal and always there.

Jared started to walk to the door and turned back to Emma. It bothered him to see Trey so concerned about Emma and know she was keeping Trey at a distance. Trey was a good friend, and it was plain he loved Emma. "Hope you know Trey only wants to make sure you're okay. No need to keep him at arms length."

Emma flushed. "I...I just..."

Jared hesitated, wondering how much he should meddle, but he knew Trey wanted to help. "Trey's as good as they come. I can tell you mean a lot to him. It's driving him near insane that ever since he ran into

Greg, he's barely seen you. Just think about that," Jared said.

He turned to look at Susie. Her lips were swollen and curls tousled. He wasn't anywhere near ready to think about what was going on inside of him, but the mere sight of her and his heart clenched. He wasn't sure what to say. Susie flushed and lifted her chin. "I'll have your quarterly audit to you by the end of the week. Thanks for helping Emma. Will you call if you find him?" she asked softly.

Jared had to fight the urge to walk over and kiss her before he left. "Of course. Soon as I know anything, I'll call." He turned away quickly and left Susie's office.

He did a quick circuit through town and followed up with a call to Darren when he didn't see any car resembling the one Emma described. "I got nothing," he said as soon as Darren answered. "You?"

"Nada. It doesn't help to have so many tourists around. We'll keep an eye out and give you a call," Darren said quickly before hanging up.

Jared immediately called Susie. He wanted to ask her if they could have dinner again, but couldn't bring himself to. She repeated everything he said to Emma, so he figured it was just as well. He drove home, his thoughts circling around Susie. When he went upstairs to shower and noticed he hadn't bothered to make his bed, all he could think about was her…in his bed. He'd known it last night when she suggested it *—before he knew she was a virgin—*a one-night stand was not a good plan for them. The state of his mind today was clear evidence of what a bad idea that had been.

CHAPTER 9

Susie grabbed her laptop and a few files when she pulled up at Misty Mountain Café. She'd run out of coffee at her house and after trying to grit through the day, she'd given up to come here for a while. She quickly snagged a corner table once she had coffee in hand. The café was crowded, but she enjoyed the hustle and bustle. Fortified with coffee, she got started on monthly reports. She was so focused that she jumped when she heard her name. She looked up to find Jared standing beside her table. Her pulse rocketed, and she flushed inside and out. The effect he had on her had been bad enough before, now it was worse. Ever since the other night, she'd been forced to come to terms with how ridiculous it had been to think a one-night stand would get him out of her system.

She met his green gaze, avoiding the impulse to look away. He searched her face, a hint of uncertainty in his eyes, which gave her a tiny bit of satisfaction. She didn't want to be the only one thrown asunder by what happened between them. His black curls were wind blown. He wore faded jeans and a black t-shirt, both molding to his muscled body—a body she was quite familiar with now, though if her body had anything to say about it, she'd get even more familiar with it as soon as possible.

"Hey," she finally replied when he arched an eyebrow. "What brings you here?"

"Coffee," he said bluntly. "Probably same reason as you."

She nodded and took a sip of coffee. Her heart pounded and butterflies unfurled in her belly.

"I'll be right back, gotta grab my coffee," Jared said before turning on his heel to walk to the counter.

After he paid, he was stopped three times by different women who greeted him flirtatiously. Susie recognized only one of the women as local and assumed the other two were tourists. She'd watched this dynamic play out time and again with Jared, along with his brothers. They would be handsome anywhere, but drop them in the middle of coastal Alaska, and they were magnets.

"Hey Susie! I haven't seen you in weeks."

Susie turned to find her friend Cammi smiling at her. Cammi had grown up in Diamond Creek and was an old friend. Cammi had a lithe build, short honey brown hair and bright blue eyes. She tended to dress in flowing clothes, and today was no exception. She wore a gauzy skirt that hung loosely from her hips paired with a poet blouse. She leaned down and gave Susie a quick hug, enveloping Susie in the flowery scent she usually wore. She leaned her hip against the table. "So what's up?"

Susie gestured to her laptop. "Working. I just

needed a pick me up. What brings you here? Don't you get enough coffee?"

Cammi owned and ran Red Truck Coffee, a tiny coffee shop housed in an old bread truck by the harbor. Cammi only kept it open in the summers, so it was rare to see her away from it. Cammi shrugged. "My busy time is early in the morning. Once all the boats are out on the water, it's errand time for me. I haven't had anything from the bakery here in weeks so thought I'd drop in."

Susie saw Jared get waylaid by yet another woman. Cammi followed her eyes and shook her head. "Poor Jared. He still hasn't figured out his best defense would be to get himself a girlfriend," Cammi said with a soft laugh.

And he just loves that no-strings attached attention.

"Oh, I'm sure he enjoys the attention," Susie replied, her tone sharper than she intended. She tried to tamp down the flare of jealousy.

Cammi glanced to her, her eyes wide. "Seriously? Look at him. He's stoic about it, but I wouldn't say he enjoys it. He looks like he'd rather be anywhere else. I can't believe he hasn't noticed that now Luke and Nathan are married, they don't have nearly as many women drooling over them."

Susie studied Jared for a moment. His smile was tight, not a dimple in sight. His shoulders were tense. She breathed an internal sigh of relief. *What is wrong with you? You and Jared are not a thing. Why do you care at all if other women are into him?*

Cammi was oblivious to Susie's internal turmoil. When Jared finally reached her table, Cammi greeted him as sweetly as always. "Hey, Jared! How was your coffee this morning?"

Jared's smile was wide this time. "Cammi, you know I love your coffee. It was perfect and kept me going all morning."

He and Cammi bantered a few more minutes before she said her goodbyes and left. He met Susie's eyes. "Mind if I leave this here while I run to the restroom?" he asked, lifting his cup of coffee.

"Of course not," she said quickly.

He set his coffee down and headed to the opposite side of the café where the restrooms were. Susie took a deep breath and shook her head. She needed to get a grip and now. She forced herself to focus on the screen on her laptop, but all the numbers blurred. Her throat tightened. She hated that Jared turned her into an idiot. The one thing she'd decided after she'd almost been date-raped was she would make sure she was in control when it came to men. It had been easy to do. Until now. Jared made her feel out of control. He made her *feel* way too much. She didn't like that her heart raced, her breath got shallow and her stomach rode a roller coaster whenever he was near. It was supposed to get better once she'd gotten it out of her system. But...that's not exactly how it was working out. Her mind kept flashing back to the feel of his hands on her body. For God's sake, yesterday Emma had almost caught them kissing because they couldn't keep their hands off of each other.

She started typing rapidly to try to get her mind on anything other than Jared when he said her name. She jumped. She was so irritated with herself that she glared at him and tried to keep typing. He shifted on his feet, silent for a long moment. "Okay if I sit down?"

She closed her eyes and nodded quickly. He sat

down across from her and took a gulp of his coffee. "Trey's coming this way," he commented.

Relief washed through her. Right now, she needed a chaperone for purposes of distraction when it came to Jared. Once they got through the hellos with Trey, Susie jumped right in. "So Jared swears you're a good guy. For the most part, I trust Jared's judgment…"

Jared interrupted her. "For the most part? Seriously? Do I get any credit?"

Susie glared at him, fighting the flush she felt creeping up her neck. "I just gave you some credit! It was a turn of phrase. I didn't actually mean there are times when I don't trust your judgment. For God's sake, don't be so critical."

Jared shook his head and waved for her to continue.

Susie gave Jared a pointed look before turning her focus back to Trey. "So Jared swears you're a good guy. I just want to make sure you know that if you do *anything* to hurt Emma, I'll make you regret it," she said emphatically.

Trey, of course, gave the right answer—for the second time—and Susie wished Jared was as easy to deal with as Trey. She was distracted from this when Trey pointed to the parking lot and called Darren to let him know Emma's ex was there. Susie started to get up from the table, and Jared laid a hand on her arm. "Susie, don't run out there. Let's get Darren on his way at least."

Susie wanted to shake him off, but she knew he was right. She experienced a moment of satisfaction when Jared latched onto Trey's arm next and stopped him mid-stride. Trey shook his arm, but Jared held firm.

"Come on, man, let me go," Trey said.

Jared gave him a hard look. "It's better for Susie or me to follow him. He knows who you are. Seeing you might end with him taking off again." Jared looked to Susie. "Now that we know Darren's on the way, let's head over. But you can't run over and make it obvious."

Susie could barely stand to have him directing her, but what he said made sense. She couldn't hold back a huff, but she nodded. Jared's bossiness raised her hackles. Not to mention that she wanted to run over and punch Emma's ex. When they started walking, she managed to stay at his side for a few strides before she tried to move more quickly.

Jared grabbed her arm. "Susie," he said, his tone edged with warning. "Don't make this obvious. Walk at a normal pace."

She forced herself to breath slowly. "I'm not running. Let's just try to get there a little quicker." Once again, she picked up the pace. Once again, Jared grabbed her arm, this time tugging her hand into his and holding on. She glared at him. "Aren't you just Mr. In-Charge," she said under her breath.

"Heard that," Jared replied.

She glared at him. "Why do you have to be so bossy?"

He didn't even look at her. "I don't think now is the time for this conversation. I'm not being bossy, I'm trying to keep you from making a scene."

"I'm not making a scene," Susie argued as they pushed through the door into the drugstore across the parking lot from Misty Mountain Café. They immediately veered to follow Emma's ex down the aisle he'd turned into. Ten minutes later, after combing the entire store, it was obvious they lost him.

As they returned to the parking lot to let Trey know, Susie couldn't help herself. "Told you we should have gone faster."

Jared came to a stop and turned to her. "We never lost sight of him before we went in the store. Unless you planned to accost him, there was no point in going any faster."

"I wasn't going to accost him!"

"So what exactly were you planning to do if you ran after him?"

"I don't know!"

Jared took a deep breath and held her gaze. "Could we just check in with Darren and then you can have it out with me?"

It was all she could do not to slap him. All Jared had to do was exist in her presence, and she became flustered and wanted him so desperately, she couldn't even think. Anger was the only emotion she could grab hold of to try to get control. She closed her eyes and forced herself to breathe. She nodded and started walking. A few minutes later, Trey handed over her bag with her laptop and papers. She returned to Misty Mountain to get her coffee before she left. Jared followed her quietly. She wasn't sure if he thought they'd talk now, but she was too out of sorts. This *thing* with him discombobulated her in every which way. She wished she could be like her friends and find a man who was just right for her. Definitely not one who infuriated her, made her heart pound, her insides topsy-turvy, and made her lose control.

Susie walked quickly to the table where she'd left her coffee and purse, smiling wryly when she realized

Trey had enough sense to keep her laptop with him, but had left her purse. It sat untouched on the table. She grabbed both items and walked out, promptly colliding with Jared who was waiting outside. Papers floated to the ground while she scrambled to keep hold of her laptop bag. Without a word, Jared picked them up and handed them to her.

"Thank you," she mumbled, not quite ready to look at him.

She finally forced her gaze to his. Those amazing green eyes looked back at hers. His expression was unreadable. His shoulders rose and fell with a deep breath. After a long silence, he cleared his throat. "Well, let's have it. You've been pissed off at me since the minute I saw you today. Mind explaining what's going on?"

As she held his eyes, a flicker of uncertainty flashed in the depths of green. Her anger—the anger that even she couldn't make sense of—softened. With it, her sense of control waned. She was beginning to realize how much her irritation with Jared kept her feelings for him at bay. She forced herself to take a breath. Anxiety bloomed in her chest. This situation with Jared had left her unmoored and confused.

She shook her head. "I'm not pissed off..." She paused when Jared arched a brow.

"Coulda fooled me," he said sardonically.

By some miracle, she managed a rueful smile. "Okay, maybe I can see I might have seemed pissed off. I'm just...I don't know..." Her words trailed off, and she shrugged.

She hoped Jared would say something here, but he held silent, his eyes focused intently on her. She fortified herself with another deep breath. "This..." she gestured between them "...is, um, kind of confusing." Words tumbled through her mind. *I can't stop thinking about you. You drive me crazy with just a look and now I know how it feels to have your hands on my body. And you make me feel like I'm losing control and that scares the hell out of me.* Just thinking about the other night and the kisses in between brought a swirl of heat to her center and a flush from head to toe.

Jared finally nodded. "Right. Confusing. That's one way to put it." He looked away, his eyes staring out toward the bay. When he finally turned back, his eyes were uncertain. He cleared his throat again. "So do you usually act pissed off when you're confused?"

Susie couldn't help it, but she giggled. "I guess I do. Not always, but sometimes."

Jared's teeth flashed in a grin. Her stomach somersaulted when his dimple flashed.

He nodded slowly, his smile fading. "Good to know. I'll keep that in mind next time you seem pissed off at me. But seriously..." his eyes sobered and his words were measured "...there was a reason I didn't think your one-night stand idea would work."

Susie tried to shut her brain off, but now that she'd had a taste of what it was like to lose herself in Jared, all she wanted was more. One night with him hadn't even come close to quenching her desire. Looking at him, flashes drifted through her mind—his lips closing around her nipple, his finger sliding into her wet channel, the feel of his cock sliding in and out of her. *Stop!* Her body's reaction to the mere thought of what it felt like to be with Jared was so strong, she became wet in seconds.

Jared glanced around. They were in a busy area, tourists and locals alike coming in and out of the coffee shop and other shops across the parking lot. "It might be better if we have this conversation somewhere more private," he said, turning back to her.

Susie nodded quickly. Jared reached over and carefully lifted the bag that held her laptop and the papers she'd stuffed inside. Wordlessly, he tidied it and threw it over his shoulder. "Where to?" he asked, his green eyes expectant.

"Um…my office?"

Jared shook his head. "Nope. Too many possible interruptions."

"We need to talk now?" Susie was getting more nervous by the second. She'd kind of hoped they could just blow by any talking about what was going on.

Jared gave her a long look. It felt like he could see right through her. "It's not like I *want* to talk, but it doesn't seem like pretending like nothing happened is getting us anywhere. We can't avoid each other. You're my friend, Susie. I don't want to avoid you. Not to mention that even if we wanted to avoid each other, it would mean avoiding all of our friends. So the way I see it, we have to try to be adults about this."

Susie knew her cheeks were bright red about now, but she managed a nod. "Okay if not my office, do you want to stop by my place?"

Jared nodded. "Perfect. I'll follow you." He immediately turned and walked to her car. His black truck was parked beside it. He carefully set her bag on the passenger seat. He opened his truck and grabbed a pair of sunglasses from the dashboard, slipping them on before looking her way. Flustered, she hopped in her car and started driving.

* * *

THE WHOLE WAY HOME, Susie's mind ran laps on its hamster wheel. By the time she got home, she'd convinced herself she would simply tell Jared the whole thing had been a mistake and surely they could move past this whole 'can't keep our hands off each other' thing if they agreed not to let anything else happen. After the first time they kissed, back when she'd taken him home after he and his brothers were airlifted off their flooded boat, they'd managed to tamp things down no problem. They could do that again. Now they knew they just needed to make sure not to touch each other. The touching was the big problem.

Jared parked behind her car and followed her inside. He'd been to her house a number of times when she had small parties with friends. Jasmine twined around their ankles before racing outside. Susie looked around and wished she'd known Jared would be here. She left things a tad messier than she'd have liked him to see. A haphazard stack of books sat on her coffee table. Her robe was thrown over the stair railing.

Jared immediately walked to her front windows. He stood with his hands tucked in his jeans silently looking out. Susie set her purse on the counter. Her stomach was knotted with tension. Jared's voice startled her.

"The view's different everywhere. You get a better look at Augustine than me."

"Oh. Right. We're a little higher up here," Susie replied, walking to his side.

Silence fell again. She snuck a look at Jared. He

instantly glanced her way and locked eyes with her. He oozed unconscious, confident masculinity. Her temperature rose just standing beside him. *Don't touch him. It's the touching that's your problem. Remember you're not doing this again. It's crazy, he makes you crazy, and...*

Her internal lecture ran out of steam. The problem was her mind didn't seem to be in charge when Jared was nearby. She forced her eyes away from his by sheer willpower and took a few steps back.

"Do you want anything to drink?" she asked.

Jared shook his head. She could feel his eyes tracking her as she walked to the kitchen. Heat spiraled inside and dammit if her heart didn't start racing. She had to get this under control. And he wanted to talk. She blurted out. "So I've been thinking about this. All we have to do is stop. We can do that."

His eyes widened. He walked slowly toward her, coming to a stop by the small island in the kitchen and leaning against it. She poured a glass of water for herself and completely failed at getting her heart to slow down. When she turned around, she ran smack into his heated gaze. All this silence from him was getting to her.

"Well?" she asked sharply. She took a sip of water and set the glass on the counter.

"So you think all we have to do is stop?"

She nodded vigorously. "It's quite simple."

Those green eyes searched her face. She flushed under his scrutiny.

"So you mind filling me in on why you didn't bother to tell me you were a virgin?"

His blunt question threw her. Much as she wanted to look away, she didn't. "I already told you. It was kind of an accident." She paused and tried to gather herself. Her face was heated and her pulse racing. His nearness made it hard to think.

"An accident?"

"It wasn't like I was saving myself or anything. It just so happened I was still a virgin because..." she paused, trying to figure out how to explain without prompting more questions. She couldn't say what the truth was. That she'd probably have lost her virginity a few years back had she not been almost date raped, which altered her basic sense of herself and set her on a path to avoid intimacy. If she couldn't trust her instincts, she couldn't trust enough to let anyone get too close. This train of thought startled her because she realized she trusted Jared. Completely. She'd been so busy convincing herself she couldn't help herself when it came to him because of her highly inconvenient attraction to him. But...she knew perfectly well she'd have never let it go anywhere if she didn't trust him. *Susie, what the hell have you gotten yourself into?*

"Were you planning to finish that sentence anytime soon, or is this some game where I'm supposed to fill in the blanks?"

Susie swung her eyes back up from the floor, which had become remarkably interesting. "Uh, no. Like I said before. It just hadn't happened yet. That's all," she finally said.

Jared nodded slowly. He looked away for a moment and turned back to her. "Okay. It would have been nice to know ahead of time. Especially since you're all about how we can just pretend like nothing ever happened."

"I didn't say that!" Irritation rose inside. She clung to it. The prickle of the feeling anchored her.

"Maybe you didn't say that precisely, but you said all we have to do is stop." He snapped his fingers. "Like that." He eyed her speculatively for a long moment. She shifted on her feet and fought the urge to move away.

"I'll take your explanation by the way, but I'm no dummy. There's more to the story."

Now she was seriously getting pissed. "Are you implying I'm not telling you the truth?" she asked indignantly.

"I think you're being vague and leaving a lot of information out. I don't want to get stuck on it, but it's not exactly fair to suggest a one-night stand and neglect to mention you're a virgin. I'm no angel, but I don't run around having one-night stands with virgins."

Anger flashed through her. She was furious, in part because he had a point. And she hated it. She glared at him. "You're turning this into something it wasn't. I'm not some simpering idiot who was saving myself. Get over it."

Jared pushed away from the counter. "I didn't imply you were a simpering idiot. For what it's worth, I believe the gist of what you're saying. I just think there's more to the story. Could we drop it for now?"

Susie's temper notched higher. It infuriated her that he had to go and point out she was being vague while he seemed all calm and collected. Meanwhile, she could hardly stand her body's betrayal. Her hands itched to feel him again. Desire buzzed through her, a soft hum running through her veins.

Before she knew it, she'd walked right up to him, hands on hips. "You don't get to decide when we start and stop a conversation," she declared.

He finally started to look annoyed, which pleased her immensely. "You wanted to talk, so we're talking," she continued.

Jared pushed away from the counter, eyes pinned to hers. "I didn't decide we were ending the conversation. I asked. Big difference," he said pointedly.

Oh did he know how to spark her anger! He just had to go and be reasonable. Even when he was annoyed, he managed to stay calm, which made her want to shake him. He stood inches from her now. She felt the heat from his body and an answering call from hers. Her breath became shallow. Looking up, she was mesmerized by his green gaze. He didn't look away as he took a step closer to her. He spoke with deliberation. "Just so we're clear, I don't want to stop." Then he kissed her. And she forgot everything else.

CHAPTER 10

*J*ared didn't hesitate, he tugged Susie against him and poured his frustration into their kiss. All afternoon, she'd alternated between being angry one minute, and vulnerable and guarded the next. He'd done his damnedest to keep his own temper in check. His brain was clear out of thoughts when it came to Susie. He simply repeated the same train of thought. She made him crazy in more ways than one. He had tons of reasons why he didn't want a relationship with anyone, much less Susie. But damn if he didn't want her like he'd never wanted anyone in his life. The fact that she'd been a virgin burrowed into his brain and perhaps his heart. All he knew was he was strangely pleased she hadn't been with anyone else, and he couldn't stand the idea that she might move on to someone else now. *That* didn't work for him.

Out of options, he kissed her. The anger and irritation she so easily elicited burned out in the fire of lust he felt for her. Desire swirled around them. He slid his hands down to cup her bottom. He groaned at the feel of her soft, lush curves. She slipped her hands under his t-shirt, coasting them up his chest. He tore his lips from hers, blazing a trail down her neck. All afternoon, he'd had to force his eyes up and away from her breasts. She wore a soft cotton shirt that hugged her body, but then everything she wore seemed to accent her curves. He got lost just looking at her. And now, finally being able to feel her...he had to force himself to keep control.

Susie didn't help one bit. He smiled against her skin when she swore and tugged at his t-shirt. He stepped away and tossed it off. Her eyes were dark and her lips swollen. He lifted his hand and traced down the side of her body, caressing the curve of her breast, the soft dip at her waist and the roundness of her hips. Her breath hitched, and his pulse ricocheted. He hooked his finger under the edge of her shirt and slowly lifted it. She lifted her arms as he raised the shirt up and over her head. It fell to the floor.

She stood in front of him, so close he could see the fluttering pulse in her neck. Her black lacy bra barely held in her breasts. Her nipples were taut. He trailed a finger up her abdomen and traced the curves of her breasts. His heart hammered in his chest, his vision blurred, and his cock hardened even more. He loved her penchant for front-clasp bras and slipped his finger under the tiny clasp between her breasts. With a flick, it came undone, the black lace fell away, and her full breasts fell out. Undone, Jared yanked her against him, his mouth melding to hers.

As he'd discovered already, her fiery temperament was intoxicating in combination with the inferno that encompassed him the second he touched her. He started slowly walking backwards, bringing her with him. Her lush curves felt so good, he could barely breathe. Somehow, he got them to the couch. She was twined so closely against him, his knees collapsed. He thudded onto the couch, a lapful of Susie coming with him. Her moist heat pressed against his cock. He tried to rein himself in, but it was damn near impossible surrounded in the sensation of her.

Her breasts caressed his chest. He broke away from her lips and pushed her back slightly. He paused to take in the sight of her. She straddled him. Her bra had fallen on the walk to the couch. Her breasts were heavy and full, her nipples pert and begging for his mouth. Her hair was a riot of brown curls tumbling every which way. Her lips were parted, her breath shallow, and her eyes dark and wild. She wore a soft twirly skirt—something she did often and he loved it —and it pooled around her hips. He ran his palms up her thighs, savoring the feel of her silky skin. She had random freckles scattered on her body, a sweet surprise he'd discovered.

His thumbs met at the juncture of her thighs where she wore something that could barely be described as panties—a mere scrap of black lace. He held her eyes as he slipped a finger under the edge of the lace and softly traced around her clit. Her breath hitched. His cock throbbed. He forced himself not to rush. He traced circles in her wet, slick heat before finally sliding a finger inside her channel. Her head fell back on a gasp. He finally gave in and leaned forward to lave a nipple, sucking it into his mouth and softly biting.

"Jared..."

"Mmmhmm?"

"Please…"

"Please what?"

He felt her irritation flare and damn if that didn't turn him on even more, though how that was possible, he didn't know. He slid another finger inside her and started slowly drawing them in and out, turning his attention to her other nipple as he did. Susie whimpered and ground her hips against his hand. Suddenly, she shifted and tore at his jeans. In seconds, she freed his cock. She stroked it slowly in her palm. When he groaned, she spoke softly. *"It's only fair…"*

Jared lifted his hips and shoved his jeans down, kicking them off his ankles. Susie was small enough, he managed this easily with her on his lap. He leaned over to fumble in his jeans pocket for a condom when she spoke softly. "I'm on the pill."

He met her eyes, her cheeks flushed. She shrugged. "It just seems silly if you don't need a condom."

With any other woman, he would have hesitated. But this was Susie and for reasons he couldn't quite contemplate, removing another layer between them was so tempting, it was all he wanted. He nodded. She settled on his lap again. His control leashed with the barest thread, he pushed the thin scrap of lace out of the way, sliding against her slick heat. A soft sigh fell from her lips when her head fell back. She slid back and forth against his cock.

He curled his hands around her hips, lifted them and positioned her over the tip of his cock. She shifted restlessly in his grip, but he held firm, bringing her down in increments. She flinched—just barely— and he registered she must be sore. He kept his hips still and allowed her to sink onto him. Sheathed in her slick warmth, he forced himself to wait, to allow her to adjust to him. Tenderness arced through him. For a blinding moment, he realized how this felt for her was far more important than how it felt for him. For her to remain a virgin as long as she did, accidental or not, he simply wanted every experience she had with him to be amazing.

When she finally sank fully on him, he couldn't hold back a groan. His cock throbbed inside of her, desperate to shift and thrust in her heat. She sighed again, and he slid a hand up her back, savoring the feel of her skin every inch of the way, and threaded his hand in her curls. He tilted her head toward his and brought their lips together.

"Is that okay?" he asked, his voice raspy.

"Mmmhmm."

Jared shifted subtly, altering the angle of his hips to push more deeply inside of her. A soft hum came from her throat. Her lips smiled against his. Her hips began to lift and fall. He couldn't help but smile in return as he shifted again, beginning to move in soft slow strokes, attenuating his motion to hers.

Her head fell back again as she began to move more vigorously. He gloried in the sight of her. Her skin dewy in the late afternoon light, her curls tumbling as she moved against him. The feel of her tight sheath pulsing around him brought him to the edge of his control. He tried to slow her pace, but she ignored him and rode him with the same passion that she approached everything—wild and fiery. She called his name when she began to climax, pulling him with her. He surged deeply into her, his release rushing through his entire body, her name a shouted prayer. She fell against him, a bundle of lush curves completely relaxing in his lap. He slid both arms around her and held her close, hanging on as he caught his breath.

As his pulse finally began to slow and conscious thought returned, Jared decided he didn't give a damn whether this was convenient or messy. He didn't know where this would lead, but he was done trying to talk himself out of being with her. This was too good, too amazing, too…everything.

Several long moments later, Susie finally stirred in his lap. She leaned back and tilted her head. With her mussed hair, swollen lips and dark brown eyes sated with pleasure, she took his breath away. When she began to look like she was thinking, he decided to head her off at the pass.

"Let's just get one thing straight. I have no intention of trying to keep my hands off of you anymore," he said bluntly.

Susie's mouth fell open, but she quickly closed it. Her eyes narrowed as she studied him. He trailed a hand around her side and under her breasts. He couldn't resist touching her, not when she sat almost bare in his lap. Her breath caught and then she giggled. A blush stained her cheeks. "I guess we'd be putting a lot of energy into something that seems like it's a waste of time—the keeping our hands off of each other, that is. This is more fun," she said with a grin. She wiggled her hips and dragged her hand across his chest, her soft touch lighting fires in its wake.

He hadn't realized he'd been almost holding his breath while he waited to see how she responded. He chuckled. "Definitely more fun…" he paused when he heard a faint scratching sound. "What's that?"

"Jasmine wants to come in. I should get up."

Vulnerability flashed through her eyes quickly.

She cleared her throat. "So I'll be getting up now," she said, glancing down at his hands, one curled on her hips, the other cupping a breast.

Jared slowly shifted and guided her hips up and off of his cock, immediately missing her moist warmth and realizing he could easily go another round right now. He had to remind himself she'd been a virgin a few short days ago.

Susie stood and tugged her skirt into place before walking over to the door to let Jasmine in. She didn't bother picking up her clothes. She turned to him. "Shower?"

* * *

A FEW DAYS LATER, Susie sat in the living room at Tess and Nathan's house trying to get up the courage to talk to Tess about Jared. She'd ruled out talking to Hannah or Emma. Emma had enough on her plate, and Hannah was wrapped up in that. Tess was just as worried as the rest of them, but she had a little more distance from the situation. Plus, Susie wasn't quite ready to admit to Hannah she might have had a point about Jared. Jared, Nathan and Luke were out all day on a fishing trip, so Susie knew she'd have a chance to talk without interruption. She desperately needed someone's perspective outside of her own. Jared had spent the last few nights with her. She floated along in a wash of sensation when she was with him. When they were apart, she felt as if she was spiraling out of control. She wanted the impossible—to have a chance at a real relationship with Jared—knowing she shouldn't even go there because Jared had made it abundantly clear for years that he had no interest in such a thing. On the heels of those thoughts, she beat herself up for letting her physical attraction to him get out of hand.

Tess came over to the couch with two cups of coffee in hand and set them on the coffee table. She plunked down on the couch by Susie, tucking her feet under her and tugging a pillow on her lap. "Okay, spill it," Tess said.

"Huh?" Susie asked, knowing full well Tess had picked up on her tension.

Tess rolled her eyes and picked up her coffee. Her honey gold curls caught the sun coming through the windows. "I may not know the details yet, but you'll tell me. You're so tense, you're practically vibrating. I'm sure you're worried about Emma, but we all are. That's kind of a constant right now. But you have something else on your radar. So spill it."

Susie looked at Tess, meeting her warm ginger eyes. Despite her sarcasm, Tess was clearly concerned. Susie was so glad Tess had moved here to be with Nathan. Aside from the fact that they were perfect together, Tess was an amazing friend—warm, kind, funny, and bright. And Susie *really* needed someone to talk to. Susie picked up her own coffee and took a fortifying sip.

"Okay. I'll spill it, but before I do, you have to promise me this won't leave this room. Everyone else will find out eventually, but I'm not quite ready. I need a little time, but I need some advice first."

Tess nodded slowly. "Of course. Are you okay?"

"Oh yeah. I'm fine. It's nothing like that. It's just...Jared."

A grin slowly spread across Tess's face. "Jared?"

Susie knew she was blushing like mad, but she nodded. "Um, we kind of have…a thing."

"A thing?"

"Oh my God. You're making this as hard as you can, aren't you? Fine. We can't keep our hands off of each other. We've been together the last three nights. I told him not to come over tonight and now all I can think about is why the hell I told him that. So I feel like an idiot because you were right about us. And now he's driving me crazy in two ways—the good way and the other way. And I don't know what to do. I can't talk to Emma and Hannah about it because, well, they have a few other things on their minds. So I just need someone to tell me what to do." The words tumbled out of her mouth, but she felt an immense relief once they were out. She wasn't purposefully keeping Jared a secret, but she was damn embarrassed her friends had predicted this, and they'd turned out to be right.

Tess's grin lingered, but her gaze was sympathetic. She nodded slowly. "Okay, I won't say I told you so."

"You just did," Susie replied wryly.

"I guess I did, but I didn't mean it to be snarky. So back to Jared…I'm not really sure what you need my advice for."

Susie sighed and set her coffee down. She put her face in her hands with a groan before looking up at Tess. "I don't know. I don't know what to do. Don't get me wrong. I will finally admit he's hot as hell. And oh my God is he amazing in bed! But I don't know where this is going to go. I don't want things to get weird. He's my friend first, and we have all the same friends. For as long as I've known him, he's been all about how relationships are messy and he doesn't want anything to do with them. I guess I just don't know what to do."

Tess took a sip of coffee followed by a deep breath. "I forgot about this part."

"What part?" Susie asked.

"It was all fine and good when we teased you about Jared. Truth? Before I even got to know you, the minute I saw you and Jared in the same place, I assumed you were together. When I realized you weren't, it was plain as day you two belonged together and hadn't figured it out yet. The part I'm talking about is this stuff," she paused and waved her hand around. "The end game is easier than this. It's like before I could just admit I *really* wanted to be with Nathan and couldn't imagine life without him. My head was all over the place—one minute, I'd convince myself we were moving too fast, the next I couldn't imagine not being with him—lather, rinse, repeat. Now you and Jared have to go through that part. If my first instinct about you two is right, it'll sort itself out. But for now..." Tess shrugged and gave Susie a soft, knowing smile.

"So basically you're saying I'll feel half crazed for awhile and somehow it will be fine anyway?" Susie asked wryly. "I was looking for something a little more concrete than that."

Tess giggled. "It's kind of hard to be concrete when you start with how hot Jared is."

Susie blushed and started giggling. She sobered quickly. "Seriously, I'm not so sure things will be smooth for me and Jared. You and Nathan are... different. My God, Nathan was enamored with you from the moment he laid eyes on you. Not to mention that he doesn't have the emotional hang ups that Jared does. He's always been easy-going. Jared's pretty much the opposite."

Tess shrugged. "Sure, they're different, but everyone's different. Trust me, I have hang ups, along with everyone else. My thesis on love is it hinges on three things: enough chemistry to make you forget yourself long enough to fall in love, loving the whole package, faults and all, and whose crap you can put up with."

"Whose crap you can put up with?" Susie asked.

Tess nodded vigorously. "Yeah. We're all messed up one way or another, so if you have the first two, and you can deal with someone's baggage and bad habits—you know, their crap—you're good to go."

"Got it. So I have to figure out if I can put up with Jared's crap then."

Tess shrieked, startling Susie so she almost spilled her coffee.

"What the hell?"

"That means you know you're in love with him!" Tess exclaimed, grinning madly.

Susie heart stuttered and her mind raced over her last words. She hadn't dared let herself even think the word love in the vicinity of thoughts about Jared and shied away from Tess's declaration. "What do you mean?"

Tess sighed and swatted Susie with the pillow on her lap. "The three things were chemistry, love, and putting up with crap. You said you had to figure out if you could put up with Jared's crap. Naturally, I assumed you meant the other two were already covered. You already admitted the chemistry is more than enough," Tess said with a grin.

Susie's face heated and her pulse leapt. Just

thinking about Jared like this—attaching the real idea of feeling something for him—was terrifying.

"Hey, I didn't mean to freak you out," Tess said softly.

Susie looked up into Tess warm ginger eyes. Her throat felt tight when she nodded. "I'm okay. I just… ugh…this is why I need some advice. I don't know how I feel. I hate admitting this, but I'm kind of scared to let myself put too much into this. Jared, well, he's Jared. You know him. When it comes to women, he doesn't do anything serious. I don't know what I am to him. All I know is we can't seem to keep our hands off of each other anymore."

Tess nodded slowly. "Right. But here's how I see Jared. He likes to keep his life under control. I don't really know the details, but Nathan says Jared wasn't always like this. He thinks Jared decided to steer clear of relationships because he got dumped right before he was going to ask a girl to marry him."

"Really?" Susie asked.

Tess nodded. "That's what Nathan says. It happened back in Seattle. Nathan says Jared's not hung up on this girl, but ever since that happened, Jared decided it was easier not to bother with relationships. Jared's a sweetheart underneath his serious side. I think he just needed to see you for who you are."

Susie's mind whirred over what Tess told her. She couldn't have imagined someone had broken Jared's heart. It made her sad to think about it. Whatever she thought, and her thoughts were quite muddled, she knew Jared had a good heart. It saddened her to think someone didn't appreciate him for who he was. This piece of his history fell into the puzzle he was.

It made him a tad less intimidating. And made her want things she'd been trying desperately not to consider.

Susie looked to Tess. "Interesting to say the least. You make it sound easy. Jared just had to see me for who I am? Seriously, Tess? Even if, and that's a pretty big if, it's that simple and we're about to ride off into the sunset, you're missing a few steps. Like Jared admitting he might even want a relationship. And me figuring out what I want."

"I didn't say it was already sorted out, but I think it will be. As for what you want, I think you already know," Tess said firmly.

Susie's mouth fell open.

Tess smirked at her. "You do. You wouldn't be here asking me anything if you didn't care a lot. Maybe you're not ready to call it love, but you two are way ahead of the game there. You've been friends for years now."

"And that's part of the reason this is complicated."

Tess eyed her. "If you think it needs to be complicated, it will be. Here's my advice: relax, have fun, don't worry about keeping your hands off of him now that you've finally let yourself have a taste, and try not to overthink it. Overthinking is dangerous."

Susie sighed. "Don't I know it." She looked out the windows that faced the bay. The mountains she knew so well sat tall and silent against the sky. The wind was up with whitecaps dotting the bay. Boats moved in and out of the harbor. Tess and Nathan's yard was filled with wildflowers. A pair of magpies sat on the deck railing pecking at a birdfeeder, the iridescent green and blue in their feathers catching sparks from the sun.

Susie finally turned back to Tess. "I excel at over-thinking," she said flatly.

Tess threw her head back when she laughed. "Me too! I don't have any great advice on that one. But I bet Jared can get your mind to stop spinning its wheels," she said with a mischievous grin.

Susie blushed, but she smiled. "Yeah, he's pretty good at that."

Tess sobered. "I wish I could give you the concrete advice you want. If you want to talk more, call me anytime. Meanwhile, just remember Jared's a good guy. Whatever happens, he's not going to be an ass about it. If you want to know, I would have bet Jared would be the one to discover how much you meant to him before you."

"Why do you say that?"

"Don't take this the wrong way, but you're pretty, um, prickly when it comes to men. I love you to pieces and you're the absolute best kind of friend, but I can't say I haven't wondered about that."

Susie took Tess's words in. A flash of defensive-ness flared, but she knew Tess was right. She didn't have to like it, but she could acknowledge it. "Prickly, huh?"

Tess eyed her cautiously and nodded.

Susie felt tears prick behind her eyes. Dammit, she didn't used to be like that. Not until she met the asshole who tried to rape her and didn't even have the nerve to do it while she was conscious. To this day, for some bizarre reason, it infuriated her that he had drugged her. The constant wonder of what she didn't remember haunted her.

Susie sighed and looked over at Tess. "I can see

that I might come across as prickly. I don't mean to be that way."

Tess searched her face. "You okay?"

Susie nodded. "I am. I just wish this was easier." She brought the topic back to Tess's point. "So you thought Jared was an easier mark than me?"

Tess chuckled. "Yup."

"Fine then. Now that I've gotten this off my chest, how are you?"

Susie spent the afternoon with Tess before heading home. As she drove home, it occurred to her that she assumed she'd see Jared tonight even though she'd explicitly asked him not to come over. The expectation unsettled her because she was beginning to unconsciously count on seeing him everyday.

CHAPTER 11

"*D*amn. That was a little too close for comfort for me," Jared said, glancing over at his friend, Darren. Darren was the local cop who'd been handling the investigation related to Emma's ex. Darren's partner, Charlie Brooks, gave a quick wave before climbing into his patrol car and driving away with Emma's ex cuffed in the back seat. Emma was standing in Trey's arms. As far as Jared could tell, Trey had no intention of letting Emma go anytime soon.

Darren shook his head and sighed, running a hand through his hair. "I'll say. Really glad you got up here as fast as you did."

Jared nodded. "Me too." After Trey had called him earlier, he'd raced up here because he was closer to Emma's house than anyone else. He'd found her truck wide open and purse spilled on the ground. Greg, her ex, was dragging her around the back of the house while his new wife sat frozen in their rental car. The next few moments unspooled rapidly. Jared found himself trying to talk Greg down, matters made much worse by the fact that Greg was waving a gun around.

Jared was relieved beyond measure that Emma was okay. She and Trey had just finished giving statements to Darren. Jared looked around the yard. It was a beautiful afternoon, the sun bright with a soft breeze. Emma's yard was bucolic with scattered spruce and birch trees, and fireweed starting to bloom in the field nearby.

He looked back to Darren. "Thanks for getting here as soon as you could. I thought Trey and I could handle it, but it was dicey once I realized he had a gun."

Darren nodded. "Hey, that's what I'm here for." He glanced to Emma and Trey. "I should head on down to the station now. We gotta get rolling on the charges for this. Think I'll leave those two be for now," he said with a low chuckle.

Jared followed his eyes to Trey and Emma who were twined around each other. The intimacy between them was so palpable, he felt he was intruding. He looked away. "I'll second that. I'm thinking we should maybe go," he commented wryly.

As he followed Darren down the road, Jared couldn't help but think of Susie. Witnessing the intimacy between Trey and Emma gave him pause. Trey had been beside himself with worry about Emma the last few weeks. Jared tried to imagine how he'd feel if Susie were in any kind of danger. Even contemplating it was so disconcerting, his mind shied away from it. *Don't go there. Just focus on what works.* Frustrating thing was that about the only time he wasn't obsessing about Susie was when they were skin to skin.

Jared hung his keys on the hook by the door and immediately grabbed a beer out of the refrigerator. He'd convinced himself he needed to *not* see Susie tonight. They'd been seeing each other almost every night the last few weeks. He wasn't sure what it represented, but he was uncomfortable with it. He turned his phone off and flipped the television on. He needed to re-establish his usual evening patterns. Phone off. Television. By himself. Nothing messy to worry about. An hour later, he sent Susie a text.

My place or yours?

Polite way of saying you want to see me tonight?

Sure.

Were you planning to call me? Worried since I heard about what happened this afternoon. Tried calling but no answer.

Huh?

Hannah called. Said Greg finally got arrested and you were there.

Come over. Will fill you in.

See you in a few.

Jared set his phone down and grinned. He'd concluded it was stupid to avoid Susie when things were fine between them. She hadn't given any hint she expected anything from him. They had amazing sex, and she was funny as hell. He was convinced they could keep it light, and he wouldn't have to worry about the potential ramifications.

Susie arrived minutes later. After a quick knock, she walked in, her brown eyes furious. Without preamble, she leapt in. "Why didn't you call me? Oh my God, Hannah told me Greg had a gun and had Emma in a head lock!"

Jared wasn't accustomed to anyone worrying

about him, so it hadn't occurred to him to call Susie. He figured he'd update her when he saw her and that would suffice. The look on Susie's face indicated otherwise. He silently swore, realizing he could have headed this off with a simple phone call, but instead, he'd turned his phone off. Aware Susie was going to demand a response if he didn't give one, he took a breath. "Sorry about that. I figured I'd let you know what happened tonight."

Susie shook her head, her curls swinging. Damn, he loved those curls. "Are you okay?"

"I'm fine. Don't I look fine? If you want to worry about someone, try Emma."

Susie's eyes widened. "Jared, he had a gun, you could have gotten killed!" She threw a glare at him.

Though he knew that was technically possible, it hadn't crossed his mind. He was rapidly recognizing he could have saved himself some trouble if he'd called her earlier. "Susie, I suppose it could have been that bad, but it wasn't. Could we focus on what happened instead of what didn't? I'm fine. Emma's probably more shaken up than me."

"Hannah said Emma was okay," Susie said, a question to her tone.

"She's fine. I just meant it was pretty scary for her. That's all." Jared filled Susie in on the details. Of course, she wanted a blow by blow, so he gave it to her. When he was finished, he looked over to see her eyes glisten with tears.

Before he could ask what was wrong, she threw herself at him, climbing on his lap and hugging him. "You are so good! If you hadn't gone up there to help, Emma could have gotten hurt." Her words tumbled out. She leaned back to smile through her tears and then peppered his face with kisses.

Jared couldn't help but enjoy her over-the-top display of affection. She seemed to think he saved the day. He rather thought it was a combination of factors, himself just one, but he didn't mind having a lapful of Susie showing her appreciation. Somewhere in the midst of her soft kisses, her lips collided with his.

* * *

DESIRE CURLED like smoke around them. Susie hadn't meant to start this, but the moment her lips met Jared's, she wanted nothing but him. Her heart felt full, her emotions too close to the surface, heating her skin, morphing into a sheer force of yearning. Jared's tongue delved into her mouth, and she welcomed it. She needed to be overpowered, needed to lose herself in the passion between them. Because thinking about how she felt this afternoon when she heard Jared had been at Emma's, and Greg had been waving a gun around—well, she couldn't go there in her mind. It was enough to be worried about Emma and relieved she was okay. But Jared...it was too much. But this— this living, breathing flame that crackled to life between them whenever they were near each other— she could dive into it and lose herself.

She shifted on his lap, straddling him, her skirt sliding up around her hips. Jared growled softly and rocked his hips into her. She ground down against him, savoring the heated length of his cock through the rough fabric of his jeans against the silk of her panties. She nipped at his lips. He tore his mouth from hers.

Dear God, Susie. She felt his words against her skin as his lips traveled down her neck. He hooked his finger under her tank top, whipping it up over her head. She sighed in relief when he unhooked her bra and roughly shoved it off her shoulders. The feel of his lips on her nipples—licking and softly biting—sparked the banked fires within. She was burning, desperate for him. Heat spiraled inside.

She tugged at his shirt, pushing it over his head, and sighed at the feel of his skin against hers. She could barely breathe when he slid his warm palms up her thighs and teased her through the damp silk of her panties. Suddenly, he lifted her off his lap and stood. He kicked his jeans off and turned back to her. The brief separation only notched her desperation higher. Jared pulled her up from the couch and tugged her skirt down. It pooled on the floor around her feet. She stepped out of her sandals, looking up at him. His eyes were dark. His gaze trained on her, he lifted her palm and turned to drop a kiss in its center. Her breath caught in her throat.

In a flash, he turned her. She fell on her knees on the couch. His warm hands caressed down her back, curling around her hips, the roughened skin leaving a trail of goose bumps in its wake. She trembled with want, dripped with need. His lips coasted down her back as he slid one finger and then another in her channel. By this point, she was near out of her mind. She moaned.

Please...

Please what?

Need you...inside...now

Susie felt the tip of his cock at her entrance. He nudged inside and slid back out, teasing her. She pushed her hips back into him. He finally surged inside, driving deep and pausing when he filled her completely. She almost sobbed with relief. He kept one hand curled on her hips, the other slipped up her back to thread in her curls. With the slightest pressure, he tugged on her hair and began a rhythm of strokes, looping in and out of her. She careened into sensation, losing hold on all thought. Her climax built slowly and exploded in ripples through her body. She felt him thrust deeply one last time and then convulse inside of her.

Jared's hand loosened in her curls and rested for a moment between her shoulder blades, the warmth anchoring her and bringing her back to herself. He slowly pulled out of her, turning to sit on the couch and pulling her onto his lap. She curled into his chest. Her heartbeat slowed and her breath finally settled to normal. She must have dozed off because she woke in Jared's arms as he carried her upstairs. The last thing she remembered was him tucking her against his body.

* * *

Jared came awake slowly. Sun fell across the bed. Susie was sound asleep in his arms. He thought he could wake to the feel of her soft curves every day and never get enough. He lifted his head and glanced at the clock. As soon as he saw the time, he groaned. He'd overslept by more than an hour. This was becoming a bit of a habit with Susie. He considered getting up immediately, but couldn't quite bring himself to do it. It felt too damn good to cuddle with her in the bright morning sun. But then he couldn't believe this was even happening. He hadn't cuddled with anyone in years. Cuddling represented something he'd decided he couldn't have. Cuddling was far more intimate than sex. And yet, here he was, cuddling with Susie. And loving it.

He flung the covers back and practically leapt out of bed. Susie rolled over. He walked into the bathroom and immediately stepped into the shower, not even waiting for the water to warm up. Several moments of cold water, and he could think clearly again. When he came out of the bathroom, Susie was propped up on the pillows. He could see her dusky nipples through the thin white sheet. He had to shake his head and force himself to remember he had a schedule today, and it did not involve a romp in bed with Susie first thing in the morning when he was already an hour behind.

She smiled at him, her curls in tousled disarray, her brown eyes sleepy and warm. "Good morning."

His chest was tight, and he didn't know why. He forced himself to try to act normal. "Morning. Sorry to rush, but I need to get to the harbor soon." He intended to walk past the bed and downstairs, but he stayed where he was, staring at her.

She nodded, hopefully oblivious to his internal confusion. "I figured. I have to get to the office. I'll head home to shower," she said.

She climbed out of bed, and Jared had to bite back a groan at the sight of her. He, who prided himself on his control, lost any semblance of it at the sight of her body. She was curvy and soft all over. Her breasts spilled out, bouncing with each step she took. Her bottom was round and lush, perfectly curved in a heart shape with little dimples at the top. He loved that she was so short and so much of a woman. If he were poetic, he'd admit that she was nothing short of a goddess. For now, he had to close his eyes to regain control. He could not yank her against him and throw her onto the bed like he wanted. He would be in control.

"Oh! All my clothes are downstairs," Susie said with a giggle.

He opened his eyes to see her hips swaying as she walked back past him and down the stairs. He took several long breaths and had to walk back to the bathroom and splash cold water on his face to get a grip on himself. When he finally walked downstairs, she was standing by the door in that ridiculous flouncy skirt and tight red tank top. Her hair was mussed.

She looked at him, a hint of uncertainty in her eyes. "So I guess I might see you later," she said.

Jared considered the mere hour he'd attempted to spend alone last night and whether he wanted to try that again tonight. He couldn't really contemplate it, but he knew he didn't want to spend an evening without her, so he shoved away his doubts and walked over to her. He dropped a kiss on her lips, forcing himself to immediately step back. "I'll see you tonight," he said firmly.

He leaned against the door with a sigh once she left. He didn't know what he needed to do, but somehow he had to get a grip.

CHAPTER 12

*S*usie kicked her boots off when she stepped inside. She was running late, but what else was new. She wasn't much of a schedule person. Working for herself didn't help matters in that area. Just as she was about to close the door, Jasmine raced by her. She paused to shake furiously, drops of rain flying off her smoky gray fur, arcing in a circle around her. Susie stepped into the small laundry room off the kitchen, grabbed a towel and briskly rubbed Jasmine with it.

"Damn, she sure can purr!"

Susie whipped her head up to see Jared sitting on the couch in her living room.

"Oh! I forgot you were meeting me here. Sorry I'm late," she replied.

Jared glanced at his watch and back at her. "Well, you're exactly an hour behind schedule, which is par for the course. I suppose I should start showing up an hour late whenever we plan to meet," he said with a tight smile.

Susie gave Jasmine a last rub and dropped the towel on the floor where Jasmine promptly curled up and started grooming herself. She looked over at Jared. His smile was tense as his eyes traveled to the boots she'd haphazardly kicked to the floor and followed the raincoat she tossed across the back of a stool by the kitchen counter.

"I lost track of time," she replied, thinking Jared would consider that insufficient planning since he was reliably punctual. Feeling defensive, irritation rose inside.

Jared shrugged. "It's okay. With the rain today, we cut our trip short. I've been back a few hours. I brought my laptop with me since I wasn't sure if you'd make it on time. Did you still want to go out to dinner?"

Susie walked over to the couch, feeling out of sorts. This *thing* with Jared had been going on for almost a month now. They hadn't spent a night apart the last few weeks. But aside from Tess, none of their mutual friends knew about it. It wouldn't surprise Susie if Tess had told Nathan about it, but Nathan wasn't one to talk. As such, Susie was starting to feel like they were sneaking around. She didn't know what Jared thought and if he wanted anything other than what they had. Which was the most amazing sex she'd ever had. Of course, her experience with actual sex was limited to Jared.

Jared had suggested they have dinner at Diamond Creek Brewery. When she'd pointed out that they'd yet to be public about themselves, he'd shrugged and said it wouldn't be obvious because they were friends anyway. His comment grated on her. It made her feel like he didn't want anyone to know about them. And yet she was far from certain about what she wanted when it came to Jared. It was too confusing. She pushed the thought away and sat on the couch beside him, resting her feet on the coffee table. When she looked over, his green gaze was focused on her, dark and intent. His black curls shone in the light cast by a nearby lamp. She could happily look at him all day. He quirked a brow, and she blushed, realizing she'd been staring.

"We can go to dinner. Are you ready to go now?" she asked.

Jared nodded and lifted his laptop from his lap to set it on the table to the side of the couch. "Yup. I'm starving. Do you need a few minutes?"

She ran a hand through her curls. They were damp and in disarray. But a few minutes wouldn't change that, so she shook her head. "Let's go. Who's driving?"

Jared stood and held his hand out to her. "I'll drive."

Susie placed her palm in his, savoring the warmth. She was chilled from the rain. As he tugged her up, his warm grip sparked a buzz of desire. He didn't let go when she stood, pulling her close for a kiss, ratcheting up the heat flaring to life inside of her. Flustered, she was blushing when he pulled away. She shook her raincoat quickly and looked around for something other than her boots to wear. She finally eyed a pair of clogs on the floor by Jasmine's water bowl and slipped them on. She watched, bemused, when Jared picked up the boots she kicked off and set them in the small shoe tray by the door. Of course that's what a shoe tray was for, but she rarely used it.

A short drive later, they dashed through the rain into Diamond Creek Brewery. As usual in the summer, the brewery was hopping. The brewery occupied a refurbished plane hangar. Though the space was expansive, it felt warm and homey. The back end of the building comprised the brewery part of the business, which was separated from the restaurant by a brick wall. Elaborate model planes hung from the ceiling of the hangar, replicas of the small six-seater planes still used frequently in Alaska. Windows had been added to the hanger offering the view of an adjacent field with Kachemak Bay and the mountains in the distance. The restaurant had booths lining the walls and clusters of tables in the center. Bright fabric wall hangings and colorful rugs softened what could have been a noisy space.

Susie glanced around to see if anyone she knew was here. Cammi was at the bar with her friend, Dara. Hannah and Luke were in a booth together in the far corner. Susie sighed internally. Somehow, she and Jared had to figure out if they were going to just let whatever this was between them go, or stop trying to pretend it wasn't anything. Susie was tired of holding back from her friends. She'd had a reason a few weeks ago while everyone was worried about Emma, but now...it was starting to feel like she and Jared were being juvenile. Problem was, she wasn't sure how Jared would feel if she let their friends know what was going on, although that was only one element of the bigger picture. There was also the rather glaring issue that Jared had been a committed bachelor for years. She gave her head a sharp shake. Now was not the time to think about this.

After a short wait, they were escorted to a booth. Susie breathed a sigh of relief when she realized they wouldn't have to walk past Hannah and Luke. Cammi's back was to the room at the bar. They might get lucky, and no one would notice she and Jared were here together. Though she knew Jared was probably right, they were friends and had been for years, she wasn't so sure Hannah wouldn't pick up on something. Hannah knew Susie better than anyone and would sense something was afoot.

After they were seated, Susie quickly scanned the menu before setting it down. When their waiter approached, she ordered a glass of red wine while Jared ordered a beer.

"Wine at a beer brewery?" Jared asked with a grin.

"I'm in the mood for wine tonight," she replied with a shrug.

Jared nodded. In moments, their waiter returned and took the rest of their order. She took a welcome sip of wine. Between the ever-present buzz of desire she felt when Jared was near and her self-consciousness about whether their friends would notice them, her nerves were high. She was so busy trying to talk herself into relaxing she jumped when she felt Jared's hand on her thigh. He reached under the table and dragged his fingertips in lazy circles on her knee. Her pulse ricocheted.

"What are you doing?" she whispered fiercely.

He grinned and took a swallow from the beer held in his free hand.

Susie watched as Hannah and Luke got up from their booth and turned toward them. Hannah nudged her shoulder against Luke's and gestured to Susie and

Jared, following with a quick wave and walking toward them.

Susie glared at Jared. "Stop it!" she hissed.

He feigned innocence and toyed with the edge of her skirt before pushing it further up her thighs and walking his fingers up the inside of her thigh. She'd complained before about how the booths here were too small and never knew how right she'd been. Jared could easily reach under the table and drive her mad, just as he was doing right now. Her panties were already wet, and he'd barely touched her. She tried to close her thighs together. Jared ignored it and applied gentle pressure to one of her knees while tucking one of his legs between hers.

Hannah and Luke reached their table. "Hey there," Hannah said. "What are you two doing here?"

Being driven absolutely mad by Jared, that's what I'm doing here. Oh...my...God... Susie almost groaned aloud when Jared slipped his hand further up her thigh and stroked the damp silk. She was about ready to dissolve into a puddle. She tried her damnedest to smile normally and flailed internally for an innocent explanation.

"I stopped by Susie's office to go over some reports. We were both hungry, so here we are," Jared replied nonchalantly.

Hannah and Luke appeared to accept that explanation though Hannah's eyes were questioning. She glanced at Susie, but didn't say anything. Susie was busy trying to keep her face from flaming. *Dammit Jared!* She surreptitiously glared at him when Hannah looked at Luke for a second. He ignored her. She tried to shift her hips back, but there was nowhere to go. The motion only heightened what her body wanted, her hips rocking against his fingers.

"Called you last night, but you didn't answer. I was hoping you could help me with some work on our shed," Luke said to Jared.

"Sure," Jared replied, ignoring Luke's comment that he didn't answer his call last night.

Jared traced circles over her clit through her panties. Susie thought she might melt on the spot. She was furious with him. He knew he was driving her mad and making it decidedly difficult for her to pretend like they were simply friends out for dinner. Her breath hitched when he slid a finger under the silk and stroked through her swollen folds, dipping into her slick cleft.

Luke and Hannah both looked at her. Her face was on fire, but she schooled her expression to blank. Luke turned back to Jared. "Mind coming by in the morning? I'm hoping to shore up the pilings and put some shelving in."

Jared nodded. "No problem. We don't have any more trips scheduled this week, so I can come by any day. What time?"

"Not before nine, but anytime after that," Luke replied.

Hannah caught Susie's eyes and lifted her eyebrows in question. Susie knew she was wondering what was up. Susie lifted her eyebrows in return and shrugged. Luke slipped his arm around Hannah's shoulder.

"Make sure to try this week's brew, it's amazing," Luke said to Jared. "We gotta get going. John's with Emma and Trey tonight, but we promised them we'd pick him up before eight."

Hannah glanced to Susie. "I'll call you later," she said pointedly.

Susie nodded. "Sure. I'm headed home soon. How about I call you?"

At Hannah's nod, she and Luke turned to leave. Once they were out of earshot, Susie looked at Jared and opened her mouth to tell him off—right when he slid a finger deep into her channel. She gasped and then glared at him. She again tried to close her knees, but it only increased the friction of his hand. Another finger joined the first and he stroked his thumb across her clit, tracing circles in her wetness.

"Jared…" she choked out. "Please stop, we're in the middle of a restaurant!"

He grinned. And dammit if he didn't make her forget where they were—he was deliciously and dangerously attractive and so in tune with what her body craved. His eyes turned a dark shade of green when he was focused on her. That combined with the dimple that flashed whenever he grinned, and she forgot everything but him. Susie couldn't believe she'd ever wondered what other women saw in him. And if they'd even had a small taste of what he was like in bed…she had no idea how they managed to walk away. She was tumbling further and further into whatever lay between them. Its force was over-whelming.

She closed her eyes when he slid his fingers slowly in and out of her channel. She was so wet, her thighs were damp. He knew what she liked now and didn't hesitate to make use of his intimate knowledge. He teased her folds and dove in again with his fingers, his thumb picked up its pace, coasting over and around her clit. In spite of, or perhaps because of, their public location, Susie was more turned on than she could have imagined. She bit her lip to keep from crying out. She didn't want him to stop anymore. Her hips shifted into his hand. In seconds, her climax rushed through her. Her hands flexed against the edge of the table. She forced herself to remain silent as the aftershocks rippled through her.

Jared slowly stilled his hand. He carefully withdrew it and put her panties back in place. He took another swallow of beer. His grin was finally gone. He looked as shaken as she felt.

"Give me your hand," he said, his voice low.

"Huh?" Her thoughts were muddled. The awareness of where they were was finally sinking in again. He tapped her knee.

"Under here."

Unsure of what he meant to do with her hand, she slipped it into his palm, feeling the moisture from her on it. He tugged her hand under the table and pressed it against his jeans. His cock was hard and hot through the rough fabric. He pressed her palm hard against him and then released it, bringing his naughty hand out from under the table. He dipped a napkin in his water and quickly wiped his hand. His expression was fierce when he looked over at her.

"Just so you know what you do to me," he said bluntly.

Susie nodded jerkily, resting her elbows on the table. She was flustered beyond measure and forced herself to look away, trying to get her bearings.

"I'm not sure we can keep doing this and act like nothing is going on," Susie said. She hadn't planned on saying that, but her feelings were intense and raw right now.

Jared nodded. "I know."

"What should we do?"

Jared eyed her, his eyes inscrutable. "I don't know."

Susie sensed now definitely wasn't the time for this conversation. She felt Jared putting up walls and wasn't ready to sort through how she felt and what to do. She shrugged. "Let's eat and worry about it later."

CHAPTER 13

*J*ared knelt down and looked under the shed. "Oh, I see what you mean," he commented to Luke. "The piling on the far side is rotten." He rested on his heels and looked up at Luke. "So what's your plan?"

Luke leaned against the side of the shed. "I have a replacement piling already cut to size. We need to jack the corner up and switch the pilings out. With your help, we can get it done pretty quick."

Jared nodded and stood. "You got the house jack from Nathan?"

"Yup. He dropped it off this morning."

"All right, let's get going."

A while later, they were almost done with the project. Jared was on his back under the edge of the shed, adjusting the bolts on the piling when Luke made a comment that made him glad Luke couldn't see his face.

"So Hannah's near convinced you and Susie are

together. If you were hoping nobody would notice, forget it," Luke said bluntly.

Jared considered deflecting, but he knew it was pointless. Plus, he figured he could use Luke's advice. He just needed a minute to gather himself. "Give me a sec," he replied, slowing the pace at which he was tightening the bolts to buy a minute or two. The nights with Susie were stacking up. When he wasn't with her, he'd try to persuade himself he could go a night without her. By the time evening rolled around, all he did was think about her. When they were together, he forgot about his reservations about relationships. But then, they didn't quite have a typical relationship. And yet, it had gone on long enough now he knew he needed to either make it stop or... something else.

Almost every morning, he found himself behind schedule. She didn't use an alarm, or appear to have any type of schedule. At least, not what he would call a schedule. Her days seemed to be guided loosely. She had meetings with clients and was reliably punctual with those, but otherwise, it was a free for all. He'd taken to mostly staying at her place because she tended to leave a trail of disorder in her wake when she stayed at his. The physical disorder was strangely like the emotional disorder he felt. He was constantly trying to straighten up behind her in the hopes his life would feel in order again. It was in vain.

For instance, he found a random shoe of hers in his kitchen closet yesterday. Just one shoe. He was still puzzling over how someone could misplace a single shoe and not notice it days later. A few days prior, he found a thong under his bed. When he'd returned the items to her, she didn't seem the least bit bothered she'd lost track of anything. While she was unperturbed, he was unsettled. He liked his world organized and prided himself on keeping it that way. Even more unsettling—when he thought he should close the door on this madness with her, he couldn't conceive of doing that.

He finished tightening the bolts and shimmied out from under the shed. Luke extended a hand to pull him up. Jared handed Luke the tools, dusted himself off and leaned against the shed.

"I figured you'd notice at some point," Jared said, looking over at Luke.

Luke chuckled and tucked the tools and his work gloves in the back of his truck, which was parked right beside the shed. He shifted to sit on the tailgate and looked expectantly at Jared.

Jared sighed and rolled his head around, loosening the tension in his neck. "I hate admitting you were right, but I have to. Susie's been driving me half out of my mind for a while now. About a month ago, I got tired of fighting it. Since then, we've been together almost every night." He paused for a breath. He wasn't sure what he needed, but he knew he needed a perspective other than his own. "And damn if I know what to do about it. Any advice?"

Luke gave him a long look. "I wish it was more fun to be right. Having you fess up this quick is kind of anticlimactic," he said with a short laugh.

"Sorry I couldn't make it more satisfying. When you're right, you're right. You're the one who pointed out that I couldn't keep my eyes off her. Now I can't keep my hands off of her. All this time, I kept telling myself to steer clear of Susie. She's a good friend. I respect her. Our lives are all tangled up with the connections we have. And now..." he trailed off and leaned his head against the shed.

"Was there a question in there?"

Jared shrugged. "Probably not. Look, you know I've said for years I didn't want a relationship. I didn't. But I can't treat Susie like some passing fling. And I can't believe I'm about to say this, but I'm not sure I want to." Simply saying that aloud, Jared's heart kicked up a notch. Whatever lay between him and Susie intimidated him. His penchant for control was shattered around her.

He looked over at Luke to catch his mouth hanging half-open. Luke closed it and shook his head slowly. "I may have been right that you couldn't keep your eyes off Susie. But I did not predict this. So let me get this straight: you—my older brother who has told me for years he has no intention of having a relationship—is saying he just might want one."

Jared couldn't help but laugh, even though he was embarrassed. "I'm seriously considering the idea. If this relationship thing hinges on how compatible we are in bed, well then we have it made. Problem is, she drives me damn near crazy in other ways. Remember how Nathan used to be when we all lived together?"

"You mean how he never really had a schedule, at least not the kind you liked, he left things around the house and parked half out of the garage sometimes?"

Jared nodded. "Exactly."

Luke threw his head back with a laugh. "Okay, I'm the middle brother, so I got the whole picture. Sure, Nathan isn't the tidiest, most organized guy. But when it matters, he's on the nose on time and takes care of whatever needs to be done. You? You're so organized, you're practically a walking spreadsheet. Falling somewhere short of that isn't a bad thing. Don't forget you lived with Nathan most of your life until he got married. You worked it out with him. After I moved out, it seemed like you two got along even better. If that's the kind of thing driving you crazy with Susie, you'll get over it."

Jared eyed Luke who couldn't keep the grin off his face. "I know it's funny, but it's also not funny. You've been on my case to get over myself and consider a relationship. I tell you I am, and you can't stop laughing."

Luke sobered. "Fair enough. I know it's not easy. You saw what I went through with Hannah. For different reasons, I was in a similar boat, so I get it. What does Susie want?"

If Jared knew that elusive answer, he'd feel better about his own uncertainty. But he wasn't sure what Susie wanted. In some ways, she was far more relaxed than he was about this. In other ways, she held herself at a distance. "Not sure I should tell you this, so promise me you'll keep it to yourself." He met Luke's eyes, so similar to his own. Luke nodded, his expression somber and quizzical.

"She was a virgin. And damn if I know what it means that she decided to let me be the one to change that little detail."

Luke looked somewhat underwhelmed by this detail. His expression was carefully blank. Too carefully blank.

"I'm guessing maybe Hannah knew and mentioned it to you, huh?"

Luke nodded.

"And I'm getting the sense you know something I don't."

Luke shifted on the tailgate, looking uncomfortable. "Don't read too much into it. Why don't you ask Hannah about it?"

"So I finally fess up about what's going on with me and Susie and now you want me to share this with Hannah and ask her why the hell Susie was still a virgin? I only mentioned it because it kinda blew my mind."

"I think Hannah could shed some light on a few things," Luke replied.

"How come you can't?"

"Because I don't know Susie the way Hannah does. Those two have been best friends since elementary school. Since you're looking for advice, you might as well talk to her."

Jared pushed away from the shed. "Okay, let's do it." He quickly glanced around to make sure he hadn't left any tools on the ground. "We're done here, right?"

At Luke's nod, Jared turned and walked to the house, Luke walking at his side.

* * *

HANNAH WAS WALKING into the kitchen when they came through the door. She immediately walked up to Luke and gave him a kiss. For a moment, Jared envied their comfortable intimacy. All this time, he'd been pleased his brothers settled down because it took the pressure off of him. He'd never once experienced any envy. Oh, Hannah was beautiful, intelligent and warm, and he could appreciate that, but that's as far as it went. But this last month with Susie made him long for the kind of comfort he saw between Luke and Hannah.

Hannah turned to him with a grin. "John was not happy you two didn't get back inside sooner. He wanted to see you before I put him down for his nap. Needless to say, he got fussier and more tired, so he's asleep now."

"I'll stop by tomorrow when he's up," Jared replied.

Luke headed straight for the refrigerator and grabbed two beers, gesturing for Jared to sit at the kitchen table. Jared listened to Hannah and Luke banter for a few minutes. Hannah joined them at the table after putting some chips and salsa out for them.

Luke glanced between Jared and Hannah. "So I suggested Jared might want to talk to you about Susie. You guessed right about them, but don't give him too much grief because he fessed up right away," Luke said with a wry grin.

Hannah's mouth fell open and then she squealed. "Oh my God! I can't believe you two have kept this under wraps."

Jared shifted in his seat. He met Hannah's eyes and smiled ruefully. "I think she wanted to say something sooner, but with everything happening with Emma… To be fair, I wasn't ready to talk about it, so she went along with that. I hope you won't hold it against her."

Hannah grinned and shrugged. "Oh no. Susie doesn't have to answer to me. Lord knows, I don't always tell her everything right away. But I have to admit to being ecstatic about this. I told her I thought you two would make a good couple!"

Jared shifted again, uncomfortable with how

excited Hannah was when he didn't even know which end was up with Susie. Hannah's grin faded as she looked over at him.

"Okay, what's up? You don't look too excited," she said quickly.

Before Jared could reply, Luke interjected. "Hon, I told Jared he should talk to you, but he wasn't exactly running in here. He's, uh, not sure what to do. I thought you might be able to give him some insight into, uh, why Susie hasn't really been with anyone in a while."

Hannah looked between Luke and Jared. Luke looked as uncomfortable as Jared felt by this point. "You thought I'd give him some insight into…?"

Jared set his beer down. "For crying out loud, I'll explain. I'm in over my head here. I can't think straight when it comes to Susie. I never, and I do mean never, planned on another relationship, but I'm having serious second thoughts. I can't tell what Susie's thinking, and I'm still pretty freaked out she was a virgin. She acts like it was some kind of random accident, but that's not the vibe I get and why me? Why the hell did she decide to lose it with me? I have no idea what she wants, if she wants anything from me, and I don't know what to do." Jared ran his hands through his hair and groaned. Susie had gotten under his skin so much, he'd just unloaded on her best friend and utterly embarrassed himself in the process.

He looked up and met Hannah's eyes, which were soft blue and filled with concern and understanding. Which somehow made him feel worse. He was not the guy who women looked at with understanding and a hint of concern. Luke took a gulp of beer and shook his head. "You're in deep," he said wryly.

Hannah glared at Luke. Jared was so emotionally out of sorts, he appreciated her protectiveness. She turned her gaze back to Jared and sighed. "So it sounds like things might be kind of…serious?"

Jared shrugged. "I don't know. I thought we could get it out of our systems, but it hasn't really worked out that way."

Hannah burst out laughing. Jared rolled his eyes. "Luke just laughed at me too. Could you lay off here? I get that it's kinda funny, but I'm serious."

Hannah stopped laughing and shook her head. "I wasn't laughing at you, I swear. I laughed because Susie said almost the same thing before anything actually happened. She had this idea she'd have a one-night stand with you and get it out of her system."

"Yeah, it was her bright idea. I don't know why I went along with it. I damn sure wouldn't have if I'd known she was a virgin," he said with a sharp shake of his head.

Hannah nodded slowly.

"Could you maybe shed some light on that?" he asked.

This time, she shook her head slowly. "I think you need to talk to Susie."

Jared threw his hands up. "I did! She said it was an accident. Don't get me wrong, it's not like I thought she shouldn't be a virgin, it's just not how she acted. She's the one who suggested the one-night stand. Not that I have lots of experience with virgins—make that one—but I sure as hell didn't expect a virgin to propose a one-night stand. She was all casual about it, which doesn't make any sense." He groaned and ran his hands through his hair again.

Hannah was quiet for a long moment. "Here's

what I can say. Susie used to date pretty regularly and was a bit of a flirt. Something happened to change that. It's not my place to talk about it, but since you care about her, you should ask her. And don't take her excuses for an answer."

Jared looked at Luke. "So why exactly did you want me to talk to her?" he asked, gesturing to Hannah.

Luke looked at Hannah. "Could you maybe give him a clue how Susie's brain works? He's lost over here."

Hannah chuckled. "If you hadn't figured it out already, Susie's a passionate person. She's loyal as hell. I figured she'd be with someone long ago, but..." she paused and shrugged "...that's not how it's worked out. I think she's forceful enough that it scares some guys away. They're too stupid to know what they're losing. That's why I thought you two would make a good couple. You're not going to be intimidated by her. And she's not intimidated by you. The one-night stand thing, that's not typical of Susie. I think she's just as freaked out by how she feels about you as you are about her. So go talk to her. Now."

Jared rolled his head around, again trying to loosen the tension in his neck. He looked at Hannah for a long moment. "I was hoping you'd tell me what I should do."

"I just did. Go talk to her," Hannah replied with a grin.

Jared had been hoping for a shortcut, but it was becoming clear he'd have to swallow his confusion and talk directly to Susie. Which terrified part of him —the part that had decided years ago that relationships were too messy. Susie was beginning to matter far more than he'd gambled. He finished his beer in a long swallow and stood up. "Guess I'll have to."

Luke gave him a sympathetic grin while Hannah smiled encouragingly.

CHAPTER 14

*S*usie walked onto her deck and set the groceries she had on the small table by the door. She walked to the front of the deck and sat in one of the chairs. Jasmine was seated on the railing, grooming. Susie looked out at the familiar view, trying to settle herself inside. It was early evening and the sun had started to dip down toward the horizon. The water was calm in the bay, the light from the falling sun rippling on the water. Mount Augustine was haloed with clouds, light filtering through them in shafts of gold and rose. The field in front of her house was filled with fireweed, which was close to blooming, the tips of the tall flowery weed bright fuchsia with buds. A raven called from its perch in a nearby tree, another immediately answering.

Susie took a slow breath. Jared had texted a while ago, saying he'd be over soon. She'd convinced herself they needed to stop this madness. She'd known long before she'd fallen under the spell of this intense attraction for Jared, he didn't want a relationship. Not to mention that she didn't know what the hell she wanted, and the closer she got to Jared, the more exposed she felt, which was decidedly not comfortable. She also sensed she was grating on him, which annoyed her beyond measure. Oh, he didn't say anything, but she knew it drove him nuts that she wasn't as tidy as he was and didn't stick to a schedule the way he did. Precisely why he drove her nuts with his insistence on precision. She appreciated precision when it mattered—like with math and accounting— but otherwise, she found it unnecessary and annoying. She'd decided tonight she'd explain they needed to end this. She figured cold turkey was the best approach. Otherwise, they couldn't keep their hands off of each other.

Jared's truck pulled into the driveway. As he walked to the deck, she soaked in the sight of him. His black curls were windblown. His stride long and loose. He wore faded black jeans and a t-shirt, practically a uniform for him. The way they molded to his fit body started a fluttery heat in her belly and moisture between her thighs. His teeth flashed in a grin, his dimple winking at her. He walked up to her side and leaned over to kiss her. Just a quick kiss and her heart started pounding so hard she was surprised he couldn't hear it.

"Hey," he said simply.

"Hey yourself."

He leaned against the railing and looked out at the view. When he turned back, his green eyes locked on hers. He looked serious, which made her nervous.

He started to speak and paused. He cleared his throat. "I told Luke and Hannah about us. Before you get pissed at me about it, I was looking for advice. I don't know what's happening here, but I don't want it to stop. But I have no idea what you want…"

"How come you didn't ask me?" she asked, irritation flaring.

He threw his hands up. "I'm asking you now, okay? Look, we've been friends for a few years now. It's not like you don't know that I didn't plan on having a relationship. But…" he paused, his face reddening "…I'm not so sure anymore. I'm not ready to put the brakes on this, but we haven't really talked at all."

When he paused for a breath, she opened her mouth, but he held his hand up. "Let me finish."

She bit her lip and leaned back in her chair.

His eyes traveled over her face, searching for what she didn't know. He looked so serious. Anxiety beat its wings in her chest.

"I don't know how to say this without it being awkward, so I'll just say it. Something happened and I don't know what it is. It has something to do with why you've never dated ever since I've known you and why you were a virgin. Before you go thinking I care about whether or not you were experienced, I don't. I was confused because you didn't bother to tell me. If you're wondering, proposing a one-night stand creates a different impression. Something doesn't fit. And if you're gonna let me be the guy who takes your virginity and claim it was an accident, you could at least explain a little more."

Susie's heart was about to fly out of her chest and her head hurt. She did *not* want to explain this to Jared. But she knew he would keep asking. She wondered if he'd tried to talk to Hannah. "Did you ask Hannah about this?"

Jared nodded. "Don't go thinking she gave

anything away. She told me to talk to you. She was downright bossy about it, so I figured I might as well."

Susie nodded and sighed. Of course, Hannah didn't say anything. Susie knew if she didn't tell Jared the whole story, Hannah would also tell her she needed to tell the truth. Though she'd convinced herself it didn't matter, she figured she might as well spit it out. Jared definitely had a stubborn streak, so he'd keep asking.

Par for the course, she decided blurting it out was the quickest way. "Not long after you guys moved here, I almost got date raped..." She paused long enough to gauge Jared's reaction thus far. His eyes were dark and focused intently on her. A muscle ticked in his jaw, but he was silent. "It was in Anchorage. I met some guy at a bar. He must have slipped something in my drink. Next thing I knew, I woke up and he was on top of me trying to take my clothes off. That's as far as it went. I might have been out of it, but I was pissed." The memory made her anxious, her throat was tight, tension slid stealthily through every muscle. She gave herself a shake to break it. "He took off with a few scratches and bruises, leaving me with a few myself. Before then, I'd decided it was high time to get rid of the whole virginity thing. But I'm kind of picky. After that, I don't know. I haven't dated anyone since. I suppose trust might be a bit of an issue."

Jared's eyes remained trained on her. His hand was curled on the edge of the railing. His fingers clenched the railing so tightly his knuckles were white. His shoulders rose and fell with a measured breath. "Do you have the asshole's name?" he asked, his voice dark and low.

"Tim. That's it. I don't have his last name. I'd just

met him at the bar. I don't even remember leaving." Her pulse pounded in her ears. "Jared, I'm fine. It was almost four years ago. He didn't actually rape me. He just tried."

"Susie, the guy drugged you. I don't care if he didn't actually rape you, attempted rape is kind of a big deal, not to mention that he definitely assaulted you."

Susie wasn't sure what she'd expected, but this protectiveness from Jared was definitely not it. As exposed as she felt telling him this, it was strangely comforting to sense his concern for her. She searched his face. His eyes were dark, his mouth tight, his hand still clenched on the railing. She stood up from her chair and walked to the railing, leaning against it beside him.

"I'm not saying what he did was okay. But it was years ago, and there's nothing to do about it now. He was from out of state, just another tourist. We can't do anything with a first name, so let it go. I have."

"You can't act like this had no effect on you. You haven't dated anyone since then. You've practically lived like a nun. There's got to be something you can do about it. Did you talk to the cops? I can call Darren and ask him about it."

Susie's throat was tight, and emotion welled inside. Jared's wish to make this right meant so much, she was utterly overwhelmed. She shook her head and turned to face him, knuckling tears out of her eyes. "It means a lot to me that you want to fix this. But it's not worth it to me. Even if, and that's a huge if, we could track Tim down, it would be my word against his about something that almost happened. I may not have talked much about it, but I did look into it. This kind of thing almost never leads to any kind of legal charges. Dredging it up this many years later won't go anywhere, and it will make me miserable."

Jared looked skeptical though the tight lines around his mouth eased, if only a little bit. He lifted his hand from the railing and brushed a few loose curls away from her cheek, tucking them behind her ear. The gesture was unexpected and so intimate it shot straight through to her heart.

"Are you going to get mad at me if I look into it myself?" he asked softly.

Susie thought about it for a long moment and shook her head. "Not as long as you don't mention my name. Hannah knows about it, and she probably mentioned it to Luke, but I'd prefer not to tell the free world."

Jared nodded slowly. "Okay. No names."

He grasped her hand and tugged her in front of him, pulling her into his arms. During their brief conversation, weariness had fallen over her. She leaned into his embrace, resting her head against his shoulder with a sigh. One of his hands threaded into her curls while the other moved in slow circles on her back. They stayed like that for several long moments. She felt relieved and vulnerable at once.

The sound of Jasmine's purring made her giggle. Jared leaned back, and she lifted her head to look at him. "It's Jasmine, can't you hear her?"

He glanced to where Jasmine had sidled over and was rubbing her head against his side. He chuckled. "Hard not to."

Jared met her eyes again. His gaze had softened, the hard edge gone. Her stomach growled. "Dinner?"

Susie nodded and stepped out of his embrace,

missing the warmth and certainty immediately. As she walked into the house, she remembered that she'd planned to tell Jared they needed to end whatever it was they were doing. But she couldn't bring herself to, not right now.

* * *

Susie awoke with Jared curled beside her, his arm thrown across her waist. His breathing was slow and even. Sun splashed across the bed. She'd forgotten to close the shades last night. She lay still, savoring the feel of Jared's body against hers. A soft breeze coasted through the window, ruffling the edge of the sheet. The quiet was broken by magpies chattering outside. Jared shifted and rolled away from her. She glanced at the clock. It wasn't quite six yet. She silently cheered. Jared hadn't overslept, which meant he wouldn't be grumbling about being behind schedule.

She thought back to last night. It had been a simple night. After she'd blurted out what happened, Jared hadn't brought it up again. He'd insisted on making dinner, which consisted of grilled salmon burgers. They'd watched television afterwards. It was the first night they'd spent together when they didn't have sex. It had been...comfortable. Now in the bright light of morning, the anxiety she'd kept at bay fluttered inside. She felt vulnerable and exposed. Jared was starting to see parts of her she didn't want anyone to see. Much less a man who elicited feelings she'd never experienced before. Even contemplating what it meant hiked her anxiety. She liked to feel in control, and it seemed every day her control on her own emotions floated further and further away. Restless, she rolled over and climbed out of bed.

One hot shower later, she toweled off and slipped her robe on. When she turned to leave the bathroom, Jared was leaning inside the door. His curls were tousled, his green eyes sleepy. Even rumpled with sleep, he set sparks alight in her. His boxers hung low on his hips. His sculpted body was a sight to behold. He ran his hand through his hair and tugged her into a sleepy embrace.

"You beat me out of bed," he mumbled into her hair. She could feel his grin against her curls.

She leaned back and looked up at him. "I usually get up early, but you've been keeping me up too late so you haven't noticed it yet," she said with a shrug and a smile. "Coffee?"

Jared nodded, his arms falling as he stepped to the shower and kicked his boxers off. She forced herself to turn and walk downstairs.

Later that day, Susie pulled up at Glacier Pizza. Hannah was meeting her here for lunch. Susie figured it was high time she talked to her about what was going on. When she walked in, Hannah was already waiting at a booth. Glacier Pizza was a utilitarian restaurant, low on frills and with amazing pizza. The brick oven stove sat center stage with an open kitchen surrounding it. A counter with stools circled the cooking area and booths lined the walls. Decorations consisted of photos from locals and tourists alike lining the walls, along with various license plates from all over the country.

Susie waved her greetings to the kitchen crew and slid into the booth across from Hannah. "How long have you been waiting?"

"Not long. Just got here a few minutes ago. I already ordered for us – got the Greek pizza because it's your favorite. How's it going?"

Susie tried to smile, but it wobbled.

"Hey, are you okay?" Hannah asked, concern lacing her voice.

Susie brushed her curls away from her face and sighed. "I don't know. Jared told me he told you and Luke about us."

Hannah nodded slowly. "Just yesterday. I guess I thought it was a good thing?"

Susie sighed. "Yes and no." She paused, trying to gather her thoughts. "Okay…the sex is phenomenal," she said, unable to repress a grin. "I mean, I don't have anything to compare it with, but I had gotten really close to the finish line before and trust me, it's good."

Hannah shook her head and smiled. "Well, well. That does not surprise me. You two have been circling each other like cats for the last year or so."

Susie blushed so hard she was surprised her hair didn't turn red. But this was Hannah, her best friend for forever, and if she was going to tell it the way it was, she had to give her the whole story. "So there's that. And then, there's the rest. You know Jared. He said for years he didn't want a relationship. And like I told you before, I didn't think we'd be a good couple because he drives my batshit crazy with how organized he is. That's still driving me nuts, though the sex helps. But now things are getting…I don't know… intense. He's acting like he wants to try to actually have a relationship. Then he wanted to know how come I haven't dated anyone in years and how come I was a virgin. So I told him and now I'm freaking out."

Hannah was quiet for a moment, which had the

effect of cranking up Susie's anxiety. "Would you say something please?" Susie demanded.

"I was just thinking. Let me start at the beginning. So the sex is amazing, Jared is still uptight and annoys you, and he asked you how come you hadn't dated in a while. Have I got it right so far?"

Susie nodded.

Hannah took a breath. "Jared stopped by yesterday, and Luke wanted him to talk to me. He was wondering how come you were a virgin and didn't bother to tell him. I think he was worried it was a big deal and you weren't talking to him about it. I didn't tell him anything, just told him to talk to you. What did you tell him?"

Susie sighed. "Same thing I told you. I didn't want to, but you know him, he's like a dog with a bone. He was great about it, honestly. He was sweet and supportive and all that. He also wants to ask Darren if there's anything he can do about it. I tried to tell him there's not because I looked into it, but you know him. He likes to solve problems. He promised me he wouldn't give my name, so I figure let him find out himself what I already know. Date rape almost never goes anywhere, especially when it didn't actually happen. It almost happened."

Hannah gave her a long look. "I get that it would be hard for anything to be done, so I'm not going to push. But don't pretend like it was nothing. You were drugged and assaulted. Don't think I'm trying to dredge this up and make it worse, but you're making it seem like it was nothing. I don't blame Jared for wanting to do something about it. Let him ask his questions and come to his own conclusions. How did it feel to talk to him? When he was over yesterday, he said he didn't know what you wanted. To be honest, he seemed kind of lost. I felt bad for him."

Susie's throat felt tight, and her head felt like it was going to explode. She didn't know how to make sense of what she felt, but she felt more vulnerable than she ever had in her life and she could hardly tolerate it. "It was okay to talk to him. I just..." she shifted in her seat, crossing and uncrossing her legs. "I don't know what to do. I didn't really talk about it, but I was okay being alone. I had come to terms with that. And then Jared just had to get under my skin. It's confusing and I can't think straight."

Their waitress walked over and efficiently set the pizza down and filled their water. The break allowed Susie to gather herself. A few bites of pizza, and she felt more grounded.

She looked over at Hannah. "I'm not sure I'm ready for this. You know me, I'm the romantic. It's nice that Jared says he wants to maybe try a relation-ship, but that's not quite enough for me. If I'm going to be all muddled and freaked out, I need to feel like he's in it for more than a 'maybe' kind of thing." Her words held far more confidence than she felt.

Hannah set her slice of pizza down and leaned her elbows on the table. "So you get to lecture me, Tess, and Emma and just about anyone else who crosses your path that we need to give love a chance and put up with the fact that it's kind of messy and not so easy —and you're going to cop out this fast?" Hannah's blue eyes flashed.

Susie was taken aback and uncomfortable with how close Hannah's words hit home. Her feelings for Jared were messy and overwhelming, and she didn't want to deal with it. Not when she couldn't be sure of where he stood. But to hear Hannah put it like that…

"I can see why you might say that, but I'm not copping out. I'm just saying I'm not sure."

Hannah took another bite of pizza and leaned back. After she finished chewing, she spoke again. "Of course you're not sure. That's part of how this works. Just don't go thinking you can try to slink out of this without us calling you out. You're my best friend, and you deserve to be happy just as much as anyone else. Even if you won't admit it, I think you and Jared have a lot more going for you than most. I'm not going to sit by and be quiet because it's more comfortable for you."

Susie nodded, abashed. "I'm not going to slink out of it." She paused and sighed. "I wish I had a better sense of what Jared wanted. That would help."

Hannah tilted her head, a small smile tipping the corners of her mouth. "I don't think that's all that's going on with you."

"What do you mean?"

"Oh I'm sure it would help if Jared hadn't said for as long as you've known him that he didn't want a relationship. But I think it's hard for you not to be in control. Relationships, the ones that matter, make it hard to feel in control, especially at the beginning."

Susie grabbed onto the one thing that was making her feel the most uncertain. "That's just it. I don't know if Jared can even get past how much he needs things to be a certain way." Saying the words out loud sent her doubts screaming. It was precisely what she feared most with him—that she'd open her heart and start to hope for something, but when things began to get serious, he'd try to box her back into a tidy friend corner. A corner she didn't know if she could ever inhabit again with him.

Hannah was quiet for a moment. "Okay, I don't doubt that's something he's got to figure out. But control is a thing for you too. It's hard for you to let go, and it's definitely hard for Jared. So maybe think about that," Hannah said softly.

Susie felt herself flushing again. She knew Hannah was right, and it annoyed the hell out of her. She wrinkled her nose. "Fine. I'll think about it. In the meantime, could we talk about something else now? I've fessed up way more than I ever wanted to, so cut me some slack. How's John?"

Hannah grinned and instantly shifted topic. Precisely why they'd stayed friends as long as they had.

CHAPTER 15

A few days later, Susie decided to stop by Jared's house on her way home and surprise him. Once again, she'd tumbled into seeing him every night despite how unsettled she felt whenever she allowed herself to think about it. She knocked quickly on his door and stepped inside. Jared was sitting on a stool at the counter, focused intently on his laptop. He didn't appear to have heard her come in.

"Yoo-hoo," she said with a wave.

His head whipped up, surprise flashing across his face. She kicked her shoes off and walked to the couch, plopping down on it. "Thought I'd stop by. Seems like we're at my place all the time. What's up?"

Jared turned on the stool to face her. "Working on some planning for our next commercial trip. I was gonna call you in a bit and head your way." He glanced at his watch.

He didn't make a move to come over to where she sat, which irritated her. She knew she was interrupting, but she didn't care. She wanted him to shift gears

"

and go with the flow. "Why don't we stay here tonight?" she asked with a bright smile.

"Don't you have to feed Jasmine?" he countered.

"She's a cat, Jared. I filled her food and water before I left today."

"Does she need to go in?"

"Is Jasmine the only reason we always stay at my place?" Susie asked sharply.

Jared's expression was inscrutable, carefully blank. He shrugged. "I guess so."

"Well then don't worry about it. Jasmine will be fine for one night. What should we have for dinner?" she asked. She purposefully grabbed one of the throw pillows and tucked it behind her and then dragged the throw, so precisely placed on the back of the couch, over her legs.

Jared's mouth tightened. He glanced at his laptop and back at her. "I need a little time to finish up what I was working on. Do you want to pick up some pizza while I finish up?"

Susie shook her head. "Nope. I had pizza for lunch today." A complete lie because she hadn't had pizza since she had lunch with Hannah a few days ago, but Susie was determined to stay at Jared's place and make him tolerate her interruption. A sense of perversity had been building. Jared had gotten under her skin, so she planned to get under his.

"Can I cook something?" she asked, standing quickly. She tossed the pillow to the floor and allowed the throw to slip off the couch, hanging haphazardly. She couldn't have planned it better. Jared's eyes traveled to the errant pillow and throw and back to her. His eye twitched, but his expression remained carefully controlled.

He didn't reply, but turned away. He quickly saved whatever he was working on and closed his laptop. She walked over and leaned on the counter beside him. When he swiveled to face her again, she grinned. "So what can I cook?"

His green eyes searched her face. "I'd rather go somewhere," he replied.

Susie felt downright mutinous. "Not in the mood," she said, pushing away from the counter and walking to the small pantry in his kitchen.

Jared moved quickly and followed her to the pantry. He leaned against the doorway. Her pulse revved and desire slid stealthily through her body. She batted the feeling back. She didn't like feeling out of control and wanted to shake Jared up.

"Mind telling me what's going on?" Jared asked.

She ducked under his arm, getting out of the tiny pantry. The close proximity to him made her thoughts fuzzy.

"I want to cook, and I want to stay here. We're always at my place. How come you don't want me here?"

His eyes narrowed, but he remained silent, which annoyed her further. "You know what I think?" she asked, her tone sharp.

He shook his head.

"I think you don't like it when I'm here because you can't keep everything perfect." Her temper was rising. She was determined to get him to be honest. She didn't like to think about it, but Jared's tendency to keep their relationship contained to her house represented what she feared—that he didn't want this to be anything other than convenient for him. While he was willing to entertain the idea of a relationship, he didn't mean for it to be anymore than it already was. Meanwhile, her heart was in too deep, and she knew it.

Jared eyed her carefully, his jaw was tight, his eyes dark. He shook his head slowly.

Susie ignored him and walked back over to the couch. She threw the rest of the pillows in a heap on the floor and picked up a book and tossed it on the floor. "What are you gonna do now?"

Not waiting for his reply, she flounced up the stairs. Inside, she was spiraling. She felt too off kilter, too vulnerable and too uncertain about what was happening between them. Jared was starting to matter *way* too much. A tiny voice in the corner of her mind tried to get her attention, but she ignored it. Instead, she stormed into his bedroom and tore the covers off his bed. She whirled around and stomped back down the stairs. To find him leaning against the kitchen counter, arms crossed.

"What?" she demanded.

"Just wondering when you'll be done with..." he paused and waved a hand around "...whatever this is."

Her chest was tight, her heart hammering. If blood could boil, hers did. "This..." she replied, imitating his hand wave around the room "...is you being way too in control. You can't stand having anyone over here because it's not perfect. Well, life is messy. Relation-ships are messy. Sometimes, I'm messy."

Jared's nostrils flared as he took a sharp breath. "I am not too in control. You forget. I lived with my brothers for years. Have you met Nathan? No one could ever accuse him of being a neat freak. Don't make this something it's not."

Susie didn't know how to reel herself in. All she

knew was she couldn't get Jared out of her head, she couldn't get her body to behave, and he was burrowing into her heart. Meanwhile, he stayed calm, cool and collected. He was gracious and polite, but he kept her at a distance...except in bed when the intimacy and passion was so intense, she almost burned in its flames.

She stared at Jared. "What am I to you?"

His composure split for a second, uncertainty flashing through his eyes. His mouth opened and closed. "What is this about?"

"You didn't answer my question," she said flatly.

"Susie...you mean a lot to me. I told you, I'm not sure what this is but..."

She cut him off. "Yeah. You said that before. What I see is a guy who's more than happy to spend time with me as long as it's at my place only and as long as it involves sex. It's like you want to keep everything tidy, just how you like it. That's not how it works! If you want more than some passing fling, it might not always be convenient. You can't have it both ways," she said, hearing her tone and hating how bitter she sounded. "Why don't you call me when you have some kind of clue?"

She didn't wait for his answer, she was too afraid she would burst into tears in front of him. She slipped her shoes on, snatched her purse and ran out of the house. When she started to pull out of the driveway, she saw Jared standing on the porch. He'd followed her out, just as he had that rainy night when he'd kissed her the first time. Her vision blurred. She forced herself to drive away, tears rolling down her cheeks.

CHAPTER 16

Jared walked into Luke and Hannah's kitchen and froze when he saw Susie sitting at the table. She held John in her lap and was making silly faces at him. John giggled. Susie's throaty laugh made his heart clench. Her curls fell in a tumble around her shoulders. It had been three days and nights since she'd stormed out of his house. He'd tried calling her once, but when she hadn't answered, he hadn't tried again. He steeled himself to get through the next few minutes. He silently cursed Luke who could have told him Susie would be here.

Hannah looked up and smiled. If she had any idea what was going on with them, she hid it well. "Hey Jared! Come on in. Luke'll be right down."

"Hey Hannah, how's it going?" he asked, striving to sound normal while his heart pounded so hard, he could hear every beat.

"Good. We had a busy morning with errands.

Susie babysat for us," Hannah replied, her eyes glancing Susie's way.

Susie finally looked up. Her brown eyes met his, a tinge of defiance in them. Jared knew she was angry with him, but he was too confused about his own feelings to know what to do about hers.

Susie nodded tightly and smiled. Her eyes, usually so warm, were guarded. "How are you?" she asked politely.

He nodded. "Fine," he replied, not trusting himself to say more. He felt untethered. He'd been doing his damnedest to come to terms with the reality of how he felt about her. He'd finally started to get grounded and accept he was going to try to do the one thing he'd sworn off doing—have a romantic relationship. And then she'd blown it up in his face. He missed her on a visceral level. Seeing her…he just wanted to tug her to him and tell her to give him a chance to figure this out. But he couldn't do that in front of Hannah, John gurgling on Susie's lap and Luke about to walk in any minute. So he waited stiffly, his mind afire. Luke came downstairs moments later, and they headed for the harbor.

* * *

LATE THAT AFTERNOON after they returned a happy tourist family to the harbor with a cooler full of halibut, Jared climbed in his truck and drove to the police station. Before Susie had stormed out, he'd left Darren a message to call him. Jared was determined to find a way to track down the Tim who tried to rape Susie and hold him accountable. Darren had finally called him back today, apologizing for the delay because he'd been out of town.

Though Jared didn't know what would happen with him and Susie, he wasn't going to drop this. He strode into Darren's office. Darren looked up from his computer and leaned back in his chair. "Hey man, how's it going? Have a seat," he said, gesturing to the chair across from his desk.

"Going okay. The usual busy season," Jared replied as he sat down. "You?"

Darren chuckled and ran a hand through his sandy brown hair. "Same here. We're ten times busier in the summer with the tourists. Last night, there was a hell of a party at Midnight Sun Lodges. We're still processing everyone this morning. A crowd of underage drinkers who found our accommodations not quite as nice as their hotel."

Jared shook his head. "You had to arrest them all?"

Darren rolled his eyes. "When the hotel refused to let them stay, it was the quickest option. College kids, most underage. Too much alcohol, some property damage and a few assaults. They're all out now. But that's not why you're here. You said you needed some help. What's up?"

Jared took a breath. "I have a hypothetical. That okay?"

At Darren's nod, he continued. "What are the options for a woman who met a guy at a bar and woke up later, half out of it, with the guy crawling on top of her, trying to get her clothes off? She thinks she was drugged and managed to drive him off, but not without a few bruises."

"This is just hypothetical?" Darren asked, his eyes concerned.

"I don't have permission to tell you who. But it really happened a few years ago. All I have is a first name."

Darren sighed. "I'd love to tell you there are options, but cases like that are a dime a dozen and damn hard to prosecute. Without good evidence, most prosecutors won't touch 'em with a ten foot pole."

"Seriously? That's bullshit. There have to be some options."

Darren shrugged and shook his head slowly. "I wish I had a different answer. Cases like that happen all over the place every day. Ever since those undetectable date rape drugs started floating around, guys use 'em like candy. Women don't even know what happened, if anything. If women even come forward, prosecution is a nightmare. Their memories are fuzzy, it's 'he said, she said.' There's your reasonable doubt right there. I'm not saying I agree. I'm just telling you how it is."

Jared pictured Susie's face the other night when she'd told him about it. Tense, embarrassed, anxious… and scared. He couldn't keep the vision of what she told him out of his head. He heard her insisting she was fine. He believed she was, but he didn't believe it was okay for some guy to do what he did and walk away, most likely to do the same thing with other women.

"So that's it then?" Jared asked. "I'm not liking your answer."

Darren met his eyes and leaned forward, resting his elbows on his desk. "I hate my answer because it's crap. It's not a fair situation for women, and the way things are right now, it's damn difficult for these cases to go anywhere. In your hypothetical, with only a first name, our options shrink to almost zero. I'm damn sorry. Trust me, I am."

Jared sighed and ran his hands through his hair. "Okay, I hear you. For now, I won't pound your door down."

Darren chuckled. "I wouldn't blame you if you did. I hear about those situations all the time. I just hope karma comes back around to bite those guys…hard."

Jared stood to go. "You and me both. All right, man. Thanks for taking a few."

As he drove away, his hand went to his phone. His instinct was to call Susie. But they were barely speaking. Jared whipped his truck into the parking lot at the post office and came to a quick stop. "Dammit!" he pounded his fist against the steering wheel. Darren's answer pissed him off. His heart hurt at what Susie went through, and he was infuriated there was no recourse for her. He leaned his head against the steering wheel. He wanted to hear her voice. He missed their banter, her frisky texts, her warm brown eyes, her wild curls and lush little body. He missed *her*.

* * *

SUSIE WAS SO focused on the report she was working on, she jumped when Emma said her name.

"I didn't hear you come in!"

"Yeah, you seem really interested in whatever you're working on," Emma replied wryly.

She half sat on the edge of Susie's desk. Emma's resemblance to Hannah was still startling at times. She shared a similar tall, willowy build, dark hair and blue eyes. Her manner was more understated, and she was generally more measured in her responses. Susie chalked that up to her being a therapist.

Susie saved the report she was working on and closed her laptop. "Are you here to follow me over to the car place and fetch me for dinner?" she asked. Her car had needed a tune up and new tires, so she'd texted Hannah, Emma and Tess, hoping one of them would give her a ride home after she dropped her car off to pick up again tomorrow. They'd cajoled her into dinner at Sally's.

Emma grinned. "Yup. I'm your taxi girl tonight. Ready?"

After Susie dropped her car off, she climbed into Emma's truck and they headed to Sally's. Susie glanced over at Emma. "You look great! How's it feel now that it's been a few weeks since that scare with Greg is finally over?"

Emma took a deep breath and smiled. "Better than I could have guessed. It's such a relief."

Susie leaned across the console between the seats and half-hugged Emma. "I'm so happy! And now you can relax and have fun with Trey," she said with a grin, shifting back into her seat.

Emma blushed. Susie pushed on. "When are you just going to admit you love him and move in?"

"How about you let me figure that one out while you figure out what you're going to do about Jared?" Emma countered, pulling into the parking lot at Sally's.

Now Susie was blushing, but she kept her composure. "I'm working on it," she said, hoping it wasn't obvious that the mere mention of Jared stirred her up.

Emma glanced her way as they walked inside, but

she didn't comment further. Tess and Hannah had snagged a booth already. After dinner was ordered and drinks arrived, they toasted Emma and caught up.

Hannah was in the middle of a story about John's antics on the boat this morning when the door swung open, and Jared walked in with Nathan. Susie looked to Tess immediately. "You didn't tell me they were coming here," she hissed across the table.

Tess shrugged. "Nathan doesn't tell me everything. He and Jared were working on some boat repairs on the big boat today. He knew we were meeting here, he probably thought he'd surprise me. I doubt he thought he had to ask for my permission. You can't avoid Jared forever," she said pointedly.

Nathan and Jared had started to head their direction, but were sidetracked by a group of tourists, likely a group they'd hosted on a fishing trip. Susie watched as one of the women in the group flirted shamelessly with Jared. It made her insides twist and her face hot.

Hannah caught her eyes. "Tess has a point. The other morning was not pretty," she said, referencing the agonizing minutes when Jared had stopped by Hannah and Luke's house and Susie was there. Susie had had to force herself to look at Jared. It physically pained her to see him, just as it did now. She knew she'd been a fool the other day when she'd torn through his house and basically pitched a fit. She felt stupid and embarrassed and missed him like crazy. But damn if she was going to be the one to make the first move. Even if she hadn't handled it well, her feelings mattered. Jared hadn't been letting her be a true part of his life. He kept her in a compartment that separated her from much of his life. If they were really going to try to do something other than have mind-blowing sex, he had to include her in his world as much as she included him in hers.

She met Hannah's eyes defiantly. "Maybe it wasn't pretty, but it's up to him to reach out to me. If he thinks I'm going to pretend everything's fine because it's more comfortable for him, he underestimated me."

"Maybe you could meet him halfway," Emma said.

"I was meeting him halfway. He wasn't returning the favor. It was like he only wanted me in his life as long as I was contained where he wanted me," Susie countered. She was irritated and hurt. She wanted her friends to agree with her. She glanced toward Jared and Nathan. They were still occupied talking to the group. The flirty woman had shifted closer to Jared and was smiling up at him. Susie wanted to vomit. The last thing Jared needed was some simpering woman. *You're just jealous. If you don't want Jared to notice anyone else, maybe you should do something about it.*

Susie mentally swatted at her taunting thoughts. Jared was going to have to at least try to talk to her. Emma nudged her with her shoulder. "You're staring."

"I know. I might sound pissed, but I can't help it," she said with a sigh.

Tess waved to Nathan when he turned back in their direction. "Well, you'd better get your game face on because here they come." She threw Susie a sympathetic glance. "If it helps, he's as miserable as you, according to Nathan."

Susie's heart lifted the tiniest bit at that. Nathan leaned over to plant a lingering kiss on Tess's lips when he reached their table. He stood and grinned when he finished. "Hi ladies."

Susie experienced a pang of envy witnessing Nathan's unabashed adoration of Tess. Jared arrived at the table a few steps behind Nathan. He leaned against the side of the booth, his hands tucked into his jeans. His eyes were bracketed with weary lines, his hair rumpled from the wind. He was polite, yet distant. His eyes passed over her. She wanted to grab him and force him to see her. She wanted to sit by him, rub his shoulders and ease his weariness. Her heart pounded, her stomach was in knots, and she felt hot and flustered.

Their friends carried on a normal conversation while she and Jared watched from the sidelines. The tension between them was obvious, but Susie didn't know what to do about it. She wanted to run her hands through his curls and kiss his sculpted lips. She wanted to feel the caress of his green eyes when he watched her the way he did. Instead, the distance yawned between them. Nathan cracked jokes, teased Tess and filled the space created by their tension.

Susie caught Emma's sympathetic glance and wanted to cry. She quickly stood and excused herself. She had to brush past Jared to get by. The heat from his body was a magnet for hers. It was all she could do to keep moving. She walked briskly to the restrooms, which were situated down a hall at the back of the restaurant. She splashed water on her face and took a long look in the mirror. Her curls were a mess, but they usually were. Her face was paler than usual, her eyes looked tired. She sighed and leaned against the sink for a long moment, marshaling her composure.

When she stepped out of the bathroom, Jared was leaning against the wall in the hallway. He looked up —vulnerability flashed in the depths of his eyes. He kept his eyes trained on her. Her pulse raced, her belly fluttered and anxiety arced through her.

"Hey," he said softly.

"Hey."

"I was hoping we could talk."

Susie didn't want to talk just now. She wanted to burrow against his hard body. But she nodded, unable to form words.

"I, uh, I've been thinking about some of the things you said the other day..." he paused when someone walked by. Once they exited through a door at the end of the hallway, he ran a hand through his hair. "Look, this isn't the best place to talk. I just wanted a chance to say I was listening to you. This whole..." he gestured between them "...relationship thing is more than I bargained for and I'm not too good at it."

Her heart leapt, practically hammering its way out of her chest. She opened her mouth to reply, only to fall silent when a cluster of drunken tourists came down the hall. Two women stumbled into the bathroom while another waited outside. She glanced up at Jared, relieved to see his deep green eyes looking back at her, sparks of heat circling in their depths.

"I heard you might need a ride home," he said gruffly.

Susie nodded. She couldn't seem to form words to reply. After a long moment, Jared pushed away from the wall, his eyes shuttering. "I only wanted a chance to talk. I guess that's too much to ask," he said, his eyes hurt.

Her voice finally kicked into gear. "No! Don't go. I just...couldn't seem to talk." She glanced to the woman who was leaning against the wall. She didn't appear to be paying attention, but nonetheless. "Let's go," Susie said, tucking her hand in Jared's arm and tugging him down the hallway. She made a beeline for the booth to grab her purse. Nathan had taken her seat and started to get up. "You stay. Jared's giving me a ride home," Susie said firmly. Hannah, Emma and Tess grinned in unison while Nathan didn't seem the least bit surprised.

"So do I get your dinner?" Nathan asked with a chuckle.

"Sure. I got the salmon burger with fries."

Nathan winked as they turned to leave.

* * *

HOURS LATER, there had been very little conversation. Susie fell back against the pillows on Jared's bed and rolled her head to the side. He lay beside her, his chest rising and falling rapidly, his pulse beating visibly in his neck. His skin was damp. Her eyes traveled down his body, glorying at his muscled chest and abdomen. He lifted a hand and stroked along the curve of her hip and down her thigh. Her breath slowed, and the delicious exhaustion she had come to associate with Jared stole through her body. Her eyes fell closed.

Sometime later, she felt the covers being tucked around her. The lamp was switched off, and Jared curled behind her. His breath quickly evened into the slow breath of sleep. She was facing the windows that looked out over Kachemak Bay. The moon was a curved sliver resting just above the mountain range. The late sunset of the summer night left its mark with deep red, gold and orange fading into the inky sky. The colors shimmered in the rippled water. She'd known this view for so long, it was etched in her memory. Yet, she never tired of it. It comforted her in its quiet presence. She tumbled into sleep, lulled by the comfort of Jared's warmth around her.

She woke before Jared and took advantage of the moment to observe him. He slept with abandon, so unlike how he was in his waking hours. One arm was flung above his head, the other resting on his abdomen. Her eyes traveled down the planes of his body, and she couldn't help but lean over and nudge the sheet off his body. It slipped away, and she gave in to the temptation to stroke her hand down his chest, across his abdomen and over his cock, which lay innocently against his thigh. The slightest caress from her, and it came to life. She enjoyed the velvety feel of the skin, sliding her fingers slowly up and down in a soft glove.

Jared moaned and shifted his hips, his pelvis arching into her hand subtly. He'd yet to awaken. She stealthily straddled his legs before leaning over to take him in her mouth. His hardness filled her mouth. She took her time, savoring his sleepy state. He often took control during their lovemaking. Not that she minded one bit, but in this state, she could take charge before he realized it was happening.

She knew the moment he came awake when his hands laced into her curls.

"Susie…Dear God…feels so…good…"

Susie picked up her tempo, sucking and stroking, clasping him in a wet grip. Jared arched deeply again, a guttural groan following. "Let me…" he said, starting to shift up.

She pushed him back down. "No," she said firmly, enjoying a moment to boss him.

He chuckled before groaning again when she took

him fully into her mouth, the head of his cock pressing into the top of her throat. In moments, his hips flexed reflexively, and he came into her mouth. She sat up and grinned, pleased for making him lose control for once. Jared's eyes opened, his green gaze still sleepy, but bright.

"Good morning," she said with a wide smile.

He laughed and tugged her against him. After a quick kiss, he dragged her into the shower.

CHAPTER 17

*O*nce again, Susie found herself tumbling back to where she'd been with Jared. She couldn't stay away from him. Though he'd said he heard her concerns, they still hadn't really talked and in a few short days, they had already shifted into the same pattern. They stayed mostly at her place. Oh, Jared tolerated her stopping by, but he was tense unless they were skin to skin. She kept trying to find a time to talk, but something always interrupted. If she was honest with herself, it was easier not to talk. Today, she'd spent the day fishing with her friends and couldn't keep Jared off the hamster wheel in her mind.

"Hey!" Susie exclaimed when an eagle swooped right in front of her and snatched the salmon she'd taken off the hook and set by the cooler.

She stood and watched the eagle lift in the air, her salmon firmly in its talons. Tess was walking toward her on the beach, a salmon in hand. "You just gave him lunch," she said with a grin.

Susie's eyes tracked the eagle as it flew a short ways down the beach away from the cluster of people fishing and immediately started tearing into the salmon. She sighed and peeled her gloves off. An errant curl blew loose from her ponytail across her forehead. "That was supposed to go in my freezer. Oh well," she said with a shrug.

"It's not like we haven't caught plenty today," Tess said as she reached the cooler by Susie. She flipped it open and tossed the salmon safely inside.

Susie promptly sat on the cooler. "Oh yeah, we did. Are you about done? I'm getting tired."

Tess nodded and sat down on another cooler. Her honey curls blew wild in the wind coming off the bay. They'd come to one of their favorite beaches this morning to fish for silver salmon. Hannah and Emma were still standing in the water's edge. The beach was less busy with tourists since it took a short hike down a steep cliff to reach the water. It was within view of Otter Cove Harbor, nestled between two cliff sides where a stream ran down the middle feeding into the ocean.

Susie leaned back on her hands, watching the boats coming in from the bay into the harbor. She thought she could see Jared and his brothers, but she wasn't sure. Sun sparked on the water. "Is that The One that Didn't Get Away?" Susie asked Tess, referencing the name of the brothers' guiding business and its boat.

Tess shaded her eyes, following Susie's gaze. "I think so. They should be due in soon." Tess grinned at Susie. "So how are things with Jared? Nathan gave him all kinds of grief yesterday when he stopped by to pick up some gear. He's happy for you two, but he can't let it go that Jared swore for years he'd never have another relationship."

Susie's heart fluttered. "What did Jared have to say?" she asked, striving to keep her tone casual. Her romantic side, the side that pushed her to nag her friends until they fell head over heels and found their happily-ever-after, was impatient and skittish. Jared pretty much held her heart in his hands, and yet... Susie didn't know if he was ready to take the next step or not. *Perhaps you should try to talk to him? You know this isn't all on him, you're avoiding too.* She almost rolled her eyes at herself.

"Jared took his lumps from Nathan. He's been pretty open that if it wasn't for you, he'd still be swearing up and down that he'd never be in a relationship," Tess said.

After a long pause, Tess cast a knowing glance Susie's way. "You're worried about something. What's up?"

Susie sighed and bit her lip. "That obvious, huh?"

Tess grinned. "Susie, you're always obvious. Which, by the way, is one of the best things about you. You're so straightforward."

Susie rolled her eyes. "I suppose there are some benefits."

Tess tilted her head, her eyes expectant.

Susie took a breath and blurted out what was on her mind. "I don't know what's next with Jared. Things are...really good." She paused, a blush flaming her cheeks. "You know I'm a romantic..."

Tess burst out laughing. "How could I not? If I hadn't seen the light about Nathan, I'm pretty sure you'd have come to North Carolina and dragged me to him yourself!" Her eyes softened as she looked at

Susie. "Not so easy on this side, is it?" she asked softly.

Susie shook her head. "He doesn't say anything about what's next. I feel like I can't say anything because it's such a big deal for him to be in any relationship. Expecting more might scare him off."

Tess came and sat beside her, sliding an arm over Susie's shoulders for a hug. "You've gone from bossing the rest of us around to realizing how terrifying it can be when it's your own foot in the shoe," Tess said with a chuckle.

Susie butted her shoulder against Tess's. "Fine. I suppose it's funny. How about a suggestion for me here?"

"The way I see it, you have two options. Boss Jared around like you do everyone else. Or wait and see. If you want my opinion, I think Jared's completely in love with you, and it might do you some good to wait and see for once in your life."

Hannah and Emma arrived to hear the tail end of Tess's comment. Hannah chimed in. "You want Susie to wait and see? Let's place bets on that!"

Emma merely laughed. Susie threw a wet glove at Hannah. "Only if I can bet too. I'll make sure I win!"

"What are you trying to wait for?" Emma asked.

Susie groaned while Tess laughed. "To see what might happen next with Jared," Tess replied.

Emma, the quietest of the group, nodded and smiled, but left it alone. Hannah put her hands on her hips and tilted her head. "It only stands to reason after you had your say about all of us that you'd find it's not so simple when it's you."

Susie blushed, but held her chin high. "I only stuck

my nose in your love lives because I cared. I never thought it was easy."

"Right. Let me know how long you can wait," Hannah said with a sly grin. "Did that eagle fly off with one of our fish?"

* * *

LATER THAT AFTERNOON, Susie walked into the kitchen at her parents' house. Faye stood by the counter, methodically chopping rhubarb. She set her knife down and wiped her hands when she saw Susie.

"Hey there, didn't know you were stopping by. Coffee?"

"I meant to call on my way over, but I dropped my phone in the car," Susie replied with a grin. "Yes to coffee."

Susie sat down at the round kitchen table, her eyes immediately traveling to the view outside the window. The sun slipped in and out of view today, clouds floated across the sky, casting shadows on the mountains. Faye set a cup of coffee in front of her and sat down.

They sat quietly for a few minutes before Faye spoke. "So, Jared?"

A blush flamed up Susie's neck and face. She bit her lip and grinned. "Figured you'd hear something by now."

Faye grinned. "Oh, I heard something a few weeks ago. Care to fill me in on the details?"

Susie shrugged. "We're seeing each other."

"Hannah seems to think there's a bit more to it than that."

"Oh my God, Mom! You're pumping Hannah for information?"

Faye nodded emphatically. "I have no shame when it comes to my only daughter. Once I heard a few rumors and saw your car over at Jared's place..."

Susie cut her off. "You drove by to see if I was there? Mom!"

Faye shook her head, her curls swinging as she laughed. "Did you forget June lives on the same road?"

June was an old friend of her mother's. Susie sighed. "Oh, right."

"So I asked Hannah about it. Don't get on Hannah's case. You know I babysit for her whenever she needs it. I cornered her when she stopped by to pick John up the other day. So what changed your mind?"

"About?"

Faye rolled her eyes. "About seeing anyone."

Susie thought about last night—about how she felt exploding in Jared's arms and curling up against him later when she fell asleep, about how what used to annoy her with him mostly made her laugh now, and about how she still wasn't sure where they stood. The last thought danced in the shadows of her mind. Faye cleared her throat.

Susie shrugged. "Well, I don't know if I consciously changed my mind. This thing with Jared just...happened."

"Hannah thinks you two are in love," Faye said bluntly.

Her blush, which had finally faded, came roaring back. Her face aflame, Susie shifted in her seat and took a sip of coffee. When she glanced her mother's way, she gave up. "I don't know how I feel, Mom," she said, a tinge of defiance in her words, annoyance at her mother and Hannah flaring.

Faye chuckled, her eyes warm. "You never did like anyone thinking you might be vulnerable. If I read the situation right…"

"What are you reading tea leaves now?"

Faye rolled her eyes and gave a slight shake of her head. "Never mind. Maybe you should stop worrying so much about guarding your heart and relax and enjoy it."

Susie took a sip of coffee and chewed her lip. She thought about when her dating life had come to a screeching halt, how vulnerability seemed too high a price to pay, and how impossible it had become to deny what Jared meant to her. "I'll work on that," she said simply.

Faye gave her a long look. "There are never any guarantees, honey. The best you can hope for is you happen to fall in love with someone who loves you too and who's going to try. That's it. We all screw up. Lord knows, your father and I have been together going on thirty years now and we still have our moments. I'm happier than I want to admit that you've let down your guard at all. Plus, Jared's damn easy on the eyes," she said with a grin.

Conversation shifted to lighter matters. Susie left a while later with a bag of fresh rhubarb in hand. She immediately called Hannah. "Did you tell my mom what I told you about?"

"She asked me about Jared, and I answered. I wasn't aware it was a secret," Hannah replied indignantly.

"I didn't mean that, I meant what I told you about before Jared and I even got together." Susie's mind had been spinning with worry that Hannah mentioned anything about what happened in Anchorage, the start to her not-dating life. Her mother's comment about her letting down her guard had her on alert.

"No! Susie, I wouldn't do that," Hannah said, her voice exuding hurt.

Susie bit her lip, instantly chagrined.

"Why would you think that?" Hannah asked.

Susie sighed. "I don't know. Mom said some stuff about me letting my guard down, and I got paranoid. It's fine you talked to her about Jared and me. I'd rather she got her gossip from you than someone else."

Hannah mumbled something.

"What did you say?"

"Oh, just trying to get John back in his car seat. Can I call you back?"

"Sure. I'll be at Jared's later on," she said before hanging up.

* * *

JARED WALKED into Sally's with Nathan where they were meeting Trey. Susie was picking him up later since he'd ridden into the harbor with Nathan today. He spied Trey at a booth once he walked in and made his way there.

A good meal and a few beers later, he and Trey were chatting with a group of tourists. Nathan had already left. Jared impatiently checked his watch. Susie had texted that she'd be by soon. Jared watched, bemused as Trey deftly fended off one flirtatious woman after another. He'd been busy doing the same, but it was a new experience. For years, he'd been content to enjoy the temporary liaisons offered by female tourists enamored with the idea of a fling in Alaska. Ever since he'd touched Susie, he wasn't the least bit tempted.

Susie pushed through the swinging door into the restaurant and caught his eye. She started to thread her way across the room, but was intercepted several times on the way by friends and acquaintances. Maggie and Jason, a local couple, stopped by to chat with him and Trey. Maggie and Jason were high school sweethearts who ran a construction company together. They were a study in contrasts, Maggie with her short dark hair and bubbly personality, and Jason with his shaggy blonde hair and low-key quiet manner.

"Hey guys! How's it going?" Maggie said, ever enthusiastic. Jason merely nodded and grinned.

The conversation shifted onto how busy summer was when one of the women who'd just been flirting with them walked right up to him and handed him a piece of paper. She was flat out gorgeous—tall and curvy with bright blue eyes and dark hair that fell almost to her waist. "I'm in town another two nights. In case you need some company..." she said with a wink over her shoulder before walking away, her hips swinging.

Trey burst out laughing while Jason shook his head. Maggie, known for being the opposite of tactful, said, "Well Jared, she's your dream woman. No strings attached and she handed you her number."

Susie arrived at the table in time to hear Maggie's comment. Jared internally winced. He had zero interest in the woman beyond an objective appreciation of her beauty. Susie's eyes breezed past his while she cheerfully greeted Trey, Maggie and Jason.

He wanted to reach over and yank her to his side, but he didn't. Their relationship had been not so public for its brief existence. Jared felt uncertain in this situation, and Susie's reserve wasn't helping. He remained polite through the remainder of social chatter with Maggie and Jason and breathed a silent sigh of relief when they said their goodbyes.

Susie finally looked at him for more than a passing glance. "Are you ready to go?" she asked, a little too politely for his comfort.

At his nod, she waited while he stood and walked at her side on the way out. Trey walked with them, easing the tension for a few moments. Once they were in her car, heavy silence fell.

Susie was quiet on the ride home. Once they got to his house, he watched her carefully, but her face was guarded. She stood to the side of the couch, looking out the windows. Summer was fading fast with the sun starting to set earlier every day. All that was left tonight were faded streaks of pink in the darkening sky.

"Is everything okay?" he finally asked.

A flush spread up her neck and face. "Where is this going?" she asked. Her voice was high, and her words rapid.

"I'm not sure," he said carefully. He sensed whatever he said meant a lot right now.

Her eyes were bright, her pulse visible in her neck. "Well, maybe you might want to think about that. I'm not blind, I know you're pretty accustomed to the tourist flings..." her words trailed off in a mumble.

Jared waited a beat, contemplating what to say.

"Susie, it was bad timing. I wasn't even a little interested in that woman." His mind raced, trying to think of the right thing to say when the truth was, he didn't know. Susie had him tied in knots.

Susie looked back at him, her eyes bright with tears. It was all he could do not to tug her into his arms, but he sensed she wouldn't appreciate that right now. Her breath hitched. "Okay, okay. I don't know… Maggie was right. That woman was like your dream woman. I'm nothing like her. I don't look anything like her, I'm not just a passing tourist you can have a fling with."

Foreign as it was for him to navigate these waters, he decided caution wasn't working. "Come here," he said firmly.

"You're ordering me around now?" she asked, an edge of irritation to her words.

Perfect. Susie irritated with him was the start to foreplay for them.

"Yup. Come here before I drag you over here."

She whirled to look at him, her curls swinging, her eyes sparking. She stomped over to him, pausing in front of him. "I'm here."

Jared grabbed her hands and yanked her onto his lap. She fell atop him, her knees falling to either side of his hips, her skirt riding up her hips. Absolutely perfect.

He slid a hand up her back, lacing his fingers through her curls and bringing his other hand up to trace her lips. "I don't give a damn who that woman was. Am I doing this just right? Probably not, but cut me a little slack. Are we done talking now?"

Her mouth parted, her breasts rose and fell with her shallow breaths. Her hips settled over him. He could feel the moist heat of her through his jeans. He ground his cock against her. A whimper escaped her.

"You didn't answer me," he said softly. "I'll give you three more seconds and then we're definitely done talking for now."

Lust streaked through him. He forced himself to wait a beat longer. Before dropping both hands to her hips and forcing her down against him. As was the case with Susie, he was constantly on edge, confused about his feelings and hers. The internal disorder only served to stoke his lust for her beyond endurance.

Her hips shifted restlessly against him. He held her still for a moment. "Look at me," he commanded.

Her brown eyes met his, dark with passion. Her tongue darted out to moisten her lips, and he groaned. He tugged her forward, crashing his lips against hers. She met him stroke for stroke. He could barely think as he tore at her clothes. Her blouse floated to the floor. With a flick of a finger, her bra came undone, her breasts spilling out. He curled his hands around them, leaning forward to lave and suck one nipple and then the other. He traced lazy circles with his fingertip around her damp, pebbled nipples. She arched her back with a sigh, and he gloried at the sight of her. He loved how she threw herself into passion, just as she did everything.

He shoved her panties out of the way, sliding a finger into her folds, already dripping wet. He reined himself in, forcing himself to go slowly enough to work her into a frenzy. He leisurely caressed back and forth, coasting his thumb across her clit. She ground her hips into his hand.

"Jared..."

"Hmm?"

"Please…"

"Please what…"

"I need you…"

She stood abruptly and tore at his jeans, kicking her skirt and panties off as she did. When she bent over, her deliciously round bottom faced him, her pink folds winking between her thighs, he wanted to stand and sink into her right there. The temptation hardened his cock, already so swollen, sensation honed in and all he wanted was to be inside of her. She stood and turned again, navigating his jeans down his legs. She grinned and leaned over, immediately taking him in her mouth.

His head fell back with a groan. He lifted it to find her breasts swaying as she licked and stroked him, taking him fully into her mouth.

"Come here," he commanded, his voice weak with lust.

She grinned as she lifted her head. "Not yet," she whispered. Her eyes stayed pinned to his when she tilted her head to lick up one side of his cock and down the other.

His vision blurred when she leaned forward, the curve of her bottom tilting into view. Jared fought to keep the reins in his control. The warm suction of her mouth, the sway of her breasts and her hips shifting as she moved up and down…all of it driving him to the edge of wildness. He almost came right then, but he needed more. "Please…come here," he pleaded, his voice breaking.

She slowly stood with a soft smile. Straddling him, she started to sink down onto him before he grabbed her hips and held her still.

He held his cock in one hand and dragged it back

and forth in her folds, the head cresting against her clit again and again.

"Jared…I…Oh my God…don't stop…"

Now, he dragged her pleasure out. The sight of her gasping, the sheen of passion on her skin made him delirious. Barely in control, he slowly slid inside—the hot, wet warmth of her channel intoxicating. Intense pleasure streaked through him as she began to ride him, her hips moving in a rolling rhythm. He felt her climax coming and surged deeply inside just as she began to pulse around him. Her hips rose and fell as he pounded into her, shouting when he finally found release. She fell against him, her soft, cushy body instantly relaxing. As he caught his breath, he thought this might be heaven.

CHAPTER 18

*J*ared watched a shoe fly over the loft railing. He was downstairs in his house while Susie remained upstairs in the loft bedroom. It was his shoe for crying out loud. "Do you mind? If you're going to throw things at me, how about giving me a wide berth?" He hollered up at her. He paused for a breath and couldn't quite believe he was dodging running shoes.

Susie huffed. "Oh my God! Don't be melodramatic. I wasn't trying to aim at you!" The sound of her stomping across the floor reinforced how angry she was. Jared wasn't quite sure how the conversation had started, but next thing he knew, Susie had demanded to know if they were going to 'date forever' and if he'd ever thought about 'something called commitment.' He'd been taken off guard by her question, so he'd answered vaguely. They'd been upstairs getting dressed, and she'd promptly thrown her towel at him.

In the midst of her anger, he couldn't think

straight. She stormed down the stairs and marched up to him, coming to an abrupt stop with her hands on her hips. Her cheeks were bright and her brown eyes flashing. His body did what it always did around her —electricity buzzed through him. He itched to grab her and bend her over the counter right there. She glared at him. "I'm going to work. Maybe you could think about this while you're out fishing today," she said, sarcasm dripping from her words.

She whirled around, her curls swinging in a circle. She quickly searched out her clogs, one under a stool by the kitchen counter and the other by the couch, and stomped out the door. Jared glanced around the room with a sigh. There were marks of Susie's presence throughout his small house. Dishes were piled up by the sink, a bright red scarf hung haphazardly over the stair railing, and a sock stuck out from under the couch. Jared shook his head and set to work washing the dishes.

He knew they needed to talk, but somehow it was easy to avoid. Ever since he'd managed to get back in her good graces, he was afraid to bring anything up for fear she'd shut him out again. He needed someone to talk to and soon. He had to get his head clear and figure out what the hell to do.

* * *

SUSIE WAS DRIVING HOME after work when she impulsively turned down Jared's road. Nathan's truck was in the driveway when she arrived. She heard voices from the back on the deck, so she began to walk around the house. She froze when she heard her name. She hadn't come around the corner of the house yet, so she was hidden from their view.

"So what's up with Susie?" Nathan asked.

Susie held her breath because she was dying to hear what Jared might have to say. There was a long silence. Nathan spoke again. "Not really sure what that means."

"It means I'm not sure. Things are great, amazing really, when we're together as long as we're not talking about us. I still don't know where this is going. Susie's amazing and she damn near blows my mind, but I don't know. I don't know what I want long-term. She got mad at me this morning, said I needed to think about where things are going. I know we need to talk, but I don't know what to say," Jared said.

Susie's stomach felt hollow. She forced herself to stay put. She waited quietly.

"Isn't this how you two ended up not speaking to begin with?" Nathan asked.

Jared's sigh was heavy. Susie could picture him shrugging. "Yeah, guess so. I feel caught here. I can't seem to stay away from her, and now she's expecting things from me. I need a little time."

Susie couldn't stand to hear anymore. Anger fired inside. She strode around the back of the house. Jared and Nathan turned together. Jared froze in place, his hand hovering over the deck railing where a beer sat. Nathan's gaze quickly shifted from startled to concerned. His blue eyes searched her face carefully.

She pointed at Jared. "I don't expect anything from you! Because you make it perfectly clear I can't. We need to talk, so consider this our talk. We're done. You don't need to worry about me anymore."

She paused for a breath, her heart hammering so

loud she could hardly hear. Her head pounded, and she felt sick. Looking up at Jared, her heart clenched. While she may not allow herself to expect anything from him, in a tiny corner of her heart, the place she shoved her ridiculously romantic wishes and hopes, she'd fallen in love with him and wanted the happy ending. His eyes were dark, his jaw tight. "Susie…"

She waved her hands. "No, no! Don't talk, don't say something you don't mean. You said it yourself, relationships are messy. Lord knows, I don't want to make you uncomfortable." She straightened her shoulders, clinging to the remnants of her dignity. Her cheeks were hot, tears pricked her eyes, and her throat was tight. "I'll be polite when I see you and eventually this will pass. Please don't call me or try to stop by."

She turned and walked back around the house. Footsteps came through the grass behind her. "Susie, don't do this," Jared said.

She whirled around. A mistake because he was right behind her. Her eyes collided with his heated green gaze. She didn't give herself time to look long, but she could have sworn his eyes glistened with tears. "Don't tell me what to do. You had good reasons for avoiding relationships. And you're right. I do expect things. Like not to be treated like nothing more than one of your meaningless flings." She turned again and kept walking. "You don't know what you want, so let me end this. We should have done it already."

When she got to her car, Jared tried to reach for her arm, but she flung his hand away. "Susie, could we *please* talk about this?"

Susie slammed her car door and started the car.

She refused to look Jared's way again for fear she might burst into tears. She drove away. Glancing in her rearview mirror when he reached the top of the drive, she saw Jared standing in the driveway, his hands tucked in his jeans. The drive home was blurred by the tears rolling down her cheeks.

CHAPTER 19

*J*ared pulled up at Red Truck Coffee and climbed out of his truck. It was just past six in the morning. Trey was already there, chatting with Cammi.

"Morning," Jared said. "How's it going?"

Trey grinned. "Perfect now that I have a cup of Cammi's coffee," he said, lifting the bright red cup.

"Hey Jared," Cammi said with a warm smile. No matter how early he saw Cammi, she was always cheerful.

"Hey Cammi. Anyone ever pointed out that you seriously found your calling?" he asked.

She grinned as she got his coffee ready. "You mean making coffee?"

"Well, there's that and the fact that no matter how early I show up, you manage to be friendly."

Cammi giggled and handed him his coffee. "I'm a morning person. It's part of why I did this. But I turn into a pumpkin pretty early at night."

Jared chuckled as he paid. He glanced to Trey who

was leaning against the counter. "Are we waiting for Luke and Nathan?" Jared asked.

"Yup. Luke called right before you pulled up and said they'd be right here. I figure you guys can follow me over to the plane from here. Any word yet from the group you're taking over for the trip?"

Jared savored a sip of coffee and glanced at his watch. "Should meet us at your plane in about fifteen minutes. Thanks for fitting us in. I know it was short notice."

"No problem."

A few other customers pulled up, so Jared and Trey stepped to the side of the bright red, refurbished bread truck that housed Red Truck Coffee and leaned against it while they waited. For the most part, Jared and his brothers ran guided fishing trips out of Otter Cove Harbor in Diamond Creek. Once in a while, they got requests to do fly out trips to mountain lakes and rivers. Those trips were Trey's bread and butter, so he agreed to fly them in and out for the trip. They'd fly out for three days and return.

Jared was looking forward to getting out of Diamond Creek for a few days. Ever since Susie had walked off the other day, he hadn't been able to think clearly. His house, which used to be a haven of orderly peace and quiet, felt big and empty. Whenever he had a spare moment, he wanted to see her. He hadn't seen her since she stormed away and he hungered for any contact, no matter how frosty. He just wanted to know she was okay.

Trey's voice startled him. "You okay, there?"

Jared glanced to Trey and shrugged. "Been better."

Trey nodded, his gaze shifting away to start out over the harbor. "Susie?"

Jared nodded.

"Not that you're asking my advice, but maybe you should tell her how you feel."

If only I knew how I felt. Wish somebody would tell me.

An eagle swooped low and landed on the sign for the harbor entry situated just past the coffee place. The eagle carefully tucked its large wings and commenced to stare right at them. Jared had become accustomed to seeing eagles almost daily in Alaska, yet the intensity of their gaze still took his breath away. Their eyes were bright yellow, sharp and fierce. He was consistently relieved not to be their prey for if he were, those eyes would terrify him.

"That simple, huh?" Jared finally asked in reply.

Trey chuckled. "I didn't say it would be easy. But, yes, that simple. It's pretty obvious how you feel to me, so you might as well tell her."

"It's obvious?" Jared asked, his heart picking up speed at the mere contemplation of how he felt about Susie.

"You love her."

Jared knew without a doubt Trey was right, but hearing it said so simply terrified him. His brain scrambled at hearing the word he kept trying to avoid thrown out there with confidence, as if it were a fact. *He's right. You love her and you know it. Stop trying to pretend like it's anything else.* Jared's heart felt like it was going to beat its way out of his chest. He wanted to be in control, he didn't want his heart to be at the whim of love. He tried to feign ignorance. "You think so?"

Trey turned to him. "Sure looks like it to me."

Jared elected not to argue the point because Luke and Nathan pulled up. He somehow gathered himself, shoving his confusion about Susie and Trey's way-too-confident proclamation into a compartment. He couldn't think about it now. *Yeah, because it hurts too damn much to wonder if you've completely blown it.*

In short order, they were at the small lake where Trey kept his floatplane. The group they were guiding consisted of four men, all avid fishermen. Matt and Ben were brothers, and Craig and Reid were their good friends. The group had traveled and fished together frequently. Jared was pleased to learn they were fairly experienced with backcountry fishing. They were flying into Katmai National Park to fish along the Brooks River, famed for rainbow trout, arctic char and salmon. The area also boasted the single largest brown bear gathering in the world. It was one of the most phenomenal places in the world to fish. Yet it required skill and a clear understanding of the importance of respecting wildlife.

Once the gear was loaded, Trey powered up the floatplane, and they were flying across the bay and Cook Inlet. The view from a floatplane was breathtaking. It was as if one could reach out and touch the glaciers and mountains as they flew over them. A cluster of sea lions rested on some rocks near the mouth of Kachemak Bay. Trey landed the plane in a wide stretch of the Brooks River.

Several hours later, they had checked in at Brooks Camp, the official camp area for visitors to the Brooks River. They headed down to attend the required bear safety and etiquette briefing. Jared, Luke and Nathan had been here several times since they'd moved to Alaska. The experience was awe-inspiring every time.

After a pizza dinner on the camp stove, Nathan's specialty, Jared stretched out with a book in the tent he was sharing with Nathan and Luke. Their tent had a screened roof, so he could see the sun as it dropped lower toward the mountains. He wondered what Susie was doing and considered Trey's blunt point. He tried to remember how he felt shortly before he planned to ask Jen to marry him back in Seattle. He thought he loved her, but now he wasn't so sure. He certainly never felt the gut-churning sense of loss he did with Susie since she'd driven off the other day. It was worse than after the first time she stormed off. Part of what weighed on him was the sharp pain in her brown eyes, those eyes that were usually warm and held a glint of mischief.

THE FOLLOWING MORNING, Luke led the way to a fishing area upriver from the famed viewing platforms. Jared brought up the rear of their group. Once they found a quiet area to fish with enough visibility to see if any bears approached, he and his brothers got busy helping the guys with them select preferred flies and get started. The entire group planned only to catch and release for the trip. For Jared, they represented true lovers of fishing. They fished only for the love of the sport, not to keep any trophies.

Hours later, Jared rested on a log by the river and gulped down some water. Nathan sat down beside him.

"Can you hand me one of those snack bars?" Nathan asked, gesturing to the backpack resting on the ground beside Jared.

Just as Jared reached for the backpack, he saw movement in the grass across the clearing where they were fishing. A large brown bear entered the clearing trailed by two cubs. Jared didn't hesitate and stood immediately, Nathan jumping up with him.

"Hey guys, cut your lines! They'll go for the fish first," Jared called.

Luke was by the shore and moved swiftly, slicing his line with a fishing knife and turning to help Ben, Craig and Reid. Matt was furthest out in the river and didn't appear to have heard Jared's call. Regulations required they stay fifty yards away from bears once their presence was known, not to mention that any moment a brown bear was nearby, they were in a volatile situation. A mother with cubs raised the risk. The safety factor on their side was that the bears were focused on fish, not them.

"Nathan, we have to get Matt's attention," Jared said.

Nathan skipped a rock in the water by Matt, and Matt finally turned, his eyes widening once he saw the mother bear headed into the water downstream from him. He quickly cut his line and started wading in to shore. Several tense moments later, they were all clear with the bears occupied with their own fishing.

"Damn, that happened fast," Ben, the younger of the brothers, commented.

Luke nodded. "Usually does. That's why it's not optional to attend the bear safety briefing. They're everywhere around here."

Nathan glanced to Jared. "Looks like now might be a good time to grab our stuff and head back to camp for a bit."

Craig looked at them, eyes wide. "You mean to walk closer and get our packs?"

Nathan nodded. "Mama bear and her cubs are busy right now. Our packs are far enough away."

Reid piped in. "I'll help."

Jared shook his head. "Nope. You guys stay put. Nathan and I can carry everything."

Without a word, he looked to Luke who nodded. "I'll wait here."

Jared and Nathan moved at a measured pace toward the cluster of backpacks on the ground. Fortunately, every one in the party only had one fishing rod and kept them in hand when they moved away. He and Nathan slung packs over their shoulders quickly and started walking back. Nathan was a few strides ahead of him. Jared looked up once to see a look of concern flash across Luke's face. The moment he looked up, Jared tripped on a rock and fell, unable to keep his balance with the weight of the packs. As he stumbled, a sharp pain shot through his ankle, and he heard a crack.

"Jared, you need to move it!" Luke called out. "Mama bear is headed your way."

Pain shooting up his leg, Jared rolled to his good side to see. Unlike with black bears, the best defense with brown bears was to play dead. As soon as he realized how close she was, he rolled onto his stomach and lay still. He prayed Nathan or Luke would move fast and get the bear spray out. He could feel her approach and sniff the packs on his back. His heart thudded as he tried desperately to keep his breathing slow and quiet. She pawed at a pack that had fallen to his side. She seemed curious, not aggressive. He felt the packs shift on his back and suddenly a flash of searing pain. Her claws had scraped his back in her curiosity. He ground his teeth together, breathing through the pain. Another few seconds passed, and he heard the distinct sound of bear spray. The bear rapidly retreated. Jared lay still as he heard the grass on the far side of the clearing rustle and the lumbering strides of the bears moving away.

Luke's voice broke through the haze of pain. He heard Luke barking orders at Nathan and the guys with them. He grimaced and rolled on to his side. "She wasn't being aggressive, just curious," he said, between gasps of pain. "Think my ankle's broken and she got me when she was messing with the packs. She was doing what bears do."

Luke leaned over, his green eyes calm and steady. "Stay put, okay? Nathan and Matt headed back to the main camp to get help. Let me see where she got you."

Jared's breath hissed through his teeth as he tried to breathe through the pain. The area where the bear had scratched him was burning. His ankle pain dulled to a throb. Luke carefully moved the packs and checked on his back and ankle.

"Your ankle is swelling fast, and those scratches are deep," Luke said, his voice concerned.

Luke came back to his other side. "How ya hanging in there?"

"Hanging. Coulda been much worse. Can you radio for Trey to fly in sooner? You guys can stay and finish the trip."

Luke nodded. "Nathan was planning to radio Trey on his walk back to the camp."

Jared rested on his side and waited. He heard Luke conferring with Ben, Craig and Reid. Ben was a doctor and efficiently splinted his ankle and did a preliminary cleaning of the scratches on his back with supplies from the basic medical kit they carried. After that was done, Ben and Luke helped carefully prop him up against a log. Luke dosed him with ibuprofen. "Won't be as good as the heavy stuff, but it'll help with the swelling and bring the pain down some," he said gruffly.

Jared heard the concern in Luke's voice and shook his head. "I'm okay. It hurts like hell, but it's just a broken ankle and some damn deep scratches. Made me think of when you watch cats bat at things. She wasn't even trying to hurt me, but their claws are so long, it doesn't matter."

Luke nodded, but the concern didn't fade in his eyes. He tugged a small log over and sat beside Jared on the river beach. Luke glanced skyward, the lines around his mouth tight. "I'm worried about the weather. Clouding up fast. Unless it moves through quick, no one will be flying in today."

Jared hadn't been paying attention to the sky and looked up. Dark gray clouds were rolling in and blocking out the sun. It had been a mere half hour since Jared had fallen and the weather had shifted markedly. But then, that was par for the course in backcountry Alaska.

Jared lost track of time, but was relieved when Nathan, Matt and two park rangers arrived. Hours later, he was resting inside a room at one of the lodges inside the park. He chuckled when he considered the outrageous cost of staying at the lodge, but the owners had been kind enough to offer up one of the staff rooms for him to rest in. Luke's concern had been warranted. Rain lashed against the windows. Nathan had contacted Trey with their satellite phone. According to Trey, the weather was just as bad in Diamond Creek. He couldn't give them an arrival time. According to one of the park rangers, it may be at least another day or two before they could fly out. Meanwhile, Jared knew he needed medical treatment beyond the basics offered here. He was more worried about his back than his ankle. With Ben's skill, his ankle appeared properly set. Ben tried and failed to keep the concern out of his face after he got a good look at the scratches on Jared's back.

"Just tell me how bad it is," Jared said bluntly.

Ben eyed him for a moment and ran a hand through his brown hair. Ben screamed outdoorsy. He was tall, fit and lean with brown hair and blue eyes. He had a quick grin and was quiet and low key. He'd been a steady presence since he helped Luke with Jared's ankle on the beach. He let out a breath. "I'm concerned because the scratches are so deep. They need to be cleaned thoroughly, and I don't have the equipment for that here. Honestly, you're going to need anesthesia to get through the cleaning these scratches require. Keep in mind, brown bear claws can be as long as three to four inches or more. Even a casual swipe can gouge you deeply, and that's the case on your back."

Jared tried to make light of it. "At least it was close to my ass," he said with a chuckle.

Ben barely smiled. "At least."

Nathan poked his head around the corner of the door. "How about some food?"

Jared's appetite was minimal, but he knew he needed to eat. At his nod, Nathan came in with a tray. He sat on the edge of the bed and grabbed a tray stand and situated it over Jared's legs. His eyes were worried, but he did what Nathan usually did and cracked jokes to deflect.

Late in the night, Jared shifted uncomfortably in bed. He was propped on the pillows, mostly on his side, keeping the pressure off of his back. His brothers and the other guys had headed out to their tents for the night. Jared lay in the dark and thought about Susie. He wanted to hear her voice more than anything and could have used her wry humor and warmth right about now. In the long hours since his fall this afternoon, when he could think past his pain, she filled his mind. All his worries about where they were headed and how to handle a relationship had fallen to the wayside. He would give anything to be in Diamond Creek right now with her messing up his tidy world. Instead, he was afraid he'd waited too long to make sense of his feelings. For now, he had to get through this long, rainy night alone and wonder if it was too late to make sure she understood just how much she meant to him.

CHAPTER 20

*S*usie slammed the door behind her after Jasmine raced inside. Rain was falling heavily and blowing sideways with the wind. The warm summer weather had disappeared with the cold rain. She flicked on a few lamps and turned on the heat to drive the chill out of the house. After she got Jasmine dried off, she took a shower and changed. Her thoughts kept traveling to Jared, wondering how he and his brothers were faring on the fishing trip in Katmai. *Stop thinking about him. He doesn't know what he wants and you're in too deep.*

Susie's mental train of thought around Jared was a broken record. She was still furious at him, but more furious with herself for letting her desire get the best of her and opening the door to her heart. Her body craved his presence and her heart ached—though her head said one thing, her heart missed him like crazy. With a sharp shake of her head, she stomped back downstairs to scrounge something up for dinner. She was startled to hear a knock at her door. Before she got to it, Hannah came in, followed by Tess.

"What's up?" Susie asked.

Hannah tugged her raincoat off and gave it a shake before hanging it on the small coatrack by the door. Tess did the same while both kicked muddy shoes off.

Hannah gave her a long look. Susie was starting to get nervous. Hannah finally spoke. "Jared's injured and they can't fly out because of the weather. Trey says he probably can't even get clearance to fly until tomorrow at the earliest, and that's only if the weather lets up."

Susie's heart froze, and her stomach felt hollow. Fear raced through her, the only two words she'd heard were 'Jared' and 'injured'." Her mind whirled and tears welled. "What?"

Tess sat down on a stool beside Susie and tugged her hands into hers. "Jared fell and broke his ankle and got swiped by a bear. It wasn't an attack, just curiosity. Nathan called Trey to ask him to fly out as soon as he could to get them, but the weather's grounded all small planes."

"Why can't they send a helicopter?" Susie demanded, an anger driven by her fear rushing inside. She tugged her hands away from Tess and started pacing.

"Because even though he's hurt, it's not considered an emergency right now," Hannah said calmly.

"How do they know it's not an emergency?" Susie asked, struggling to keep her composure. She pictured Jared in pain and waiting in this cold, dreary weather. Her heart clenched, and she wanted to *do* something. She couldn't stand the thought of him waiting by himself in pain in this weather. Being trapped here, miles and miles across the ocean was excruciating.

"I talked to Nathan myself. He said Jared will need to get home soon, but he's okay right now, mostly in a lot of pain," Tess said evenly.

Hannah joined Tess by the counter. "Luke called me too and said that one of the guys on the trip with them is a doctor. He thinks Jared will be okay, but they need to be able to fly back soon. I'm sure if Trey can't get clearance to fly out tomorrow or the day after, they'll figure something out."

"Susie, he'll be okay. We wanted to come over, so you didn't hear from someone else," Tess said quietly.

Susie stopped pacing and leaned her elbows on the counter, face in her hands. Her throat was tight. She finally lifted her head and didn't bother trying not to cry. Hannah came around and hugged her. "Jared'll be okay. We just have to wait."

Susie pulled away and swiped at her tears. She walked into the living room and plunked on the couch, hugging a pillow to her chest and staring out at the rain. It was driving so hard, the mountains were barely visible across the bay.

"Are they waiting in tents?" she asked, picturing Jared trying to stay warm and dry in this weather.

Hannah and Tess had followed her into the living room, Tess joining her on the couch and Hannah sitting in a chair to the side. Jasmine leapt up beside Susie and nuzzled against her, purring audibly. Susie stroked her thick gray fur.

"Luke said one of the lodges in the park put Jared up in a staff room, but the rest of them are sitting tight in tents. Luke said the doctor with them has been checking on Jared regularly. He'll be okay. We just need to wait," Hannah said.

Susie couldn't seem to get her heart rate to slow down. Worry galloped through her mind. She needed to know Jared was okay. "Can we call Trey? I want to know when he thinks he can fly over."

"Susie, it's almost dark. Even if the weather was better, Trey wouldn't be able to fly over until morning," Tess said evenly.

Susie tossed the pillow to the side. "Well, can we call Luke or Nathan? Who has the satellite phone?" she demanded.

Hannah handed her phone over. "It's the last number in my recent calls."

Susie tried calling, but got no answer. The next few hours passed in fits and starts. Hannah left to bring pizza from Glacier Pizza, and Tess insisted they were spending the night at Susie's. When Susie demurred, Tess pointed out that Luke and Nathan were out in the weather too, and Hannah had dropped John off with Susie's mom so they could have a girl's night. They tried to keep her distracted with television, cards and wine, but Susie struggled to keep her mind off of Jared. She couldn't bring herself to talk about it, but she could hardly stand how worried she was. She kept replaying the last afternoon she saw him, the replay freezing when she turned around and saw tears in his eyes.

* * *

SUSIE WOKE THE FOLLOWING MORNING, temporarily disoriented. She was on the couch with a blanket tugged to her chin. When she rolled over and saw

Tess asleep in the chair nearby and Hannah crashed on the floor nestled among some pillows, she remembered Jared was injured and awaiting the weather to clear to be flown home. She wished her first slumber party in years hadn't been prompted by her friends' worry for her.

She sat up and ran a hand through her curls. She looked out the windows to see rain falling in a steady drizzle though the wind had died down. Heavy fog lay over the bay, making the mountains across invisible. Her stomach churned with worry for Jared. In this fog, he'd have to keep waiting.

There was a sharp knock at her door, and Emma stepped inside quickly. Her dark brown hair was damp. She held a small cup holder with four coffees from Misty Mountain Café. The scent of fresh baked goods wafted through the door with her. Susie stood, the blanket falling to the couch, and walked over to take the coffees from Emma.

"Good morning," Emma said with a soft smile. "Hannah told me she and Tess were staying here last night, so I figured y'all could use some breakfast. I brought spinach and cheese savories from Misty Mountain."

In short order, Hannah and Tess were up. They sat clustered in the living room. Emma nibbled on a savory and passed on the latest update from Trey, namely that he hoped to get clearance to fly out early this afternoon.

"Has he heard from Luke or Nathan?" Susie asked. "We tried calling a few times last night, but didn't get an answer. I figured the weather was interfering with reception."

Emma shook her head. "Same thing here with the

satellite number, but Trey got through by radio to the park ranger. They reported it was clearing over there and looked good for a landing by early afternoon."

"Did they have any information on how Jared was doing?" Susie asked immediately.

"Not much, other than he was stable," Emma replied softly.

Susie leaned back with a sigh, staring out the window and willing the fog to dissipate more quickly.

Emma eyed her carefully. "I thought you were mad at Jared and he wasn't worth your time?" she asked bluntly.

Susie flushed, but didn't shy away. "I was mad at him. But it doesn't mean I don't care." She paused and tried to marshal her thoughts, or more accurately, her feelings. "I don't know. I don't know how I feel."

"You sure about that?' Emma asked.

"No," Susie replied, a little too sharply. "I didn't mean to snap. I was mad at Jared because he obviously doesn't know what he wants. I can't stand to admit this, but the truth is he matters way too much to me. I can't be stupid and put myself out there when he doesn't even know what he wants. Then something like this happens...and I'm so worried, I don't know what to do."

She felt all three of her friends' eyes on her and felt too exposed. Emma nodded slowly and took a sip of coffee before replying. "Not that you're asking for my opinion, but maybe you should give Jared the benefit of the doubt. Just because he isn't sure what he wants doesn't mean he isn't going to figure it out. You've been pretty cagey about where you stand too. It's obvious to all of us that Jared loves you. Trey told me he even talked to Jared about it the other day when he flew them out."

Susie's heart leapt at Emma's words. "What did Trey say?"

"Just that he talked to Jared about you. He thinks Jared's in love with you, but he's been alone for so long, it's kind of freaking him out. The same could be said for you," Emma said.

Susie finally registered Emma's point that she'd been cagey about her feelings too. "You mean it looks like I've been as confused as Jared?"

Tess and Hannah burst out laughing together. "Are you kidding?" Hannah exclaimed. While Tess's emphatic "Yes!" joined the chorus.

Emma smiled wryly and nodded. "Pretty much looks like that from the outside."

Susie sat there, feeling foolish and abashed, a flush heating her face. Here she'd been trying to be who she thought she was supposed to be—the strong one who wasn't vulnerable, the one who wouldn't let Jared play her along—when it was obvious to everyone but her, she was getting in her own way. Her romantic side, the side she'd been frantically trying to shush ever since her desire for Jared had overwhelmed her defenses, was clamoring to be heard. *You want this, so stop getting in your own way. Don't hide how you feel. You got angry with him before you made sure he knew how you really felt.*

Susie swallowed and took a breath. She thought back to the last month or so. Inside, it was obvious to her how she felt. She was in deep and scrambling to keep her wits about her. But...she'd never told Jared what she was feeling, not explicitly. She'd expected it was obvious. She'd been mortified how fast she'd fallen and how little control she had around him.

She looked at her friends and sighed. "I guess so..." she set her coffee down with a sigh and rolled her head around, easing the tension in her neck. "I feel so ridiculous. I didn't realize how it looked on the outside."

"It doesn't matter how it looks to everyone else. I only mentioned it because you were upset with Jared," Emma said softly. "Whatever you do, remember Jared's a decent guy and no matter what, he isn't trying to hurt you."

Susie's heart raced and her stomach fluttered at the mere thought that Jared might love her. She had to see him. "Can you call Trey and see if he has an update?" she asked Emma urgently.

Emma grinned. "Uh, Susie, I talked to Trey this morning before I left to come here, maybe thirty minutes ago. He promised me he'd call me once he had official clearance to fly."

Susie sighed and rolled her eyes. "Okay, okay." She commenced to wait with her friends. The fog finally started to lift late in the morning.

CHAPTER 21

*J*ared hobbled toward the dock where Trey's plane was waiting. Ben and Nathan were on either side of him, holding most of his weight. His ankle felt better than he'd expected, but Ben was adamant he keep his weight off of it. His low back was another matter—deep, throbbing pain surrounded the area where the bear had swiped him so casually. He'd slept in fits and starts, Susie occupying his dreams and waking thoughts. He desperately wanted to talk to her, so he could explain he'd just needed some time to accept the fact that he was in love with her.

Facing the reality that he'd managed to avoid a potentially fatal situation had wiped out his confusion about how much Susie meant to him. Through the long night, alone and in pain, he kept thinking about how much time he'd wasted worrying about how he felt. He knew exactly how he felt. He wanted to wake up beside her every day and lay down beside her every night. He wanted her to know he was always,

always thinking about her and would always be there for her. And this second…he wanted to be beside her, not because he wanted her to comfort him, but because her presence was elemental to his heart. Before he could get to any of that, he had to find a way to repair the damage he'd done by being too damn stupid to face his feelings. And before that, he had to climb in a tiny plane for what would likely be a bumpy ride to Diamond Creek.

Trey waved from the floatplane dock. Luke was going to stay with Matt, Craig and Reid for another day of fishing. Nathan insisted on returning to Diamond Creek with Jared to take him to the hospital, while Ben wanted to accompany them to provide an update to the doctors once they got there. Jared tried to talk Ben out of it, but Ben claimed he'd already had an amazing fishing trip and a few days in Diamond Creek would offer other wonderful fishing opportunities.

Jared took a long look around while Luke and Matt loaded up gear. The rain and fog had dissipated in the heat of the sun. The mountains rose up in the distance. The water rolled by, the sound soothing. An eagle called nearby. Jared could see the viewing platform in the distance, brown bears clustered around the famed Brooks Falls.

He breathed through his pain while Ben and Nathan carefully walked him down the dock to Trey's plane. An uncomfortable ride later, Trey guided the plane in for a smooth landing in Diamond Creek in the lake where he kept his plane docked. Jared tried to call Susie once they were within cell range, but got no answer.

Nathan and Ben functioned as human crutches for

the walk to Nathan's truck. Nathan immediately headed toward the hospital.

"It's not an emergency guys. If it was an emergency, the rangers would have called a helicopter in for me," Jared said, hedging to buy some time in the hopes he could reach Susie soon.

Nathan shook his head firmly.

"What are you two, my keepers?"

Nathan glanced over at him. "Yeah, we are. Ben said your back needs to be looked at as soon as possible. There's no reason to wait," he said firmly.

Jared tried to look over his shoulder at Ben who rode in the back, but he couldn't quite turn around without sharp pain stabbing in his low back. Though his injuries were technically scratches, the term felt insufficient when the largest land-based predator on earth was responsible for them.

"Seriously, Ben? I can't have a little time to make some calls."

Ben chuckled. "Make your calls on the way over. Every minute you wait increases the chance of infection."

Jared sighed and tugged his phone out again. Once again, he got Susie's voice mail. He resorted to a text.

Hey, just got in. Sure you heard about what happened. Nathan taking me to hospital. REALLY want to talk to you. Not sure how long I'll be there. Please give me a chance to explain later. Miss you.

He slipped his phone back in his pocket. Moments later, they pulled up at the hospital. Nathan and Ben took their stations on either side and walked him in.

Jared tried to ignore the flushed feeling he had, worried he might have a fever. Once Nathan spoke to the nurse in the emergency room, the wheels of the hospital started turning rapidly. Jared was whisked away. The last thing he remembered was wondering when he would see Susie before fading into black.

* * *

JARED WOKE to the sound of low voices. He was on his stomach. Disoriented, it took him several moments to recall he was at the hospital in Diamond Creek.

"...concerned about infection..."

"I know..."

Jared wanted to ask a question, but couldn't. He tumbled back into the oblivion of modern pain medicine. He had no sense of time when he woke later. His room was dark. Someone must have helped turn him over because he couldn't imagine he did it himself. Even the slightest movement caused pain. His entire back throbbed. Ben had told him the scratches would need to be debrided due to the dirt and debris from the wounds. He warned that while the debriding was necessary, Jared would likely be in much more pain after it was over. "Imagine someone taking a small cut, digging around in there and scouring it with disinfectant. Hurts like hell afterward," Ben had said flatly.

His eyes gradually adjusted to the darkness. He made out the shape of someone sleeping in a chair by the window, the telltale outline of curls giving the person away as Susie. He smiled in the dark, relaxing with the knowledge she was there.

* * *

SUSIE OPENED her eyes to bright sun shining on her face through the window. She immediately turned to see if Jared was awake, cringing when her neck resisted the quick motion. He was sound asleep. She'd fallen asleep in what had to be the least comfortable chair to sleep in ever. Her neck had twisted into an odd angle during the few hours of fitful sleep. She quietly stood and stretched. She'd arrived at the hospital yesterday shortly after Jared had been wheeled into surgery. If it weren't for Ben, the ever-patient doctor whose Alaskan fishing adventure had become something else entirely, she might have made a scene.

Roughly two hours into waiting, Susie was pacing, demanding an explanation for what was taking so long. Nathan had returned to the waiting area with Ben, who was disarmingly handsome on top of being as nice as could be. With his brown hair, blue eyes, and incredibly fit body, Susie figured he was candy for most women. She could care less. All she wanted from him were answers about Jared.

"Why the hell is it taking so long?" Susie demanded, throwing her hands up and stomping away from the nurses' station.

Nathan had walked into the room with Ben right at that moment. Ben joined her as she strode back and forth in the room. "They usually don't offer much information because it's more frustrating if they give you a timeframe, and they turn out to be wrong," Ben commented evenly.

"Well, they could at least say that!" She was furious with the vague answers. They made her afraid something was really wrong, something they weren't telling her. She needed to know Jared was okay and needed to know *now.*

Ben nodded and continued strolling alongside her. "They have to debride the gouges in his back. It's tedious and time consuming. It's more important that they take the time to get the injuries clean than it is to rush."

The knots in her stomach twisted tighter. "Gouges?"

"That's the best way to describe them," Ben said with a small shrug. His blue eyes were warm and concerned. "He'll be okay, but it may be awhile. When he's out of surgery, they'll keep him here for a few days to monitor for infection. His ankle is more straightforward. It was a simple fracture, so I was able to set it easily. They'll put a supporting cast on it and that'll be it."

Susie was so tied up inside, she thought she might explode. She'd been trying so hard to hold it together, but she didn't think she could settle until she could see and talk to Jared. It wasn't sounding like that would happen soon enough. Her heart was in her throat, and anxiety coiled through her body. She needed to make sure Jared knew how she felt and that he wasn't alone in this. Though Ben's explanations helped ease her worry, it barely took the edge off. The word infection conjured a host of horrible scenarios in her mind. She tried to keep her mind on the moment. Ben's calming presence relieved some of her tension. "I'm glad you were over there," she said with a small smile.

"Me too. He'd have been okay without me, but I was glad to help. We had an amazing day of fishing too," he replied with a quick grin.

Susie rescheduled all of her appointments for work and camped out at the hospital. Jared's text had come while she was in a meeting with a client yesterday. By the time she had seen his message, he was already in surgery. Hannah, Tess and Emma joined her at different points throughout the long afternoon and evening. At present, Nathan was lounging in the waiting room with Tess. Susie finally stopped pacing and flung herself in a chair beside Tess. Ben quietly sat down beside Nathan.

Tess offered a small smile, her ginger eyes warm. "Ben knows what he's talking about. Jared will be fine."

Susie leaned her head back against the wall with a sigh. Weariness washed through her. The tight feeling that had taken up residence in her chest and throat the moment she heard Jared had been injured had yet to ease. She *needed* to know he'd be okay. Only then would she be able to relax.

"I know..." She paused, her breath catching. "I want him to be fine *now.*" A tear rolled down her cheek. She swiped it away.

Tess snagged a box of tissues from a side table and silently handed them over. Susie wiped her eyes and blew her nose, tears continuing to fall.

"This sucks," she said flatly.

Tess nodded. "Pretty much. Don't suppose it would help if I said something about how it could be worse?" she asked wryly.

"No. It would be annoying. I know it could be worse. I know he'll be okay. I just...wish I hadn't flown off the handle and told him off. Now he's in there, and I'm scared. I feel like a fool, and I still don't know how he feels. I just don't want him to think I don't care."

A sob burst forth, and Susie buried her face in her hands. Tess stroked her back and remained quiet. Tess was good at knowing when words were entirely unnecessary.

By the time the doctor came to the waiting room to report Jared was out of surgery, Jared had been in surgery over six hours. Susie barely heard the details of the doctor's report. The words "he's stable" beat through her heart like a drum. Ben had been on target with what he'd told her. The doctor explained they'd keep Jared for a minimum of three days to get him past the period when he was at higher risk to develop an infection. Whether the doctor wanted to let her or not, she quickly caved to Susie's persistent demand to stay in Jared's room for the night.

After stretching, Susie walked carefully to the bed and placed her hand on Jared's forehead. It was slightly warm, but she couldn't tell if he was feverish. She slipped on her clogs and scurried to the nurses' station, dragging a nurse back with her to check his fever.

"He's warm," Susie whispered fervently when the nurse gave her a questioning look when they arrived in the room.

The nurse in question put her hands on her hips and rolled her eyes. She was an older woman who exuded practicality. She was slender with bright blue eyes and long gray hair braided and coiled on the top of her head. "Young lady, he is sleeping. That's why he's warm."

"Please, please just check his temperature," Susie pleaded. "Don't you have one of those things you can run over his forehead, so we don't have to wake him up?"

The nurse's eyes softened, and she shook her head. "God save me from a woman in love," she said with a sigh as she tugged the very thermometer Susie had described out of her pocket. She quickly checked his temperature and turned away. Jared didn't budge. "It's slightly elevated…"

Susie cut her off. "Shouldn't you do something then?"

The nurse came over and tucked her hand in Susie's elbow, firmly guiding her out of the room. "I'm Helena, by the way," she said. When Susie didn't reply, she shook her head and continued. "As I said, his temperature is slightly elevated, but that's normal given his situation. Fever happens for a reason. We already have him on antibiotics, but it's best if we use as low of a dose as possible. A fever tells us his body is trying to do its job."

"Are you going to check it regularly?" Susie asked.

"Of course! I would have been down here to check his vitals in fifteen minutes if you hadn't come to get me. Honey, he's doing exactly how we'd like him to right now. He just needs to rest. I know you're worried, but I promise you, we'll let you know right away if there's anything to worry about."

"Okay, okay. I didn't mean to bother you," Susie said, slightly abashed. She hated how helpless she felt, awash in the push and pull of her feelings.

Helena smiled. "No bother. I've got other patients to check on. You come find me if you need to."

Susie watched her walk away and leaned against the wall with a sigh. Returning to the room, she found Jared still sound asleep. Glancing at her watch, she wondered if she could get away with showering in his room. Not bothering to wait, she rushed through a shower, feeling much better afterwards. When she quietly closed the bathroom door, Jared shifted in his sleep, grimacing as he did.

Susie raced to his side. He blinked a few times, his green eyes finally opening, landing right on hers.

"Hey," he said softly, his voice gravelly.

"Hey, how are you feeling?"

"Not so good..." he began to say.

Susie immediately reached to tap the call button by his bed for the nurse. "I'll have the nurse come right down," she said, almost frantic.

"Susie."

She looked back at him. "I want the nurse to check on you..."

"I didn't mean for you to call the nurse. I'm not so good because my back hurts like hell," he explained, the corners of his mouth tipping in a small grin. He shoved the thin cotton blanket down and reached for her hand, which rested on the bed rail.

Tears spilled over and rolled down her cheeks. The moment his eyes met hers and he reached for her hand, all the emotion she'd been holding at bay washed like a wave through her. She hadn't let herself think it, but a tiny corner of her heart had been afraid he wouldn't want to see her. His eyes were on hers, that intense green gaze boring into her, and she may not know everything in his heart, but she knew he wanted her there. At that moment, the door swung open, Luke, Nathan and Hannah coming in the room. Susie frantically swiped her tears away and took a step back.

"Was hoping you might be up," Nathan said with a grin.

Jared's smile was weak, but genuine.

"How you feeling?" Luke asked.

"My back hurts like hell. I can't even imagine how bad it'd be if I wasn't on heavy duty painkillers."

Susie stood back and let the brotherly banter commence. Hannah came to her side and slipped her arm over Susie's shoulders. "Hey there, your mom stopped by this morning with a change of clothes for you." Hannah lifted a small bag.

"I should've known she'd do that," Susie said. She struggled to get her bearings. Emotions were coasting through her, keeping her off balance.

"You okay?" Hannah asked quietly.

Susie swallowed through the lump in her throat and nodded. "Yeah. I am. It was a long night."

"I know. Tess told me they stayed until Jared got out of surgery, and it was well past midnight by then. Did you sleep at all?"

Susie gestured to the chair by the window. "In the most uncomfortable chair ever! I snuck a shower just a few minutes ago though," she said with a rueful grin.

Hannah searched her face. "Do you want to take a break from here? Maybe go grab some breakfast?"

Susie shook her head forcefully.

Hannah's eyes widened. 'Okay then. I guess you've sorted out how you feel."

Susie rolled her eyes, Hannah's droll tone taking the edge off her feelings. "I just..." she paused, her throat tightening and tears threatening again "...don't want to leave him here by himself."

Hannah lifted a brow and tilted her head. "Pretty sure he's not going to be alone for hours. Tess is headed over soon. Emma and Trey will be here. Jared's parents are flying up. The list goes on and on. You sure that's the only reason you don't want to leave?" she asked with a soft smile.

Susie couldn't leave because her heart wouldn't let her. She was tired of running from what she felt, and once the floodgates were open, she couldn't hide from it. She bit her lip and glanced over at Jared. He was grinning at something Nathan said, but his eyes were tired. She looked back to Hannah. "I don't want to leave right now. That's all. Interpret that however you want," she said archly, a touch of irritation flaring. As emotionally overwhelmed as she was, she knew she had to keep somewhat of a lid on her feelings with everyone around. As usual, her feisty side got her through it.

Hannah chucked and quickly sobered. "Though I've been just as worried about Jared as you, I also want to make sure you take care of yourself. Have you two had a chance to talk?"

Susie shook her head. "He woke up right before you all got here. And I'm okay. I just need to be here." She had to be here to know he would be okay and because what she might not have said in words yet, she had to show through her presence.

Hannah nodded in understanding and stepped closer to Jared's bed. The next few hours passed with a rotating cast of visitors. Jared dozed off and on at points. The few times when the room was without visitors were brief, or included a stop from Helena checking on Jared's vitals. Late that afternoon, when Susie thought they might finally have a moment alone, Jared's parents arrived.

Susie had met them several times before when

they were visiting. Iris, Jared's mother, entered the room in a swirl. Matthew, his father, followed at a rambling pace. Iris was tall with long black, wavy hair shot through with silver. Jared's green eyes were strikingly similar to hers. Matthew had the same lanky, lean build as his sons, his hair almost entirely silver with sparkling blue eyes. After Iris fawned over Jared, she came to Susie and hugged her tightly, stepping back, her hands on Susie's shoulders.

"How are you dear?" Iris asked, her eyes curious.

Susie didn't know what Iris knew, if anything, about her and Jared.

"I'm fine," Susie said. "I've been busy with work and the usual summer stuff. I know Jared's glad you and his dad came up today. He had a rough few days."

Iris nodded and stepped back, adjusting a wide silver bracelet on her arm. "Luke waited to call us until they were flying out." Iris shook her head. "I can't believe he didn't call right away, but he said he didn't want us to worry."

Iris paused when Matthew said her name.

Matthew was leaning against Jared's hospital bed. "Hon, I think we should go pick up some takeout for Jared. He'd love something from the pizza place. If we don't, he'll be stuck with hospital fare."

Susie caught Jared's eyes and could have sworn he winked, but she wasn't quite sure. Iris moved to Matthew's side. "Of course! We'll go right now. What kind of pizza do you want sweetie?"

Jared sighed and closed his eyes after they left. Susie sat on the foot of his bed, entirely uncertain of what to say after waiting for hours to have a moment alone with him. Quiet settled in the room, the distant sounds of the hospital muted.

"It's nice to see everyone, but damn I'm tired," Jared said.

"How are you feeling overall?" Susie asked.

Jared opened his eyes and smiled weakly. "Been better, but okay." He looked toward her. "I'm glad you're still here."

She was pinned in place by his green gaze. His eyes were intent. Her heart kicked up a notch and her breath became shallow. Against all reason, given that Jared was in a hospital bed and in absolutely no condition to do anything, her body reacted—heat swirled in her center, desire stealthily slid through under her skin, flushing her inside and out. She stood abruptly.

"Come here."

Jared beckoned with his hand, eyes still locked on her. She stepped to his side, resting her hands on the edge of the bed. Someone had let the bed rail down hours ago. He reached for her hand, tugging it into his. He grimaced. "Be careful," she admonished.

He grinned. "It's not so bad. I'm just...damn sore. It's not horrible."

His thumb idly stroked across the back of her palm, sensation chasing in the wake of each small stroke. Susie tried to keep her heart calm, but it was no use. She'd missed him so the last few weeks. Two days of the sheer agony of worrying over him had left her heart without defense. She couldn't even muster her cranky side. The tears that had started hours ago pressed against her eyelids. She swallowed them down and took a shaky breath.

"My dad bought us a little time, but it won't be much. My mom's kind of a worrier," he said softly before taking a deep breath. "I had a lot of time to think while I was waiting over there. I know you were mad, maybe you still are, but you have to know I love you." He searched her face before continuing. She was so stunned by the bare honesty in his eyes, she didn't hear much of what he said next. She was stuck on 'I love you.' Her heart started dancing, and tears rolled down her cheeks. She forced herself to look at him and try to listen. He had closed his eyes as he continued to speak. "…I didn't plan on this and obviously I'm not so great at the whole relationship thing, but if you're going to shut me out, I don't want you to do it without knowing how I feel. I want to make this work. Even if it means I screw up half the time," he said wryly, his eyes opening, meeting hers with such intensity it took her breath away.

He squeezed her hand. "Please don't cry," he said fiercely. "I don't know what it means."

Susie shook her head, her curls bouncing. She snatched a tissue from a box on a table by his bed and scrubbed the tears away. "It's not bad. I…I love you too…" her words ended in a sob, tears rolling again. Jared started to reach up, gasping in pain when he did.

"Stop it! You need to be still," she ordered. She took a shaky breath and squeezed his hand. "I was a mess even before you got hurt. And the last two days…well, they sucked. I was upset with you, but I've had lots of time to think—all day yesterday and then some—and I wanted to make sure you knew how I felt." She took a breath just as there was a sharp knock on the door. Helena entered the room, quickly checking the monitor and moving to the bed.

Susie backed away. Jared kept his eyes on her as Helena checked a few things and gave him his latest dose of pain medication. Once they were alone again, he reached for her hand. "So it's fair to assume we won't have more than five minutes alone until visiting hours are over," he said with a chuckle.

Susie grinned. "Probably."

Her heart was so full, she could hardly contain the feeling. Impulsively, she leaned over to kiss him. In a flash, she tumbled into the desire shimmering around them. Jared threaded his hand into her curls pulling her against his mouth forcefully. He made her forget his condition, tracing the contours of her lips and stroking deeply into her mouth with his tongue. She strained toward him, heavy desire pounding through her. He broke away from her mouth, his lips traveling in a heated path down her neck into the opening created by her blouse. He licked the exposed skin between her breasts. She could feel his arousal pressing against the edge of her hip and brought her hand down to cup him through the sheet. He groaned and fell back against the pillows. "Damn...I missed you..."

She looked up and lost herself in his mesmerizing gaze. His hand slowly slipped out of her curls and stroked around her ear, cupping her cheek. His thumb caressed the beat of her pulse in her neck. Shivers raced through her body. "I missed you too." She suddenly felt shy and exposed.

Jared shook his head. "Don't. We're in this together," he said softly.

Her heart beat so hard, she thought it might beat its way out of her chest. She nodded. Trying to be open and risk her heart this way was terrifying. But with his eyes pinned on hers, she couldn't ignore what she saw there. Intense yearning...and vulnerability. This was just as frightening for him. "Okay," she said softly.

"So before we get interrupted again, does this mean we're trying again?"

For a moment, she worried she'd misunderstood. Just as her mind climbed on its hamster wheel, Jared spoke her name. "I'm not asking because I'm not sure. I'm asking about you. Let me make it crystal clear. I love you, I want you, and I don't want there to be any daylight between what I feel and what you think I feel. Every day without you all I did was miss you. You said I wanted things tidy. Not anymore. Tidy almost made me miss out on the best thing that ever happened to me. And that's you."

Susie was so overcome, tears spilled over again. Joy unfurled inside when she met his eyes through the veil of her tears.

"Crying is a good thing?" he asked with a small smile.

She nodded and knuckled her tears away. "You have to know I was going to make sure you knew I loved you no matter what. I figured it wasn't fair for me to get pushy with you if I wasn't even being open about how I felt. I just didn't..." she paused and gulped in air with her words tumbling out "...didn't dare let myself hope you felt the same way."

He held her eyes for a long moment before pulling her down for another kiss. Just when he stroked his thumb across her nipple, there was a knock at the door. She pulled back, her heart light and airy as if its windows had been flung wide and sunlight flooded inside.

CHAPTER 22

"Honey, let me get those for you," Iris said, coming to Jared's side and taking his crutches from him. She set his crutches against the back of the couch.

Jared sank into the couch with a sigh. He was at Luke and Hannah's house. His parents were staying there for the remainder of the week. He'd been discharged from the hospital over a week ago and was flat tired of hobbling around. Much as he loved his mother, she was also pushing him to his limits with worrying and her barely checked tendency to get over-involved in his life.

His father sat down in an adjacent chair as Iris returned to the kitchen where she was helping Hannah cook dinner. "You're about to the end of your rope with all this hovering," Matthew said with a wry grin.

Jared smiled ruefully. "Just about. I'm hoping to be cleared to ditch the crutches by tomorrow."

"I'd better not hear from Luke or Nathan that you plan to start working again right away," Iris said, returning to the room and handing a beer to Matthew. She turned to Jared, her blue skirt swaying, and eyed him. Her hair was twisted in a bun with chopsticks. Though Jared was many years past answering to his mother, one look like that from her and he instantly felt chagrined. He'd absolutely planned to join Luke and Nathan on the next scheduled day trip.

"Of course not, Mom. I'll be working behind the scenes," he said, fighting to keep a straight face.

Iris shook her head. "Don't lie to me. You might think you can convince Luke and Nathan to cover for you, but I've already talked to Hannah, Tess *and* Susie. They won't cover for you," she said emphatically.

Jared groaned. "Seriously, Mom? I'm a grown man. I don't need you monitoring my every move."

Matthew coughed, masking a laugh. He caught Jared's eyes and shook his head. Iris kept her gaze trained on Jared. "I'm perfectly aware you're a grown man, but I know you well enough to know that as soon as you're not hobbled by those crutches, you'll push yourself."

Jared elected to avoid further discussion. "Mom, I promise I'll take it easy. Let's leave it at that. How long are you and Dad staying anyway?"

"Just three more days. We'll be back up in another few months," Iris said, sitting down in a small rocking chair on the other side of the coffee table. She pursed her lips and tilted her head to the side. "So when were you planning to fill me in on Susie?"

Luke happened to be coming downstairs, carrying

John in his arms. He glanced Jared's way and grinned. Jared had enjoyed the benefit of his brothers' respective marriages taking the pressure off of him when it came to their mother. She was an endless romantic. Having enjoyed a loving marriage for decades, she wanted all three of her sons to have the same. Jared figured his mother would have noticed something, what with Susie an almost constant presence in his hospital room.

He took a breath. "Mom, I haven't been hiding anything. Just got a little sidetracked—you know, broke my ankle, curious bear and all that."

Iris merely lifted her eyebrows.

Jared flushed. He'd actually been planning to ask his mother for some help when it came to Susie. Even though he had absolutely no doubt about what Susie meant to him, he was a fairly private person and being open with his mother made it hard to keep much private. He glanced to his father, realizing he'd get no help there with Matthew suddenly enamored with the view out the window. Jared took another deep breath. "Right. Susie. Well," he paused to clear his throat "Let me cut to the chase: I love her."

Iris squealed, her hands flew to her mouth and tears filled her eyes. "Oh Jared! Really?"

Jared flushed even deeper, but he nodded.

Iris started to say something else before her gaze softened. "Jared, you're my serious one, and you almost had me convinced for a while there that you would never give yourself a chance to fall in love. I knew it the first time I saw you and Susie together—she was the only woman I knew who had a chance to get you to let down your guard. I can tell you're about to squirm out of your chair over there, and if you could get up and gracefully walk away, you would, so I won't torture you further. I'm just happy to see you give love a chance."

Jared barely kept his mouth from falling open. "Mom, you met Susie a few years ago. We only started seeing each other recently."

Iris grinned. "I know my boys. Susie could have wrapped you around her finger early on. You might not have had enough sense, but it was clear as day you couldn't keep your eyes off of her. I like her, and she's good for you. She'll keep you on your toes," she said firmly.

Jared was flabbergasted and more than a little embarrassed. Matthew finally lost interest in the view and turned away from the window. He chuckled and took a swallow of his beer when he saw the look on Jared's face. "You just made your mom's day, and I'm damn happy for you too."

"Thanks Dad."

Iris came and sat beside him on the couch, hugging him to her side.

Jared cleared his throat again. "So Mom, I need a favor."

"Anything."

"Well, I need help getting a ring for Susie. I don't want to waste anymore time, so I thought maybe you wouldn't mind heading up to Anchorage with me before you leave to help me pick one out."

Iris squealed again, hugging Jared hard enough that he lost his breath.

"I'm sorry, I'm just so excited. Let's go the day after tomorrow. Your dad can drive," Iris replied, looking expectantly at Matthew who grinned and nodded.

Iris stood and nodded firmly before twirling around and walking briskly back to the kitchen.

Jared couldn't help but laugh and marvel at his mother. Though she could annoy the hell out of him with her interference, he knew he was lucky to have a mother who cared as much as she did.

CHAPTER 23

Susie walked into Jared's place to find him seated on the couch staring out the window. She followed his gaze. Two ravens were flying in twirling circles outside the windows against the backdrop of the bright blue sky. Sun glinted off the waves and boats dotted the bay. Glancing back at him, she saw his eyes were wistful.

"How's it going?"

He glanced up, his green eyes sparking when he saw her. "Better now you're here." He moved to get up, and she gestured for him to stay put as she put several bags of groceries on the counter.

He stood anyway and walked over to her, brushing her curls back and dropping a kiss on her cheek. She flushed instantly, warmth unfurling inside.

"I was going to come over there, you didn't need to get up," she said, turning toward him.

"How about we agree you'll stop treating me like glass?" Jared said with a grin. "I'm fine. Look, my cast came off this afternoon." He pointed to his ankle. "My back is all healed up. I'm good to go. My doctor says I need to wait another few weeks before I can start running again. I definitely don't need to sit in one place all day."

She clapped her hands. "Yippee! I know you were hoping she'd take the cast off today." She tugged him close for a kiss, which went from playful to burning hot in seconds.

She pulled back for a breath. "How about you let me finish putting the groceries away?"

Jared's dimple winked at her with his grin. "Okay. How about we grab a pizza and you let me drive?"

His hands caressed her bottom as they slid away. A shiver raced through her. She forced herself to take a step back and quickly put the groceries away. "Pizza sounds perfect. You sure you don't want me to drive?"

He sighed. "I'm bored out of my mind since my mom managed to persuade Luke and Nathan not to let me ignore doctor's orders and go fishing. Driving seems pretty exciting about now."

Susie tilted her head. "Poor you. Of course, you can drive."

A short drive later, and they sat in a booth in Glacier Pizza, which was bustling. Summer was winding down, but tourists would be out in force until well into early fall. Susie lifted a piece of pizza to her mouth when Darren approached. He and Jared caught up briefly. As Darren turned to leave, he asked, "You ever find out any more about that thing?"

His question was about as vague as it could get, but Susie's ears perked up. Jared shook his head quickly, a little too quickly. Darren walked off, and she tried to read Jared's expression, which was carefully bland.

"What's he talking about?"

Jared shrugged. "Just something I asked him about."

She didn't know how she knew, but she knew Jared had asked him about her situation. "You didn't tell him it was me, did you?"

Jared's eyes flew to hers. "No! I told you I wanted to ask around about it, but I promised I wouldn't mention your name and I didn't." His eyes darkened and a muscle ticked in his jaw. "I had to ask and see if there was anything I could do."

Her face was hot and her throat tight. She nodded slowly. "Okay. What did Darren say?"

Funny thing was, ever since she'd taken the leap and let herself feel what she felt for Jared, the ugly memories that had swirled around her heart had faded. What happened was what it was. She'd almost been raped and had gotten lucky enough to stop it. The power the incident held over her had dwindled once she stopped letting it hold her back. Though she wouldn't have chosen for Jared to ask anyone about it, she appreciated why he did.

Jared's mouth twisted and he laughed bitterly. "Pretty much what you said. What happened to you is way too damn common, and the options for legal recourse are limited. And that's when they have actual hard details." He paused and took a sip of water. "It pisses me off, but I thought about it a lot. Even if we knew the guy's last name, it would be your word against his years after the fact. If you wanted to go for it, I'd support you every step of the way. But I can see how hellish it would be. And after what Darren said... I'll never be okay with it, but I can leave it alone if that's what you want."

Her eyes were hot with tears. He reached a hand over, his thumb brushing one off her cheek. He held her gaze, his green eyes a haven.

"I won't say it didn't affect me because...you know, the virginity thing..." she paused. She couldn't half-believe she could joke about how long her virginity trailed around behind her.

Jared smiled softly, his hand coming to rest on the table. "Ahh, right, the virginity thing. Well, we took care of that."

She nodded and took a breath. "But like I told you, I did talk to the police about it later on. It didn't seem worth it. I don't think it's right that it happens so often and it's so hard for women to do anything about it. But it is what it is. I'm okay. I really am. I don't want to drag it up now. Maybe if this were way closer to when it happened, I'd feel differently. But now... I'm okay. I'd like to leave it alone," she said firmly. She felt more clarity about it than she ever had. For so long, she'd felt ashamed of what happened and ashamed she hadn't found a way to do something. But she had to deal with the hand she'd been dealt. In this case, it was a hand without much other than her own choice after the fact. So she took charge of what she could. Emotionally, she was more than fine.

She held Jared's gaze and smiled. "To moving on," she said, lifting her glass of wine.

* * *

THE FOLLOWING EVENING, Jared pulled up at Susie's office after returning from Anchorage with his parents. He'd tried to come by earlier, but every time he drove by, there were cars there. He'd finally resorted to asking Hannah to call Susie and invite her for dinner after work, so she'd plan to finish up early. Hannah had a good laugh at his expense, but she'd happily obliged him, even calling to update him what time she'd asked Susie to meet her for their faux dinner date.

He strode into Susie's office to find her bending over to reach into a file drawer. She wore one of those short twirly skirts she favored, bright red today, topped with a white blouse that barely buttoned across her breasts with a lacy silvery camisole underneath. She stood abruptly when he closed the door.

"Oh! I thought you were having dinner with your parents tonight." Her curls were bundled into a messy knot held in place with a pen. Loose curls hung around her cheeks. She glanced at the clock. "I told Hannah I'd meet her for dinner at Sally's in a few."

Jared nodded as he slowly walked toward her. He had some kind of plan, but it dissolved into the pulse of lust pounding through him. Damn if he couldn't get enough of her. He kept walking past her desk, straight for her. She backed up until her back hit the wall behind her.

He reached her and lifted a hand to brush a loose curl out of her eyes, trailing his hand down her cheek. Her breath hitched, and she bit her lip. He placed his other hand on the wall behind her. With no further preamble, he crushed his lips to hers.

* * *

Jared walked toward her, his green eyes trained on her. With his black curls and sun-burnished skin, his eyes stood out. His faded blue t-shirt stretched across his muscled chest and shoulders. He'd lost the last of his limp and strode toward her in that loose stride of his. Susie's pulse leapt and her breath became shallow. Work kept her busy, but he danced in the edges of her mind whenever she had a spare moment. He'd unexpectedly shown up, and she was practically salivating at the mere sight of him.

Lust streaked through her, suffusing her with heat. His presence was so intent she backed up as he approached, bumping against the wall. He didn't pause and came right against her, stepping into the cradle of her hips. He brushed a curl out of her face. She closed her eyes as his fingertips caressed her cheek. His lips came against hers fiercely when he rested a palm against the wall behind her. Thought fled her mind and she dove into the passion coursing between them.

His kiss set her aflame, he stroked deeply into her mouth. He roughly tugged at her skirt, shoving it up and settling against her. She gasped at the feel of his cock, hot and hard through the rough denim abrading the thin cotton of her panties. He tore his lips away, burning a path of heated kisses down her neck to trace the line of her collarbone. He paused for a moment, pulling back to look at her. She could barely breathe at the sheer *want* in his eyes.

"Just a sec," he whispered before stepping back and striding swiftly to the door.

She felt bereft the moment his heated body left hers. He flicked the sign in the window to closed and locked the door before turning back. Every step of the way, her eyes stayed locked onto his, electricity arcing along the path between them. This time, he came against her slowly, slipping a hand under her knee and lifting it, opening her up. His other hand cupped her cheek as he brought his lips slowly to hers. The kiss started gentle, but she couldn't stand it and stroked a hand into his hair, tugging him close.

Several breath-stealing moments later, he dragged his mouth in a path down her neck, tearing at her blouse as he did. He swore when the buttons didn't give easily and yanked at the fabric, buttons pinging against the floor. He shoved her camisole down. With a quick flick, her bra came undone, and her breasts—heavy and aching for his touch—spilled out. He sighed against her skin before his lips closed over a nipple. She moaned and shifted restlessly against him. She tore at his jeans, desperate to feel him closer to her. His cock sprang free after she fumbled his boxers out of the way. She lost focus when he sucked and nipped at one breast, his fingers tracing lazy circles in the moisture on her other nipple. He took advantage of her distraction to press his cock against her moist heat, rubbing across the nub of her desire. She began to arch into him when he pulled back, easing the pressure.

"Jared…"

"Mmm…"

"I need you…now…"

He chuckled, the soft laugh against her skin causing a shiver to race through her. Her skin was flushed with desire, hypersensitive to the barest touch.

He pulled back, his eyes meeting hers, dark with desire. "I'd like to make you wait, but…"

His voice broke when she grabbed his hips and arched into him, riding against his hardness.

He took a shuddering breath. "Don't know if I can..."

His hand was curled around one of her breasts, he softly pinched the nipple before dragging it down and slipping it under the edge of her panties, pushing them out of the way. He stroked lightly across her drenched folds before dipping a finger into her channel, his thumb rolling back and forth across her clit. She moaned and pressed against his hand, desperately seeking release.

He muttered an imprecation before he moved swiftly, lifting her against the wall. Her legs fell open. She was held between the wall and his hard body. His hand left her and then she felt the head of his cock sliding back and forth between her folds. If it weren't for the wall, she'd have collapsed. Desire ricocheted through her as she trembled against him. Just when she thought she couldn't stand it anymore, he surged into her, filling her completely in one deep thrust. He cupped her bottom in his hands and settled against her for a long moment.

Jared breathed her name against her lips. Her eyes opened to meet his, and she couldn't look away. His forehead fell against hers. Intense pleasure coursed through her as he began to stroke into her—long, deep, thrusts that brought her closer and closer to the brink. Lost in the blur of his green gaze, her slick channel throbbed around him. She careened into sensation as her climax began. He shuddered and pulsed into her, his eyes closing and his head dropping to her shoulder.

She rested against him, her body trembling in the aftermath. He lifted his head, his lips curved softly. He shifted her weight and turned them, bringing his back to the wall. He slid slowly to the floor, keeping her close in his arms. His knees came up behind her, her knees landing on either side of his hips as she rested in the cradle of his lap. His hand coasted up and down her back in slow strokes.

When her breath finally slowed, she lifted her head to see his rested against the wall, his eyes closed. He immediately opened his eyes and grinned. "Nice to see you."

She giggled. "Ditto. What happened to dinner with your parents?"

He shrugged. "I had something to take care of."

She suddenly realized she was well on her way to being late to meet Hannah. "Oh! I'm supposed to meet Hannah at Sally's. Probably..." she looked over her shoulder at the clock "...about now." She didn't want to get up. She wanted to simply stay here in his warm embrace. "What did you have to take care of?"

Jared shifted his weight, slipping his hand into the pocket of his jeans, which were shoved down around his hips. He fumbled a moment before tugging something out of his pocket. When he looked up, his eyes held a trace of vulnerability. He cleared his throat.

"I had this idea I was going to wait for the perfect moment, but it has to be now."

He held her eyes for a long moment, the depth of emotion present there bringing tears to her eyes. His hand was curled tight. He uncurled it between them. A beautiful ring sat in his palm, an amethyst stone set in a platinum setting and band. Her tears spilled over.

"Oh Jared!" Though they were only inches apart, she plastered herself closer, mashing his hand in between them, and feathered his face with kisses. "You were planning this and you didn't say anything?

Jared chuckled. "Only since the day I got out of the hospital, but I needed a chance to get up to Anchorage. That's where I was today. Mom went up with me to help me pick out your ring. I remembered how impatient you got with, well everyone, when they didn't take the big step fast enough. So if it wasn't obvious," he paused to clear his throat. "I love you and can't imagine a day without you. So please tell me you'll marry me because you are the *only* woman for me."

She knuckled her tears away. "Yes, yes, yes!" she said, dusting more kisses on his face. He actually blushed, which made her giggle again.

A while later, when they were standing and had reassembled their clothing, Susie remembered her dinner with Hannah. She grabbed her phone.

Jared stilled her hand with a grin. "You're not having dinner with Hannah."

"I'm not?"

He shook his head. "I asked her to ask you, so I'd be guaranteed you'd be at the office when I came by." He shrugged. "I had to make sure another day didn't go by without making it absolutely clear how much you mean to me."

* * *

JARED AWOKE to the sun slanting through Susie's bedroom window and warming the bed. He curled over, expecting her warm body to be beside his. When it wasn't, his sleepy haze cleared, and he opened his eyes. He smelled coffee and bacon. He flung the sheets back and stretched once he was standing. A quick run through the shower, and he went downstairs.

Susie stood by the kitchen counter, transferring bacon from a pan onto plates. She wore a blue silk robe, loosely tied, exposing the generous curves of her breasts. He walked over and dropped a kiss on the soft skin between her breasts. Lifting his eyes, he met her smile and warm brown eyes.

"Good morning. I was trying to serve you breakfast in bed, but I should have known you wouldn't sleep much longer," she said with a grin. She set the spatula down on the counter and tugged him close. He gave her a proper kiss—one that sent his pulse skyrocketing and ended with his hands tangled in her hair and gasping for air.

"Good morning," he finally replied. He stepped away and leaned against the counter, snatching a piece of bacon to nibble on.

"Have I mentioned you're a good cook?"

Her curls swung as she shook her head and giggled. She nudged him out of the way with her hip and carried two plates to the small round kitchen table.

"Sit," she ordered.

He happily complied and left not much later with a full stomach. He swung by his house to change. Stepping inside, his eyes traveled around. One of Susie's scarves hung on the stair railing, a few throw pillows were on the floor, and another random sock was by the couch. It occurred to him that a few months back, he'd never have considered leaving his house like that. Yesterday, all he'd bothered with were the dishes. He started laughing so hard, he had to sit on the bottom stair.

Nathan walked in to find him like that a moment

later. Nathan's eyes swept the room, landing back on Jared.

"What's so funny?" Nathan asked with a puzzled smile.

Jared shook his head and gestured around the room. "Just Susie."

Another glance around from Nathan before his puzzled smile faded. "It's like you're living with me again!"

Jared stood as Nathan came over and slapped him on the back. "How'd yesterday go?"

"Perfect."

*S*usie walked down the dock in Otter Cove Harbor. Waddle would be the more accurate word for what she did. She was seven months pregnant and had come to hate tall women in a way she'd never contemplated before. Given that two of her closest friends were staring at the six-foot mark, she'd given them plenty of grief. Hannah had barely looked pregnant until the last half of her pregnancy and even then, she didn't look like Susie did. Emma had just had a baby, a little girl named Janet, and even nine months into her pregnancy, she'd managed to move with grace. At five feet, Susie felt more like a beach ball than a person.

"Susie!"

She glanced up to see Jared waving at her from his boat. He was finishing up a day of cleaning and repairs. It was early fall with the long days of summer fading fast. She returned his wave and kept walking, a smile blooming in her heart. The sun was setting across the bay, casting filtered rays of orange, red and gold across the water. The mountains were cast in shadow, silent and looming in the dusky light. A loon called, the tide was rolling in, small waves cresting on the shore, the sound rhythmic and soothing.

Jared stepped off the boat and slung a bag over his shoulder. He met her halfway down the dock, leaning forward to kiss her. His lips met hers in a soft caress, swiftly escalating to a searing burn. He pulled away with a soft chuckle. "How are you feeling?" he asked, his hand caressing her round belly.

"Gigantic."

He grinned. "You look beautiful."

She smiled ruefully. "For a man who once swore he was no good at relationships, you have it down. I'm gigantic and you know it, yet you insist I look beautiful."

Jared merely grinned and slipped his arm over her shoulders, turning to walk toward the parking lot.

She thought back over the past year and still found it hard to believe. She'd watched her friends fall in love and get married and convinced herself she'd be content sitting on the sidelines. Meanwhile, the buzz between her and Jared got loud enough she couldn't ignore it anymore. Jared continued to surprise her. They'd married a year ago today on the fall equinox.

Susie who loved planning weddings could barely think straight when it came to her own. Tess, who'd also taken over the planning for Emma's wedding, had ably stepped in and made it a beautiful day. Susie was trying to convince her she needed to add wedding planner to her fundraising business, but Tess was ignoring her so far. For Susie and Jared, Tess had made the day amazing. She'd orchestrated a beach ceremony with the cooperation of the weather. As the sun set over the mountains, a crescent moon had made its appearance, rising through the red and gold and winking above the mountains. Jared had swept her off her feet—literally—and carried her in his arms down the dock to his commercial boat, which had been decorated with paper lanterns swinging above the railings.

They'd flown to Hawaii the following morning for their honeymoon. Her mind reeled back to the present when Jared said her name. They'd reached his truck.

"Huh?"

His green eyes crinkled at the corners and his dimple winked at her with his smile. "Lost in thought?"

"Oh just thinking about this time last year," she said softly.

Jared took a step closer and slid his hands down her back to curl around her bottom and tug her to him. "Mmmm…my favorite day."

Though her body reacted instantly to Jared's touch, desire unfurling inside and heat building, she was irritable because she felt huge and unwieldy.

"Your favorite day? Really?" she asked, her tone sharper than she intended.

He pulled back, his eyes warm, but serious. "Yes. My favorite day. It may have taken me a little while to figure it out, but *you* are the woman for me." His eyes softened and he brushed a loose curl off her forehead. "You look tired. We don't have to do dinner out tonight. I was trying to do the anniversary thing."

Her irritation faded. "I know. Let's have dinner at home. I'd rather celebrate our anniversary this year with my feet up," she said with a chuckle.

Hours later, her feet were in Jared's lap as he massaged them. Dark had fallen, rain coming behind it. She thought back to that rainy night, which felt like forever ago now, when they'd first kissed. She looked over at him, the lamplight limning his features.

"It was my favorite day too," she said softly.

He leaned over, his lips falling softly to hers. "I know."

Thank you for reading Love Untamed - I hope you loved Susie & Jared's story!

For more swoon-worthy small town romance, Risa & Darren's story is next in Tumble Into Love. Risa crashes into Darren's life - literally. Darren's the oh-so-sexy cop who rescues her after a car accident. He's panty-melting hot, and Rise can't remember why she swore off men when she lays eyes on him. Don't miss Darren's story!

Be sure to sign up for my newsletter for the latest news, teasers & more! Click here to sign up: http:// jhcroixauthor.com/subscribe/

For more swoony romance…

This Crazy Love kicks off the Swoon Series - small town southern romance with enough heat to melt you! Jackson & Shay's story is epic - swoon-worthy & intensely emotional. Jackson just happens to be Shay's brother's best friend. He's also *seriously* easy on the eyes. Shay has a past, the kind of past she would most definitely like to forget. Past or not, Jackson is about to rock her world. Don't miss their story! Free on all retailers!

Burn For Me is a second chance romance for the ages. Sexy firefighters? Check. Rugged men? Check. Wrapped up together? Check. Brave the fire in this hot, small-town romance. Amelia & Cade were high school sweethearts & then it all fell apart. When they cross paths again, it's epic - don't miss Cade's story! Free on all retailers!

For more small town romance, take a visit to Last Frontier Lodge in Diamond Creek. A sexy, alpha SEAL meets his match with a brainy heroine in Take Me Home. Marley is all brains & Gage is all brawn. Sparks fly when their worlds collide. Don't miss Gage & Marley's story!
Free on all retailers!

If sports romance lights your spark, check out The Play. Liam is a British footballer who falls for Olivia, his doctor. A twist of forbidden heats up this swoon-worthy & laugh-out-loud romance. Don't miss Liam & Olivia's story.
Free on all retailers!

FIND MY BOOKS

Thank you for reading Love Untamed! I hope you enjoyed the story. If so, you can help other readers find my books in a variety of ways.

1) Write a review!

2) Sign up for my newsletter, so you can receive information about upcoming new releases & receive a FREE copy of one of my books: http://jhcroixauthor.com/subscribe/

3) Like and follow my Amazon Author page at https://amazon.com/author/jhcroix

4) Follow me on Bookbub at https://www.bookbub.com/authors/j-h-croix

5) Follow me on Twitter at https://twitter.com/JHCroix

6) Like my Facebook page at https://www.facebook.com/jhcroix

* * *

Visit my store to purchase ebooks & fun swag!

J.H. Croix Shop

Diamond Creek Alaska Novels
When Love Comes
Follow Love
Love Unbroken
Love Untamed
Tumble Into Love
Christmas Nights
Last Frontier Lodge Novels
Take Me Home
Love at Last
Just This Once
Falling Fast
Stay With Me
When We Fall
Hold Me Close
Crazy For You
Just Us
Fireweed Harbor Series
When We Meet - free prequel!
Make You Mine
Dare To Fall - due out June 2023!
Be The One - due out October 2023!
Light My Fire Series
Wild With You
Hold Me Now
Only Ever Us
Fall For Me
Keep Me Close
With Every Breath
All It Takes
Take Me Now - due out August 2023!
Dare With Me Series

Crash Into You
Evers & Afters
Come To Me
Back To Us
Take Me There
After We Fall
Swoon Series
This Crazy Love
Wait For Me
Break My Fall
Truly Madly Mine
Still Go Crazy
If We Dare
Steal My Heart
Into The Fire Series
Burn For Me
Slow Burn
Burn So Bad
Hot Mess
Burn So Good
Sweet Fire
Play With Fire
Melt With You
Burn For You
Crash & Burn
That Snowy Night
Brit Boys Sports Romance
The Play
Big Win
Out Of Bounds
Play Me
Naughty Wish

RESOURCES

A note about Susie's story

*L*ove Untamed reveals Susie's brush with attempted date/acquaintance rape, an all too common crime. It is estimated that approximately 47% of rapists are known to their victims (Rape, Abuse & Incest National Network, 2015). In addition, it is estimated that 68% of all sexual assaults are unreported (RAINN, 2015). Of those that are reported, 98% of perpetrators will never spend a day in jail (RAINN, 2015). In writing Susie's story, it would have been emotionally satisfying for her to experience justice, however that is remarkably unrealistic. The emotional and psychological pain and shame that victims carry can be devastating. If you or anyone you know has experienced date/acquaintance rape, there are resources for help.

· · ·

NATIONAL SEXUAL ASSAULT HOTLINE: http://www.thehotline.org
   1-656-4673 (HOPE)

NATIONAL SEXUAL ASSAULT ONLINE HOTLINE: https://ohl.rainn.org/online/
   Confidential online instant messaging and online chat with trained professionals

NATIONAL DATING ABUSE HOTLINE (for teens and youth): http://www.loveisrespect.org
   1-866-331-9474

NATIONAL CENTER for Victims of Crime: www.victimsofcrime.org
   1-202-467-8700

ACKNOWLEDGMENTS

A bow to my husband who graciously listens to plot updates and continues to offer his talents to anything in need of a name. Once again, Laura Kingsley kept me on my toes with excellent editing and made sure I gave Susie and Jared the story they deserved. Many thanks to CT Cover Creations for my gorgeous cover.

Yet again…my readers! Wow, wow and wow! You are all so supportive and so gracious. I love hearing from each and every one of you! Thank you for taking a chance on my books and motivating me to keep writing. There are many more to come!

xoxo

JH Croix

ABOUT THE AUTHOR

USA Today Bestselling Author J. H. Croix lives in a small town in Maine with her husband and three spoiled dogs. Croix writes contemporary romance with sassy women and alpha men who aren't afraid to show some emotion. Her love for quirky small-towns and the characters that inhabit them shines through in her writing. Take a walk on the wild side of romance with her bestselling novels!

Places you can find me:
jhcroixauthor.com
jhcroix@jhcroix.com

facebook.com/jhcroix
instagram.com/jhcroix
bookbub.com/authors/j-h-croix